ories by

Aimee Bender

Benjamin Cheever

Michael Connelly

Sebastian Junger

Elizabeth McCracken

Rosie O'Donnell

Chris Offutt

Marc Parent

Anna Quindlen

John Burnham Schwartz

Alice Sebold

Lauren Slater

Edited by

MARC PARENT

The Secret Society of Demolition W

The Secret Society of
DEMOLITION
Writers

RANDOM HOUSE New York

Copyright © 2005 by Marc Parent

All rights reserved under International and Pan-American Copyright Conventions. Published in the United States by Random House, an imprint of The Random House Publishing Group, a division of Random House, Inc., New York, and simultaneously in Canada by Random House of Canada Limited, Toronto.

RANDOM HOUSE and colophon are registered trademarks of Random House, Inc.

Library of Congress Cataloging-in-Publication Data

The secret society of demolition writers : stories / by Aimee Bender ... [et al.] ; edited by Marc Parent.—1st ed.
    p.   cm.
  ISBN 1-4000-6264-0 (acid-free paper)
  1. Short stories, American. I. Bender, Aimee.
  II. Parent, Marc.
  PS648.S5S426 2005
  813'.0108—dc22   2004051355

Printed in the United States of America on acid-free paper

Random House website address: www.atrandom.com

9 8 7 6 5 4 3 2 1

First Edition

Text design by Simon M. Sullivan

A Note from the Bleachers
MARC PARENT

E VERY SEPTEMBER, THICK CLOUDS of blue smoke rise from a lit-up field on the outskirts of a small, northeastern Pennsylvania town. I'm told by those who would know that the smoke is most likely the result of a full-impact, lateral hit from the back end of a Chevy Impala, Cadillac Fleetwood, Olds Cutlass, or other circa 1970s brick shit-house on wheels, which cracks the block of the intended target—Pontiac Grandville, Chevy El Camino, Plymouth Hemi 'Cuda—spraying oil over a manifold that's cooking at a comfortable five to six hundred degrees Fahrenheit. White clouds indicate a radiator hit—hoses bursting with an explosion of steam that instantly fills the interior of the car and sends the driver scrambling through the side window.

Smoke is what we all come here to see. Steep metal bleachers on the south side of the field are filled to capacity with people of all ages chewing fat, dark cubes of fudge and washing them down with gulps of orange soda. We have all paid to see smoke. The local volunteer firemen want smoke as well. Tricked out in enough gear to take down a towering inferno, they sit with bored faces over the wheel wells of their rigs as they wait to shuffle across the field with a water hose toward the gas line rupture and subsequent rash of fire that would make momentary heroes of them. Their girlfriends stroke the backs of their necks as backhoe operators on the other side of the field are at the ready to hoist crumpled cars into the air and haul them away. High up in the announcer's booth, a row of men with their caps drawn low over their eyeglasses sit hunched over microphones, ready to narrate the destruction.

This is the GDS Demolition Derby; five heats of ten cars per round—two rows of five cars lined up on either side of the field, which after a countdown from three, commence to smashing the hell out of each other until there is only one left with its motor running. At the end of the night, the winners from each heat drive their nearly decommissioned vehicles into the ring for a final battle. The winner of this round takes the night—he stands on top of his smashed-up car, beats his helmet against the roof, and lets out a victory howl that the crowd in the bleachers echoes back. Then he hops off the car and walks over the muddy field like a stiff-legged rodeo rider, to pick up a trophy and a kitty worth around a thousand dollars.

Over the years, the ritual of this night has signaled the last gasp of summer for my family. My wife and I cover our kids' ears with headphones to deaden the roar of engines and fill their pockets with candy so they will last the night. We meet up with two other families and huddle together with blankets across our laps as we point to the hand-painted taunts on the cars and shout them out to one another—"Outlaw Crusher," "The Jugulator," "Eat Me," "Yo' Momma." Then the heats begin and we fall silent to watch the skill and finesse of the drivers, the reckless stupidity, the cheap shots, determination, and even bravery.

By the conclusion of the contest, after the roaring engines, flying mud, sparks, fire, and twisting metal have all come to an end, something incredible happens every year: the same guy wins. His name is Pete Hansen. You really need to see a demolition derby from the front row to fully appreciate the impossibility of this. There are simply too many variables in the random, unpredictable chaos of the competition for the same person to win every year. Yet every year, that's exactly what Pete Hansen does.

I developed a simmering obsession with the man after I saw his third win. The following year, before his fourth win, I was sure his streak would break and then watched as he reduced his competitors to smoking heaps of debris. By the fifth year I knew that if he entered he would win—decisively. The men in the announcer's booth ran down the roster for the first heat, Pete Hansen's name was called, he rolled unceremoniously into the ring, the flag dropped, and I watched as he systematically tore the insides out of every car within reach of his back bumper. He went on to do the same in the final battle and own the night. Instead of doubting him or shaking my head with astonishment as I had in previous years, I watched him closely this last time and I saw the thing that made him unbeatable. In a word: fearlessness. In a sentence: Pete Hansen drives like he's got nothing to lose.

I went home that evening thinking about the strength of that mind-set and because of what I do at my desk for hours on end, I thought about what that mind-set could do to writing. What would it be like to write like I had nothing to lose—write like

Pete Hansen drives, so to speak? Then one afternoon, I asked a friend of mine who is also a writer, "What story would you tell if no one knew it was you?" We grinned deviously at each other, and *The Secret Society of Demolition Writers* was born.

Over the next several months, I went out to other writers whose work I have admired for all variety of reasons and asked them the same question—what would you write if I could all but guarantee your anonymity? Under the cover of a dark helmet, how hard would you drive? Where would you take it? Released from the constraints of your reputation and the expectations that come with it, how far would you go? Those exact questions are answered twelve different times, twelve different ways, in the twelve different stories that make up the pages of this collection.

It's hard to believe this has never been done like this before. Hasn't everything been done before? Anonymous short stories from well-known writers make too much sense not to have been put together in a collection long ago. Nearly everyone who has written more than one book can tell you that there is a great deal of difference between writing with the knowledge of what will happen once the book is published and writing without that knowledge (if for no other reason than the moment you take after the second book to think about choosing a title that will be easy to explain to every other person who asks you on the tour). God help the writer who finds success and can finally buy the lake house but is conscripted for the remainder of his career by publishers and readers alike to the one mineshaft that hit pay dirt. Wouldn't it be nice if an author like this could somehow chuck everything their reputation stands on in order to see what else might be out there? Wouldn't it be liberating and in turn, wouldn't that be good for storytelling? While we're at it, wouldn't it be nice if well-known authors had the courage to throw out a totally new story without the support of their celebrity to influence us as we read—if they had a way to let the story stand on its own, told a story for the story's sake, so to speak?

In a sense every first book is written anonymously. The person who writes their first book can't imagine it will eventually be published, much less read by anyone. They take what is just a stack of paper and hand it to their agent, who hands it to a publisher, who finally turns it into a book, and the name printed neatly across the cover doesn't change the fact that they'd *written* every page anonymously. When I dare to look back through some of my first pages, there tucked in between passages that scrape mercilessly against my better senses, are occasional flashes of uncalculated, spontaneous freshness born directly out of the quiet, private room of anonymity. No subsequent book is ever written with the unknowing sparkle of the first—when the writer undertakes the enormous task of laying down a hundred thousand or so words with no track record to stand on, no road map to follow, nothing but a voice inside that says, hell, maybe I can do this. . . . The deficit is somewhat compensated for (hopefully) by skill and the maturity of experience, but still, there is only one time that a published author writes anonymously and enjoys within that state the unbridled freedom to do something truly outrageous: try something new.

In the stories that make up this collection, we have all tried with fits and starts (believe me) and with varying degrees of success (*you'd never believe who wrote . . . !!*) to step away from the constraints of our past and current works, our names and the assumptions built around them, as well as the small tics and quirks within our sentences and paragraphs that we have become fond of or even at times secretly depended on. Some have told me who in the group they'd like to be mistaken for. Some have tried to write in the vein of X, then given in to the sound of Y, only to turn in a perfect Z. There was high-seas drama in the creation of many of these stories. Each one in almost every case represents only the tip of the iceberg. If only I could tell you—if only I could tell *anyone*. But I have given my word to the writers that I will hold fast to the secret of our society. I will tell no one who wrote what—not agents, not family or friends, not even the publisher. No slip of paper exists that would identify the authorship of these twelve stories. The secrets in this collection are safe from everyone except the readers who accept our invitation to play the detective's game. Knowing what I do, I believe the code can be cracked, but be warned, many of the writers have gone to great lengths to steer you from the path to their discovery—there is no such thing, after all, as a clean fight in a demo derby. So watch for flying metal as you go, because at its heart, a demolition derby is all this really is.

In that vein, I would like to dedicate this book to the drivers of tonight's heat: to Aimee, Ben, Mike, Sebastian, Elizabeth, Ro, Chris, Anna, John, Alice, and Lauren—bad-to-the-bone outlaw crushers every last one of you—yo' momma. *Whose momma?—Yo'* momma! A box of fudge and a bottle of orange soda to the winner—here's mud in your eye. Pedal to the metal all—get on your boots and ride. . . .

The cars are lined up and ready. Everybody—count it down! In—

Three . . .

Two . . .

One . . .

Contents

Eggs

I T SEEMED THE SUN NEVER SANK that summer. All day long the air was thick and the river running through our town was just a dead gray snake with a sulfurous smell. Without wind, the tops of the trees drooped and when you fanned your face, the air was like a wall of water barely moving over you. People complained. Air-conditioning units banged, and the ice from a Slurpee was cool blue heaven before it melted on the pad of your tongue.

I didn't want to get a job selling Slurpees, the way so many others my age did. I certainly didn't want to be a lifeguard, hoisted high in one of those chairs with an emergency cross blazing at my back. I look *eh* in a bathing suit. I'm twenty-one, sun sensitive, my skin as white as milk in a blue china cup. I am the kind of person who seeks shady places and books; I like any book that has to do with houses and their insides. I like the old books about Boston houses—Edith Wharton and a man named James write about those—and I like the new books you get in the paperback rack in the drugstore, books where living rooms have velvet drapes and people are in love for two seconds tops. I've been in love a few times, but nothing worth noting here.

I live with my mother. In our town, most of us do. We go to the high school, a big industrial brick building with rows and rows of slick red lockers, and then we graduate up to the community college where huge elms shade the campus and there's an archway you have to drive through that says something important and Latin on it. At the community college, most of us major in physician's assistant training programs, which means you learn to draw a lot of blood and read pressure. Others do something with software architecture. I knew right from the start these career paths were not for me. I knew, and always have, that I wanted to do interior design, to make homes as beautiful as they possibly could be, to understand the subtle but serious distinction between mauve and merlot, or how to bring light to a row of wavy glass windows, to choose a carpet that complements the color of wood that soaks up the shine from the beaded chandelier, the one I chose, swinging from its root in the freshly spackled ceiling.

The summer of heat, the summer before my junior college year, my mother's cancer returned, after ten years' remission. My father left us a long time ago, for Florida. At first my mother felt just a small ache in her bones and then the ache turned into a limp and she finally had to admit the pain grinding and grinding at her hip was not arthritis. The doctor confirmed it with a

4

CAT scan. He showed us the recurrence, there on films so gray they looked covered with cobwebs, there on the furniture of my mother's bones, her architecture all wrong, chips and calcifications, black stains where the malignancy was. The body is a house. Make no mistake about it. The body is a house and the organs are the plush parts and the bones are the scaffolding and bed frames and bookshelves on which you hold your memories, your disappointments.

We came out of the doctor's office, into a blast of heat. My mother waved a rolled-up patient information sheet in front of her face, perspiration lining her lip. "I'll do the chemo," she said. I wanted to put my arm around her, draw her in close, *oh mom*, but it's not that way between us. We get along, but if you were to give us a personality test, you'd get opposite results. She's loopy and eccentric and has little sense of style. She wears bedroom slippers a lot. I shop at all the outlets for Joan and David shoes and Talbot's clothes. My mother has a knot in her hair, and instead of combing it, she just lets it get bigger and bigger until at last the lady at the salon just has to cut it out. She lives off my father's alimony and spends her days reading horoscope charts and smoking cigarettes until the ash gets so long it drops off onto the carpet. Frankly, I have higher aspirations. A woman should. I'd like, for instance, to accumulate some wealth. I say to my mother, "Don't you need a retirement plan?" and she takes a deep suck off her cigarette, her cheeks collapsing inward and says, "Whoop de doo, I'll be gone before then." I say to my mother, "Don't you want to dye that gray in your hair?" and she says, "Gray tells the truth, Cynthia." Standing close to her, I can smell decay, the same way I can smell that river that runs through our town, odiferous vapors rising up, singing tunes of sinking things and wretched things and houses taken by torpedoes.

I don't remember ever being close to my mother. I don't remember ever holding her hand or sitting in her lap. She invited me, over and over again, and I refused. I can be distant and scared. In our high school class there was once a girl named Leah Kowalski. Leah had a bad lisp and a gimp leg that ended in a prosthesis. Sometimes she'd take the prosthesis off, unbuckling the leather-and-steel contraption, removing it from where it nestled on the knee, and I'd see what was beneath. I'd see the sheen of amputation, the skin and spoke of bone, and I'd want to touch her there. Right there. Of course I never dared.

IN THE SUMMERS, in my town, most of us flip burgers or bag groceries or work in the hospital gift shop, but these things aren't for me. I wanted to make some money. My mother's cancer had returned, a boy was abducted while he walked home from the mall, his murdered body found in the weedy woods, and I dreamt of Leah Kowalski; she was saying *operator, operator* and coming towards me in an old-fashioned black dress with gorgeous buttons of pure pearl. I'd wake up shaking, the tree shadows fingering out across my bedroom wall, the occasional car swooshing by in the street outside, the heat just building like a bomb. I was in Gerry's one day, ordering a low-cal soda, when I saw the sign. It was pinned on the community bulletin board, right next to the sectional sofa for sale. EGG DONORS NEEDED the sign said. GENEROUS COMPENSATION. 21–34. Call . . . and it gave a toll free number. Now, first off, I have always loved dialing toll free numbers. Sometimes I do it just for the thrill of reaching all the way across the country, to a voice in Texas, or Louisiana, or maybe even France, for free. But it was more than that. Generous compensation. I thought here might be a way to get wealthy. Here might be a way to stockpile some cash, start a serious savings plan, and move my way up and out of this tiny town of two-room houses and poor cable reception. I'd like to live in a place with just a bit of panache. I'd like to live in a house that has a foyer. I'd like a bathroom where the tiles are white floor to ceiling, except for the thin floral band that belts the midsection, beaded with water when I shower.

So I called. We are talking, here, the difference between a $5.61 summer wage, and a GENEROUS COMPENSATION. Who knew what it would be. I was thinking, maybe a couple of hundred? I had no idea. When I say that I mean that absolutely. I had no idea at all.

HE WAS A LAWYER. He said to come on in. We made an appointment for the next day. While I was waiting for the next day, I sat on my mother's porch swing and sipped some soda. My friend Alice called and said she'd kissed a trumpet player; he had an incredible lip. My friend Marie called and said mud was good for your face. These girls I am close to, but not by much. I have always been dreamy and inward. I am always building places inside my head, rooms where quilts hang on antique racks, hallways with ceramic hands cupping candles on the walls. This world, that world, my world, where it is perfect and lonely both.

The next day, I went in to see him. He had a 1-800 number but an office just two bus rides away. I live in Troy, a tiny town; he was in Albany, big city, far but not far, if you see what I mean. His office was in a high-rise with one thousand windows. The elevator doors parted soundlessly, and I whooshed upwards, stepping into a silent hall, and then a waiting room of utter white, a carmine couch, a sleek telephone on the glass side table. He called me in. He was handsome as hell, or heaven. He said his name was Ike. Ike Devin. He had one of those faces that descend like ledges, and bead blue eyes. He wore chinos, perfectly pressed, and an excellent Oxford shirt that showed the little trigger of his Adam's apple. "Sit down," he said, and I did. "I have hundreds upon hundreds of couples," he said, and he told me the tale, the women too old to make good eggs, the couples late thirtyish, always in love. They were looking for donors "like you," Ike said, "healthy and smart," and I could feel myself beginning to beam. Of course, like me. "A young woman like you," Ike said, "has probably thousands upon thousands of genetically sound egg cells," and when he said that I thought of my mother, her genetically unsound cells, and then I thought of my stomach, its flat pale plane, the little wink where the belly button was, the way Ike looked at me, approving, a small smile on his face. "You think I'd be a candidate?" I said.

"Quite possibly," he said.

"Which couple would get my egg?" I said.

"It's what we call a reciprocal process," Ike said. "You choose them and they choose you, a partnership." Then Ike pulled out a file drawer and riffled through it. "Here are all the profiles," he said. "Here are all the couples who might want your genetic material."

"How much?" I said.

"Five thousand," Ike said.

I felt my eyes pop out like a pug dog's. "Five thousand?" I said.

"Per retrieval," Ike said. "If you do it more than once, then of course you get five thousand again. It can be lucrative," Ike said. "And for a girl your age, you have a lot to give."

I HAD TO sign on many dotted lines. I had to sign away my rights to the future child, which was not a problem, because in my mind I was not giving away a child, just an egg, and there's a difference. I had to prove who I was, birth certificate, doctor checkups, health histories, school report cards, where I've always been straight A. Three weeks later, Ike called. "You're approved," he said. I went back to his office and he fanned out the files before me. It was like picking parents. Each couple had their history, their likes and dislikes, their golfing styles, their pet status, their gardens and careers. I knew I wanted my egg to go to a certain sort of woman, one who had, say, a circular lawn, and underground sprinklers, the kind that work on an automatic timer and rain upwards just as the summer sun sinks, giving the air a lavender smell. I wanted the woman to have a lawn and a walk-in California closet and most definitely a career; she should have earned these things herself, and she should like dogs. I picked her, Janice. We would never meet, but then again, we would. I would be buried in her. She would grow me all over again. I would be born from her, born into her house, which she described as contemporary colonial, with two staircases and a shag carpet the color of cream. In the kitchen, I pictured fresh peppers hung in copper baskets; I pictured a small room painted a beautiful pale green, where the crib would be. I pictured the baby opening its eyes to see the lacquered blond spindles and the walls and a face bending over it, all shadow and jasmine scent. Janice. In her house, I would sleep in Neiman Marcus sheets. In her house, touch would be safe, mouth to cheek, finger to wrist, the skin always moist and fresh.

I THOUGHT THE procedure would be relatively easy, my mistake. They can't, it turns out, just go in there with lobster tongs and pick out an egg or two. I had to take a lot of drugs and this did not appeal to me, given that, unlike my mother, who eats meat, I am a vegetarian with insides as bright as sunny corridors. So I wasn't happy about the drug part, but the fertility doctor at the clinic, where Ike referred me, said it was absolutely necessary. The goal was to ramp up my ovaries so they spit out eggs like silver pinballs, so doctors could harvest as many as ten at a time, all for Janice. I went in for ultrasounds. The technician squirted warmed goop on my belly and said, "There they are," but when I looked on the screen all I saw were shadows and clouds. Now, at night, I dreamt of Janice. She was my mother, my sister, my friend. I could be close to her; we could be like blood relations with none of the liabilities this usually imposed. We did not share disease or death or even difference.

We were just a pure blood-bond, and she came to me in my dreams, this Janice did, her skirt a spiral of color. She held my hand. I felt I had come home.

MEANWHILE, MY MOTHER's cancer was doing the cancer thing. Once a recurrence happens, and once that recurrence goes to the bone, well, you can imagine. If you have a cancer in your breast, which is where hers started, you have it limited, because there are only two breasts on the body. But when cancer gets to the bone it has a whole sewer system to work through because bones are everywhere, and they are not durable. My mother was in pain. She knocked on a door one day and shattered her porous knuckle. She drank her chemo down. The chemo was red as Batman's cape, and left a stain on her lip. Ten years ago, when my father left her for a woman in high high heels, my mother's already graying hair finished its transformation. Her veins are very purple in her high thighs, a little like mashed grape. "I'm my own woman Cynthia," my mother tells me, has always told me. "I don't care what anyone thinks of how I look or live and it's a shame you do." She says this to me in her bedroom slippers, as she sucks on her mentholated sticks. The smoke is snarled and yarnlike. I can't believe I came out of her vagina. Sometimes I have a weird belief that the doctors never completely washed me off, so I still smell like her and what is this smell, my mother's oils, the substance beneath the stone, where the worms are?

SO, SHE DRANK her cherry red chemo and I took my fertility shots; we sort of did this side by side. "Five thousand dollars Mom," I'd say, holding the syringe in the air, plunging it down fast into my backside, feeling the Fertinex do its work, seep into my tubes, nourish my eggs, which were turning gold and perfect. Day after day I plumped out and became an Easter basket.

Day after day she did the opposite, like a bad compare/contrast English assignment we were, the basket of her body frayed and unstable. "I disapprove of this *job*, Cynthia," she'd say, and then her hair would fall out, a big clump on the rug.

IN COLLEGE, WHERE I was going to be a junior, I liked literature. It's not my major, but I am bookish and also, of course, interested in decorating magazines. That summer of unusual heat I could sit for a long time on the porch swing, one bare foot scraping against the floor, and read stories about fortune-tellers who saw strange things in the crosshatched lines, stories of men on sailing ships and old Bostonian streets lit by gas lamps while women in hooped skirts walked poodles. I read *Bed+Bath* and then this writer named Colette, who described melon very well, and then Anne Rice with her vampires. Once, in school, in my freshman year, we read a very conceptual book called *Purity and Danger*. It was all about why some cultures find some things unclean. For instance, did you know that Jewish people don't mix milk with meat because it is unclean, and the reason why is that dairy comes from a certain sphere, and meat from another, and some spheres should not touch. The same way some planets should not touch, the collision of worlds. Incest is unclean because a child is in one sphere, a parent in another, and it would be like a comet coming down, sex would. When I gave my egg, sphere shaped and wet, to Janice, would we be in purity or danger? Would we be one world, somehow separated, finally coming together, two women cut from the same cloth, separated by accident and neighborhood, or were we really two different worlds that had no business being in contact? I wondered about this, a little. I went to the library one day and looked for that book *Purity and Danger*, but the librarian said, "There's no such book, my dear." But there is. I remembered reading about the danger of pollution, but I also remembered reading about the danger of purity, how realms kept strictly separate, rigid realms where the goal is perfection unto itself, are also abominations. The craving for symmetry, the rejection of the dented world. That's possibly some sort of sin.

I WENT FOR my first egg retrieval. The clinic was chic, the waiting room filled with pained and wealthy-looking women. I enjoyed their jewelry, the tennis bracelet, the stop-sign–shaped ruby on the ring. The nurse called me in. They did a quick ultrasound and then proceeded to sedation. "Just to calm you down," they said, and I felt the pinch of the needle and an immediate coolness fill my veins, like some blue Slurpee, some sleep and relief from the heat. I saw the doctor in a dream or in reality, I don't know which. My legs were hoisted high, into stirrups, and a warm sun shone into my cleaved body. I saw a silver-sharp instrument hovering in his gloved hand, and then it went in me. Up, up, the needle nosed, up into my uterus, feeling for the stuffed sac of the ovary, *there*, the gentlest pierce possible, the tiny sweet eggs spilling down the straw and into a clean bowl, where they were then whisked away. Afterwards, I sat up. Someone brought me water. "Good job," they said. I sipped. I moved off the table, and where I lay, just a little dab of bright red paint, my body's color.

ALL IN ALL, a very trustworthy operation. One week later, a check for five K in the mail. I took my mother and said "c'mon," and we went downtown. I bought accessories. I bought glass doorknobs and ribbons. We went to the makeup counter at the mall. My mother said, "Cynthia, I'm tired." I pushed her forward. I had just the slightest soreness in my side. I said, "Can you give her some foundation, some sparkle eye shadow?" I went through one procedure, she now through another. Five thousand, four thousand four hundred and fifty.

The makeup lady, who looked like a doctor herself in a white coat, poured a promising mixture onto a cotton ball, wiped at my mother's face. Somewhere, Janice was taking my egg, they were inserting it into her; it was petaling open, a little leg cracking its fragile shell. Here we go. I felt giddy, rich, full. I felt pregnant myself, my egg there in the lining, there in the lavender-scented sprinklers, the blond lacquered crib, *shushhh* a woman says, and she holds me against a body that does not break. "I'm tired," my mother said, and the makeup doctor swabbed her and waxed her with pink lipstick and then, it was all of a sudden, my mother swiped her hand sideways so bottles went scurrying like people in a sniper attack, rattling sideways, falling onto the floor, seeking shelter under the counters.

The whole store got quiet, looking. "Leave-me-alone," my mother said into the silence. The makeup lady froze, a cotton swab in mid-descent. "You," my mother turned to me, "you are entirely without empathy." And I felt myself flush with shame, for it was true, my sin was flounce and flourish, and had it ever been any different? Once, a long time ago, I had liked to draw simple things, a star, an elephant without tusks. Return me there. "And you," my mother said now to the Lancôme lady; my mother struggled to stand up, she backed away. "And you," she said to that lady, who was holding her healing cottons and her pressed powders that in the end would do no good. That's what my mother said next: "No good."

CERTAIN THINGS BECOME compulsions. Some people drink. Some people smoke. Some people donate their eggs. Another cycle. Another five K, another chance at another woman's womb. Ike said sure. My mother got weaker. Summer finally passed, and when the fall arrived it was a godsend, cooler air from Canada, birds in a V. I went back to school, hauling myself up off my mother's porch swing, out of our smoke-stained house where the wallpaper curled, and into the classroom, where I'm straight A. Because I was a junior now, I took almost all interior design courses, to prepare me for the world. I took a course in perspective, where we studied vanishing points, and a course in textiles, where we compared cotton to twill, and I took a course in color management, where we learned what went together and what didn't. I was bad at color management. I put things together I should not have; I collided separate spheres and thought it looked wonderful. I took pale orange and put it next to a wash of violet in a virtual room; I made one wall hunter green, the floor wine red, and I thought—I still do—that this was lovely. The instructor said, "All your homes look nervous," but I couldn't tell. Color, I think, is God's way of laughing. I envision places inside me where the spectrum spreads out so every hue and tone meshes in a subtle burst of light. I picture a terra-cotta sill, a pot of pressed sea glass. Give me my floors in deep blues, my ceilings in marbleized pink. The instructor said, "Less is more, Cynthia." My instructor said, "Neutrals like coffee work well," but I couldn't see that, couldn't stand that, and so I found my flaw; it had to do with color. I got my first bad grade ever in that course. B. Minus. Look at it. B–. Like a pair of sideways breasts with a slash at the skin. My mother's cancer went to the brain. I did yet another egg retrieval and picked a couple in a farmhouse in Nyack, New York, where there was, so said the profile, a salmon-colored living room, a woman with strawberry blond hair. I began to worry that something was seriously wrong with me. Never had I been anything but good at what I did. B. Minus. My instructor said I had a bad eye.

THERE ARE THEORIES, there are stories, and there are facts. Color is all three of these things. Eggs are just facts. The fact is that a baby girl is born with over fifty thousand tiny fresh eggs in her ovaries and she loses them month by month, so by the time she's ready to have her own baby, she's diminished; she's down. I didn't know this ahead of time, but I read it in the waiting-room literature. There are other ovoid facts. For instance, every egg has a tiny little X inside it, a perfectly shaped letter, a crossroads, two fine lines jointed just right. The most amazing fact, says Ike, is none of these things. The most amazing fact is that every single one of us, thieves and terrorists and adulterers and greedy ones, every single one of us is truly a good egg. Otherwise we would have miscarried. If this is true, and it so obviously is, then why did my mother's cancer spread to the brain? Why can't I manage my color wheel? Why did I get a B minus and why was there a boy murdered in the weedy woods, where the mall parking lot stops and the crow-darkness begins?

MY LAST EGG retrieval happened on a Thursday. I didn't know it would be my last one, because I was getting rich, cash piling up as my storehouse diminished. My mother was babbling on and on at night now about angels in her tapioca pudding. I wanted them to move her to a hospice. I sometimes came to her and put quarters under her pillow, like I remember she used to do for me when a tooth fell out, and I'd sleep all night on silver. *Oh mom, what can I give you?* I couldn't kiss her, couldn't stand the feel of her skin on my lips, or maybe it was my lips I couldn't stand, the way I started to see them as earthworm pink, segmented and ominously plump.

I went for my last egg retrieval. I had two moments that are of note. That they happened almost side by side is important. Sometimes I get what I call these "flashes of notice." They can happen anytime and they never come with warnings. Sometimes it seems to me that the world steps out of its skin and shows me its original beauty, or its ugliness. On the way to the clinic that late fall afternoon, doused on drugs that were maybe making my own mind a little whacked, I saw light swimming in the top of a tree, light fractured by leaves and swimming like little fish up there in the treetop sky, and I thought, "I am looking at a mass of light." That was a moment of notice. Then I got to the clinic. I stepped in and sat down. Next to me was a woman too old to be there. She had a map of lines on her face and sunken eyes. She was, I'd say, fifty. She was wearing taste-less black-velvet leggings and a long tunic top and all in all, she had a beaten-up, trashy look. And I had a flash of notice then. I saw her ugliness absolutely, same as I'd seen the light's beauty. I saw the cells spilling down her aging face and teeth, each one a tombstone. I felt, then, a pure and rising fury. I felt a tightness in my throat, like I'd swallowed a red rubber ball. I was going to cry soon, even though, come on, come on, we're all good eggs. I sat down. Women whooshed in and out, hands placed protec-tively on their lower bellies. "What are you here for?" I said to the woman, really brazen, I didn't care. I figured she was wait-ing for a daughter, and that, it turned out, was right, in a way. "I'm here to receive my first donor egg," she said, and I felt punched in the gut, for it had not occurred to me, anyone can get a donor egg, you can be eighty years old and get one im-planted, it is never too late to harbor life, and that seemed awful and wrong to me. It seemed polluted to put a young fresh egg in an ancient vessel. It was like a taboo. I had the thought that maybe one of the women I had picked was really like this woman, looks good on paper, but dying; of course. Color is God's way of laughing. I thought of that myself. Here's some-thing else I thought of. Every moment you are with a person, you are with a dying person. There's no way around that.

I stared at this woman. "Aren't you a little old?" I said, my voice high and frantic. The woman blinked. She had so much mascara on that her blink left little black dots on the belly-bags beneath her eyes. Everyone in the waiting room turned to listen.

"Old for what?" the woman said snippily.

"Old to be getting a donor egg?" I said. "I mean," and the rage kept rising, "I mean, at some point you just have to admit, it might be too late."

The woman didn't say anything, just looked away, fiddled with the gold clasp on her purse.

"Well," I said, laughing, and I'd like to add here that months and months of fertility drugs can make you crazy, although I know it's more than that, there are many facts, theories, stories that underlie a mind, "well," I said, "I'm a veteran at this and let me tell you it sucks. It sucks," I said. "They put you on a table, spread you wide, and then blow the eggs up you like they're bubbles."

"Would you shut up," the woman said to me.

"Would I shut up?" I said. I thought of my mother then. She kept talking tapioca, angels with wet wings. Why wouldn't she shut up? Would I shut up? "Fuck you," I said. "You're too old to have a baby."

"Please," the woman said, holding up her hand, "please, stop."

"I'm just trying to tell you the truth," I said. "They spread your legs wide and stuff things inside. Like a flaxidermist."

"You mean taxidermist," she said.

"That's what I said," I said.

"Tiffany," a nurse called, coming to the door, and the woman looked up.

"Your turn," I said. Outside the plate glass windows, the trees were glorious, but I did not have a flash of notice; the glory stayed separate from me. Tiffany, old, with a big fat butt, moved off, her cells falling onto the floor with a tinkling sound, like goblets being broken. Only I could hear it. I sat there, my eyes closed, listening.

THE SEDATION, THAT last time, felt particularly fine. I was covered in a net of fluff and borne away with Winken. The retrieval needle seemed sheathed in silk, and I closed my eyes. When I opened them again, I was in the recovery room, sun streaming in, falling in bold strokes across the squeaky floor. In the bed next to mine, Tiffany was lying there, moaning. I could see her bare bottom through the sheet, the extra bags of fat. "Tiffany," I whispered, "Tiffany, Tiffany," and she turned slowly towards my sound, and opened her hurting eyes, and looked at me. "What," she said, and then, I don't know, she tried to get up, she wanted to escape me, or she just thought it was time, but in order for implantation to succeed, a woman should lie flat. "Don't move Tiffany," I whispered, "you have to lie flat for thirty minutes," but she kept struggling to stand. I should help her, I thought. I should just take her hand, lead her wherever it is she wants to go. For how long, after all, can a person dwell in a perfectly decorated sphere? My egg store was getting depleted. My colors could not be managed. There are discordancies: angels in pudding, babies in ancients, and then there's plain old pain. It cannot be helped. In a farmhouse, in Nyack New York, there are built-in bookshelves, fir floors. Janice, she could be four months along already, I'll never know. What I knew then was Tiffany, struggling to stand, so I gave her my hand, and I pulled her up, and we walked across the sunlit floor together, two people from ordinary eggs, two people taking first steps to some unnamed place. Where it was, I had no idea.

There Is No Palindrome of Palindrome

H E HAD A SHARP-CHINNED HEAD that could split wood, a nose that was merely a smaller version of his head, an angular torso. His hands, too, his flat feet, were ax-shaped and sharp. In the silver light of morning, he looked like a many-bladed knife, with all of the blades pulled out for display. At night, in the dark, he looked merely amphibious. You would have thought he was a mortician or toymaker, his hands white and muscular, made for life's hardest or gladdest work. He was a pharmacist. Of course. Look at him again, the spatulate fingers, the long limbs, the exuberant yet deadly serious mustache. Not a knife after all, not sea-life come to suck the rarefied oxygen at water's surface. Halfway between a mortician and a toymaker: a pharmacist's hands. Now he steadied a woman's chin in the L of his right thumb and index finger. He had his other hand on the back of her neck. He was looking at her tonsils. They were both at a party.

"Babe is examining tonsils again," said Mal, the evening's host. "Babe has a tonsil fetish."

"Yes?" said the woman's Dutch husband. "This is very original."

The woman had the artificial, trustworthy, fiber-optic blond hair of a CNN foreign-policy pundit, lit up with Aqua Net. Her head was tipped back. Her eyes scanned the ceiling in an attempt to make the examination seem incidental: she was thinking great thoughts, she was multiplying great sums in her head. She tried, the way you always try when being examined in a room full of strangers, to look unworried. Besides, it was hard to look directly at Babe. His eyes didn't exactly match. The left one was slightly smaller and lower than the right.

"Pretty as an Arizona sunset," he said, still peering.

It wasn't true, what Mal said. He didn't have a fetish. He just liked looking down women's throats, and when you put it that way, yes, it sounded terrible. But he felt he was performing a service. He admired women's tonsils at the drugstore (he worked for a national chain), but he preferred parties. So yes, all right, yes. A fetish. He was a voyeur and an exhibitionist, both. Sometimes he sat a woman down in a chair, to look down her throat from above. Other times he targeted a tall woman and had her lean over. Every angle had its pleasures, and every pair of tonsils had its beauty. Jealous husbands gathered, waiting to catch him in the act. Did he look down her blouse or let a hand slide somewhere it shouldn't? Maybe he was about to lean in for a kiss. No. He didn't even glance at her tongue. If he was feeling naughty he might raise his oak eyes a fraction of a millimeter to the woman's uvula. "Beautiful uvula," he'd say.

The woman with the blond hair was named Connie. She felt on her cheek twin spots of intermittent hot breath from his nose, warm and damp as her own tonsils but with a whiff of well-groomed mustache. She'd never seen her own tonsils face-to-face. Why was he so interested? She breathed in. She crossed her legs and kicked him in the shin, felt him wince, instinctively caressed the shin with the same toe that had done the kicking. He stood up.

Her mouth still hung open. She raised her eyebrows and gave a quick nod to ask the diagnosis.

Babe shrugged. His leg hurt. "I'm a pharmacist," he explained apologetically. He reached over and closed her mouth for her. He could feel her jawbone under his thumb. When she got up to leave, he saw how badly put together she was—bow-legged and pigeon breasted and spraddle elbowed—and also how pretty. She looked like the sunniest, dopiest person he'd ever met. That kick, her toes. They were the thin edge of the wedge, he'd think later.

BLACK-AND-WHITE film combined with murder makes any room look small and sordid. The corpse lowers the ceiling, the film and flash turn all the surfaces to dented metal. In this case, in this crime-scene photo, the room is large—a suburban kitchen overlooking a dining room, a cathedral-ceilinged addition to an old house—but you can't tell. There are two bodies on the floor underneath sheets. Aren't all corpses back sleepers? Not the one closest the camera. All you can see is an ear turned wrong way round, one curl of light hair. Even so, the blood on the sheet is patterned in a physiognomic way. The head's wearing a mask: a pair of dark eyes and a long nose, a stroke victim's sloppy mouth. Never mind that it's in the wrong place. The face on the sheet is singing something but failing to remember the words. It seems to be backing up in the song again and again, the way you do when you hope the chorus will remind you of the verse. The other body is visible only as a pair of men's feet, one wearing an untied shoe and the other bare. The bare foot is clean. The rest of the body is hidden behind a kitchen island.

Nothing is happening in the photo. Things happen up until the photo, then continue afterwards. For the moment, the two people under the sheets are not dying. They're alive or dead. Their pulses are beside the question, being undetectable. In this way every photo is a photo of a corpse, devoid of circulation, synaptic function, liver function, brain function, kidney function, respiration. Even the third person in the photograph, she is a body, too, her chest thrust out towards the camera and her brown eyes open very wide, a teenager wearing a Shetland sweater. The semicircular pattern across her shoulders and chest looks under the circumstances like some kind of restraint. Her complexion is tarnished, her blue jeans are hammered tin. She's pointing to the right. Her mouth is hanging open. Her name is Constance Lafferty, she is fifteen years old, and she's about to be arrested for the murder of her parents.

BABE KNEW NOTHING of this. Connie was one of Mal's strays, or her husband was, the doll-like Dutch Jules. They'd introduced themselves at the wine table in the dining room. "This is my husband, Jewels," said Connie, and Jules—pale blond hair, brunet eyebrows—said to Babe in a merry voice, "Hallo I am *Zhool.*" They seemed perfect for each other. Connie was one of those brash, intensely American women who nevertheless develop a deep identification with a foreign country. He'd known them in college, the girls who dated only foreigners. They were the girls who'd never had a date in high school. In college they'd order widely off the atlas: the chubby friendly Kenyan, the vest-pocket Malaysian Romeo, the Irish engineering student with the smelly feet, the Argentinian painter with hearing loss and a crush on his sister. These girls always had the loudest voices in the room. They'd go on dates with their foreigners, and all you'd be able to hear would be the American girl blaring out her love for all things Kenyan, Malaysian, African, South American, and the low murmur of her date agreeing. Eventually, the girl would settle on a region. She might even go to graduate school and major in it, in some way—Comp Lit with a specialty in writings of the Americas, Public Health with a focus on East Africa. Connie, clearly, had landed on the Netherlands, and here was Jules, patient and practical and Dutch, to feed her chocolate on her morning toast and listen to her monologues. Both of them seemed made out of a jumble sale, Connie with her seaworthy torso and spindly legs, Jules with his clashing hair and eyebrows. Like all mismatched couples, they seemed suited to each other. Which was why after all Babe asked to look at her tonsils. It was the happily married women he was interested in, having once been happily married himself.

He was a widower. Women felt stirred by such tender concern for a part of themselves they'd never seen straight on: tonsils—who knew? His wife had been killed in a car crash, a hit-and-run in the crosswalk in front of the stationery store where she worked. Let's be honest, he'd done the tonsil thing when his wife was still alive, and now it was unsettling, but who'd refuse him? Sad man with a mustache, unhandsome until he smiled, which he almost never did. He had a billboard cowboy's smile, open-mouthed to show his perfect white teeth. He rocked back on his heels in a silent impression of belly laughter. He even touched his stomach then, as though to ask it, *D'ja hear that, buddy?* Smiling scrunched his eyes up till they matched. His voice seemed made of pencil shavings: grubby, sneezish, insinuating. People thought he was making fun of them when he said what his name was.

His wife was seven years dead, enough time for a sense of humor to regenerate, at least a little. Babe liked puns, palindromes, horror movies. Family pleasures, in other words. What is so sad as a solitary punster? His friend Mal, a doughnut-shop owner and giver of dinner parties, cocktail parties, surprise parties, invited him to everything.

So what if Babe sometimes had a few drinks and turned to somebody else's wife and suggested, "Say ah?" So what if he put his hand on her neck and inhaled, in a professional way, her patient, personal breath. He was tactile. He was a letch, but in an old-fashioned cocktail-napkin way. Harmless.

He was a decent guy! He was still in love with his wife, poor thing. Everyone knew *that*.

THE SMALL FLOCK of pharmacy assistants filled most of the actual prescriptions. Babe checked them, argued with insurance companies, consulted with customers, gave advice, worried about the string of Oxycontin holdups in the area. Mostly the store was prey to teenage theft of condoms, pregnancy tests, protein bars, Dramamine for the dimenhydrinate, Robitussin and Coricidin for the dextromethorphan. A group of local high schoolers held a Robitussin Round Table by the dumpsters. They cracked jokes about their hallucinations, they announced they were tripping, they informed each other they were tripping.

Yo, dude: you're tripping.

I am, I'm totally tripping.

In the afternoon you could hear them laughing. Later, you could see the tiny unused cups, the plastic wrappers, and slicks of vomit.

"It's called Robodosing," said Hilary, the pharmacy assistant with the rusty-bedspring hair. She was sorting NutriNate, a chewable prenatal vitamin that smelled disconcertingly of merlot. "Or Robocopping. Or plain Roboing."

"I know," said Babe. He didn't know what was more depressing, kids getting high on motion-sickness pills and cough syrup, or coming up with slang for it. Teenagerland. Adolescent

Narcissiville. Some days Babe longed to travel there with shoplifters, look around. The land of teens, its mufti and customs, Babe understood none of it. He hadn't even when he was a teenager himself.

The teenagers never approached him. They merely squinted at him standing at the pharmacy counter as though he were the goalie of the opposing team and he better watch out for flying pucks. Then they left by the far door.

A pharmacist is fluent in mime. Fingers flutter around cheekbones to explain one kind of sinus pain. They straddle the nose for another. Some symptoms can't be articulated except by pulling faces. Some need both arms and one foot. In the fluorescent lights of the pharmacy, Connie-from-the-party had a sugar-cookie complexion. She wore pants in a lavender-based plaid and a bulky, bumpy sweater that seemed carved out of dirty snow. In her hand she held four hot-pink daisies wrapped in blue tissue paper. Babe stood on the raised flooring behind the Drop-Off counter.

"The florist said they're very masculine flowers," she said. Maybe she wanted a second opinion. He couldn't tell whether she'd be disappointed to have the diagnosis confirmed.

"They're pink," he said.

She sighed. "Pink's pink, I guess."

"A manly pink!" he answered. "The color of Sylvester Stallone's prom dress."

At this she smiled. "Yes!" she said. "They're—what's the word?" Her pink tongue tapped against her very white teeth.

"Testosteriffic?" asked Babe.

She laughed briefly, then frowned. "They're for you." She hoisted them higher. Then she put her free hand to her own throat and stroked it. She opened her mouth.

Was she crazy? Was everyone? Pharmacists weren't supposed to examine people. The roof of her mouth looked ribbed like a cathedral. You could dive down that throat. Her tonsils were inflamed but small, and for the first time Babe wondered what was past a pair of tonsils. He'd always thought of them as landmarks, just not on the way to something.

This time she steadied her own chin. He stared at her fingers. "What do you want?" he asked her.

She leveled her head but still held her throat. Her mouth was ajar. Finally she said, in her loud voice, "What do you recommend?"

"Truly?" he said, and his hands shook. "You should go to a doctor for a culture."

She shook her head. Her hair didn't move. "My mother was a doctor," she told him.

He led her to the Cough & Cold aisle. "So," he said, to indicate that *he* hadn't forgotten the facts of the matter, "how long have you and Jules been married?"

"Four years?" she asked. "Depends on how you do the math. Four years for real, but we didn't live together till about six months ago."

"Because he was in Holland?"

Connie hooted. It was an actual hoot. She threw back her head like someone impersonating a rare suburban owl. *Hoo-hoooo!* "You don't know!" she said. "Mal didn't tell you!" She looked directly at Babe. Her eyes narrowed and she leaned in. She touched his forearm. When she spoke, she was as loud as she'd ever been. "Not because he was in Holland. Because I was in prison."

"Right. OK. What for?"

At the end of the aisle an old woman pushing one of the store's pygmy shopping carts appeared. "I killed my parents!" said Connie.

"You killed your parents!" he answered, which seemed the only appropriate response to such a statement. He could hear the little old lady's cart quiver in shock. OK: Connie *was* crazy. Of course. Whenever a strange woman seemed the least bit interested in him, it turned out to be in a Rescue-Me-from-the-Space-Aliens way. The bottle of grape-flavored Chloraseptic he held in his hand—for children, she was so childlike—would not cure her problem, no matter how zealously she operated the spray pump. Haunting pharmacies, claiming to be a parricide. Very classy, to go crazy in the way of the Greek myths. Very sensible, to go crazy near a stock of antipsychotics. We will of course be delighted to meet your future pharmaceutical needs.

She raised her eyebrows and nodded. Was that *delight* on her face?

No, not quite. Babe looked closer and saw how thin the line between shock and cheerfulness was on this particular face, and how troubling the similarity had been for her, all her life.

She left with a tin of Sucrets. "I like the box," she said. "Do they work?"

When he'd returned to the pharmacy counter, the little old lady, who'd been browsing the Seasonal Items aisle, came wobbling up. The shopping cart had a long pole with a red plastic pennant at the top, to discourage theft. The woman herself had a large red mole on her forehead, an eyebrow-pencil beauty mark on her cheek, and an Eastern European accent. She rested her breasts on the consultation counter. This wasn't unusual. The counter had supported plenty of geriatric, confidential breasts. She beckoned at him though he was already very close to her and said in the voice of a spy, "She did, you know."

"Did what?" asked Babe.

"She did kill her muzzer and fazzer. I have zeen on the—" the woman drew a square with her index fingers. "Channel 5. She goes to jail, and now she leaves, maybe zix months ago."

"No," said Babe.

"Yez," said the woman. "When she is a girl, she haz kill her muzzer and fazzer. Now she haz sore t'roat." The woman shrugged. *Make your own conclusions.*

CONNIE MURDER. MURDER PAROLE. *Teenager parole. Doctor murder. Mother murder. Mother father murder.* Everything he stuck in the search box of the city paper's website sounded like the name of a bad rock band and brought up nothing.

Constance murder.

Her name was Constance Lafferty, and she had beaten both parents to death on October 11, 1982, first her mother, and then her father. First with a candlestick, then with a hammer. A two-blunt-object job. Her mother had been dead drunk, according to the autopsy; the father had been slightly tipsy, if tipsy could be applied to the dead, if that wasn't too trivial a word. The daughter, the murderer, the blond woman who that day had given him four flowers, Connie, may or may not have had a boyfriend, a drug problem, a friend in the world. The parents were loving or absentee. She'd been on the honor roll.

No mystery to who, how, when, where. Lots to why. She confessed, she pled guilty, she went to prison. She'd found God, of course. God seemed to spend a lot of time in the federal prison system. No one ever found God at Disney World.

The picture he instantly recognized: it had been famous and shocking, once upon a time. Even on a computer monitor, the gray blood looked like wet newsprint. He couldn't get the dead parents and the live girl on-screen at the same time, and wobbled them back and forth. Her hair was darker and longer, all one length.

Who took that photo? Who covered the bodies? Who called the police?

Shouldn't somebody do something?

Crime photos are usually badly composed. You get a first impression when you look—in this case, the visible ear, the wisp of hair from beneath the sheet of the female victim (the mother, *her* mother), the soft features of the teenage girl—but you'll guess wrong. The bodies look as though they were dropped from a height onto the floor, though they only fell from ordinary human height. The daughter looks as though she's just walked in the room.

He saved the file and ordered a copy from the newspaper's archives.

The newspaper stories about Samantha's death—*my* death, Babe thought, not as in *when I died* but *the death that belongs to me*—were not accessible online. In this way Babe was like a teenager. He had come to believe that a thing that was not mentioned on the Internet might never have happened at all. A search for "Samantha Kent" turned up plenty, an African American studies professor, a missing go-go dancer, a talented sixteen-year-old long distance runner in Overland Park, Kansas, a fictional character in an interactive porn story, any number of people who weren't her. He was glad for that. There was a theory in physics that, as he understood it, posited that there were endless universes with endless possibilities. You need never worry about what your life would have been like if you hadn't, say, met a chubby brunette woman who had a birthmark shaped like a blueberry muffin on her left hip, who chewed bubble gum way past bubble-gum-chewing age, who worked in a stationery store and was absent-minded enough to look left and then right but fail to look left again before crossing a street, who was hit by a midsized car, possibly according to an eyewitness a blue sedan, a woman who died instantly. In some other universe, right now, she existed but you didn't, or she existed but the birthmark didn't, or no one had invented bubble gum. In some other universe, the two of you had never met. When he idly Googled her name, which he didn't do often, he liked to pretend that all of those other people with her very common name represented the dozens of universes where she was still alive and well and had never met him, and good for her, he thought, good for her.

Babe kept the flowers, Gerber daisies according to Hilary the pharmacy assistant, on the front counter. He tried to keep them going. He changed their water daily, and when they dropped their petals to the counter, one by one, it seemed like every bad movie montage he'd ever seen that described the passage of time and the death of something ineffable.

She came back the next week, in black Mary Tyler Moore stirrup pants, and asked for antacid advice.

"I'm sorry," he said. He meant about the heartburn. She nodded as though receiving sympathy for a great deal more. She stood wide legged at the counter, bent at the waist. She shifted her hips as though she were about to swing her foot onto the counter like a limbering dancer.

"Your wife's dead," she said. She'd been doing some research of her own.

"Yes."

"*I'm* sorry."

"Why?" he said. An inappropriate joke, a tic, really, from the days back about six months after Samantha's death when he mistakenly believed his sense of humor had returned, bounced into his mouth. "Did *you* kill her?"

Connie nodded in a forward direction. "Nope," she said, "nope, that one I woulda remembered." Then she laughed her hooting laugh.

The next week it was acne medication.

Then she had athlete's foot, then rosacea, then psoriasis.

That was the summer of *there had to be a reason*. Everything was innocent, of course! She was married! He was a decent guy! There had to be a reason she killed her parents, a reason she believed in God, a reason she sought him out. Neither of them understood. They met only at the pharmacy counter in the middle of the day, when business was slow, beneath the red letters that said CONSULT. If he were in the middle of a consultation, she browsed in the makeup section. There was a brand of very cheap, highly glittered preteen cosmetics that she loved: she would stripe the back of her hand with the testers (blue, pink, lilac, the Flag of Connie) and wait for him to finish. He spoke to her with paternal caution, the kind of wary, passionate tenderness he imagined people had for their teenage children. Pride, worry, rigor, joy. She depended on him in her stunted way. They had jolly, pointless conversations.

"Hey Babe!" Connie would holler as she passed through the automatic doors near the front of the store. "How's the pill and potion business?"

She made the teenagers who stumbled through the store after school laugh, but they made her laugh, too. She couldn't get over the pants! The underwear purposely pulled up to the waist with the pants belted around the hips!

"I just want to—" She clenched her hands and mimed yanking someone else's pants down. "You know? I want to *pants* them." She hooted. "Seriously, that's what would have happened in my high school!"

A kid passed with the rolling walk that Babe attributed to overloose pants, overweight shoes, possibly shoplifted items stowed in underwear. His skin looked maloxygenated. His brown eyes looked trapped and nervous. "Can I ask you a question?" Connie asked. "I just have a question."

Babe could almost feel the pharmacy counter rise up around him. Then he realized he was dipping below the counter in embarrassment and fear.

"Why the pants?" Connie asked the kid. "I mean, come on! You can hardly walk in them."

"Oh God," said Babe. But the kid smiled, the kid displayed the great grillwork of his braces, which were paved with McDonald's French fries. He gave a hitching shrug. "They're *cool*," he said.

"Oh!" said Connie. "Yeah? What's cool about them?" She really wanted to know. She examined the drape of the leg.

"Hey man," said the kid. "They're just cool. Weren't you ever young?"

"Me?" asked Connie. She scratched her chin and winked sideways at Babe. "Not sure, *man*. I'll definitely get back to you on that one."

OF COURSE THERE were theories.

She was abused by her mother, the doctor. She was abused by her father, the head of a small Catholic charity. She was abused by her parish priest. She'd had a head injury and was never the same after that. She did drugs and had a psychotic break. She had seizures. She hallucinated. She snapped.

She was abused by her mother the doctor under the guise of medicine, in the medical office that was, like the kitchen, an addition off the back of the house: she was abused on an examination table, she was abused with medical equipment, she was made sick with medication so that her mother could get the sympathy of a sickly child, she was a sickly child. She was abused by her father, the head of a small Catholic charity, and when she told her doctor mother about it, her doctor mother refused to believe it, her doctor mother slapped her. She was on drugs. She was covering up for someone else.

She killed them for no reason.

She confessed to the murders. That was a fact. She said the same thing to everyone, the lawyer paid for by her grandparents (both sets), the police, the social workers, the psychiatrists: "There's nothing I can say."

HIS FIRST MURDERESS. His first Christian, for that matter, at least his first Born Again. Did that explain the daffy expression on her face? Maybe it was just all the corrections he'd made to his initial impression of her, a cheerful dork in a snowflake-patterned sweater. (Even that sweater seemed tragic to him now, fifteen years out of date. She clung to the knitwear of her youth.) Then an insane woman. Now a murderer, but what kind? She killed people. She believed in God. Babe didn't know which was more unfathomable. Connie of the bad sweaters, Connie of the flowers.

Connie, why did you do it?

The teenagers who hung around the store became human to him, because of Connie. She was fascinated by the boys and disdainful of the girls, like any girl who for whatever reason hadn't attended her high school prom. "They're so big and quiet!" she said of those boys. In their raised sweatshirt hoods, they were a race of muffled men, leaning hood to hood to communicate, a branch of the military service in some mumbling country, on leave here on the shores of the strip mall. They examined batteries as though they were foreign trinkets, bags of Fritos like they were the local delicacy: delicious, possibly lethal, worth the risk. They never raised their voices, except, occasionally, to laugh. One had the laugh of a movie genie. The sound could shake you apart.

Sometimes the European little old lady would ask for pharmaceutical advice when Connie was there. "Excuse me, darling," she would say, putting her hand on Connie's elbow. "Excuse me, sweetheart." She'd wedge herself in at the consult counter, using her breasts as a lever, and Connie would try to step away, but the little old lady wouldn't let her. She'd hook her arm in Connie's. "No, darling, sweetheart, a moment, I wouldn't bodder you but. Excuse me sir! I am wondering perhaps vhere is somessing for ear vax." Who knew where she was from? Maybe there had been a moment in her life when she wished she had the nerve to swing a candlestick.

"Listen," Babe told Connie later, in the hosiery aisle. "You don't have varicose veins."

"I don't? Cool!"

"No, listen. You don't have acne. You don't have psoriasis. You don't have athlete's foot. What do you want?"

"I'm just worried about you," she said. "That's all. I worry."

"I'm all right," he answered, insulted, ecstatic.

She was so *innocent*. Not technically. She'd killed her parents, no suggestion of accomplice or mitigating circumstances. As a person, though, innocent and pure of motive. She brought flowers to everyone who treated her with kindness, even the guy at the McDonald's. Imagine the guy at McDonald's, a skinny Haitian teenager with walleyes and a shy smile, receiving a bouquet of flowers! She thanked people for the smallest favor. She seemed frozen at fifteen, as though she were the one who was killed, as though Babe were being haunted by the memory of a long-ago lost child.

He tried to imagine the night of the murders and failed every time.

You'd have to be that innocent, Babe thought, to kill your own parents. How could a girl with a guilty conscience manage it!

DID YOU LOVE *your parents?*

Yes.

Did you love your mother?

Yes, I said so, I just said so.

But particularly your mother?

I loved both my parents the same.

But you killed them?

Yes.

Why?

[Silence.]

There has to be a reason.

I didn't mean to.

Constance. Connie. The murder scene—

I was there. You don't have to tell me.

Do you consider yourself a good person?

I don't consider myself anything.

Do you consider—

I don't consider myself anything. There's nothing wrong with me.

SHE WOULD HAVE told him, as best she could, though no one would understand. She didn't understand, either. If you'd asked her on October 10, 1982, if she ever could have killed anyone, she would have said no, of course not, and she would have believed it. But she was rageful. No one knew that but her parents, and even they didn't know the depths. She was fifteen and furious. At night she whipped her thoughts around until she felt she could smash through the window and fly through the streets of the town, bursting into bedrooms. People were asleep like storybook children. They never woke up or looked at her while she pummeled them to death. Usually she dreamt of one bedroom visit a night, but sometimes she flew to two or three. She flew wrapped in garbage bags because of blood splatters, in bathing caps to avoid shedding hairs, in wigs so as not to be recognized. She flew concocting alibis. Usually she was righteous, but sometimes she killed people for bullying reasons, the girls who didn't know how to dress, the boys with bad skin who made her nervous.

She understood this as fantasy. She'd always gone to sleep with dreams of flight, since she was a little girl. They were the way you calmed yourself.

What happened with her parents had nothing to do with that.

BABE WAS CONSULTING a woman who had perioral dermatitis but thought it was globally antisocial to take antibiotics. At the end of aisle six (First Aid, Cough & Cold, Pain Relievers) two teenage boys walked up to Connie.

"Can I ask you a question?" said one of the boys, the boy Connie had asked about the coolness of his pants. Only fair: of course he could.

"Sure," said Connie.

"My friend says you killed someone."

"Shut up!" said the other boy.

"Shut up!" answered the first. "No, seriously. We heard you killed someone."

Connie held still. She bit the side of her thumb. "Yeah," she said at last. "I did."

The first boy shoved both hands deep in his pants pockets: the force of the admission seemed to knock him at an angle. "Get out!" he said. "Really?"

"Yeah," she said, casually, but now she wouldn't look them in the eyes.

"Like, how?" said the second boy. He grabbed at her elbow to get her attention. "Like, with a gun?" He raised his hand to hold an imaginary gun parallel to the ground and made a consonant-rich gunfire noise, a single shot.

"Who'd you kill?"

"Or didja go psycho on them with a knife? Ee-ee-ee-ee!"

"No seriously, who'd'ja kill?"

"Or like run them over!"

"Leave her alone!" said the little old lady, who'd come to the rescue, but from a distance. She was afraid of the boys. She aimed her tiny shopping cart at them as though prepared to use it as a weapon.

"It's all right," said Connie, exhausted.

"Go away," the little old lady commanded, and the boys were about to, until Connie said, "My parents."

"Your parents?"

"Fu-*huck*."

They took a step back to look at her better.

"Darling, you don't have to tell them anything."

"She *is* a psycho," said the second boy.

"She's a fucking psycho!"

"Fuck!"

Did Connie think they'd like her, if she told them, or did she just want to testify? The boys looked at her as though—well, as though she'd just announced she'd murdered her parents. One of the boys laughed a sudden run of nervous silver laughter: a giggle really. He put his hand to his mouth. "C'mon," he finally said to his friend. "Let's book."

But they didn't turn and leave. Instead, they walked past Connie as though she'd become invisible. So invisible, in fact, that one knocked into her on either side, a girl in their way for whom there was no reason to expend any energy whatsoever, not even to step around her.

"Pharmaciss!" called the old woman. She hailed Babe like a cab. "Pharmaciss!"

Connie leaned on the end-aisle display of on-sale contact lens solution. The old lady stroked her arm. "Tugs," she said. "Common tugs, sweetheart."

"I know," said defeated Connie. The circles beneath her eyes looked like tarnished silver.

"You're a goot girl," the woman told her.

"That's not true. You know, I did it."

"Not you, sweetheart."

"*Me.* I killed my parents."

"So long ago," said the little old lady. She looked as though she were about to crawl into Connie's lap. "Not you. Someone else, so long ago. You know? Ziss is life. Pharmaciss," she said to Babe. "Cheer up the girl."

"What a command!"

"Yes, please," said Connie, and then she added, "pharmaciss."

"OK," he said.

"Good boy," said the little old lady.

HE THOUGHT OF dark-haired breasty serious Samantha, his kind, late wife. He heard her make fun of him: *you have a crush on a Christian murderess.*

"Go away," he thought, for the first time.

A person who can do that is not a person. It's not a crime of passion, a person who can do that feels nothing, least of all passion. Think about her grandparents: they lost their children, and even so they tried to save their grandchild. Can you imagine what that feels like?

No.

*She's not more saintly for having been so bad before, you know.
Real saints start out saintly and stick with the program.*

Oh, Samantha, let me have this. Surely this is the exception
to every single rule. She wants to save me. I promise I won't let
her do it, but let her try. Let her do her best.

—

Sam—
Promise.
Promise.

HE TOOK HER to the spinning restaurant on top of the Holiday
Inn, another childish pleasure for childish Connie, the defini-
tion of a place that would cheer you up. The place revolved once
an hour. Every table was its own minute hand: you could keep
time by yourself, quarter past, half past, quarter of. The diners
couldn't tell they were turning, they only knew that the scenery
changed. In his pre-Samantha youth, Babe had waited tables
there, a disaster considering his sense of direction. Eventually
he took to wearing a compass around his neck, though how did
that help? A four top would be pointing north for the appetiz-
ers, south-by-southwest for the entrées. He took Connie there
for the same reason doctors prescribed Ritalin, a CNS stimu-
lant, to hyperactive patients to calm them down. He figured
they'd be less disoriented there. Sometimes they'd look out and
see the downtown. Sometimes the highway. Somewhere there
was a universe where her parents were alive.

He thought the scenery, north, northeast, east, southeast, all
the clockwise way around, would distract them. Where's the
mall? Where's my house? Neither of them knew where the
other lived. Mightn't this be a way to explain your life in a place,
up above and rotating. There's where I was born, there's where
I get my car fixed, there's where I met my wife, there's my opti-
cians, there's where I cried, they tore down my parents' house,

there's Mal's Donuts, there's where you and I met, there's where I lost my wife, you can't really see it, but right there, you see, left of the green neon, right of City Hall.

But they scarcely looked out of the window, as though the universe were rotating around them, instead of them rotating inside of the universe, and to acknowledge this would be to interfere with the most basic rules of physics. Gravity might let up. The earth might go squealing through space like a let-go balloon.

"I didn't even know a place like this existed!"

"They used to be the rage. Can I take your coat?"

"I think I'll keep it, if you don't mind. I'm really cold-blooded. Um, obviously. Not really, bad joke. It reminds me a little of a place I used to eat with my parents. Didn't spin though."

"So it reminded you—"

"I don't know. I'm making conversation. I'm nervous. I'm depressed. Those boys, they just got me thinking. My *parents*—"

"You miss them."

"I do. Yes. I mean it's stupid, not stupid—I do, my father particularly, but both of them. And at the same time, I know they're with me, looking over me."

"Sure. No, I understand."

"Oh, I'm glad. I'm glad 'cause most people don't. I don't feel *sorry* for myself 'cause I'm an *orphan*, ha ha *ha*. But. Gosh. I'm glad you understand. I'm really, really glad you understand. Is that the courthouse over there?"

"I think so. Yeah. Connie, can I ask you something?"

". . . Yeah. Of course. What? Go ahead."

"Why'd you do it?"

"Oh God."

"I'm sorry—"

"No, it's all right. I just—I never answered this before. Not even Jewels, and he's my shrink. *Was* my shrink."

"You don't have—"

"I was mad."

"What?"

"I was mad."

"What do you mean, crazy mad?"

"No. *Mad* mad. Like angry, ticked off. I had a date, for the first time in my life, and I didn't tell my mother because I was afraid she wouldn't let me go, so I said I was going to see a movie with friends and she still said I couldn't go. If my mother said no, it was no."

"You killed your mother because she wouldn't let you go to a movie?"

"You're not listening, Babe. Because I was mad. That's all I can say. I was angry and I picked up the candlestick and I hit her twice, and I got angrier and angrier. It had nothing to do with my mother. Of course she was yelling, of course she was fighting back, but it was like I was, oh, what's the word, the girl in that movie, *possessed*. The longer it went on the angrier I got. I was angry that I was angry, I was angry that I was doing this, and then my mother wasn't my mother anymore. And then she was dead."

". . . Your father—?"

"He loved her. He loved me. How could . . ."

"Ah, ah. Okay. A mercy killing."

"Don't be mean! I sound horrible and I know it. This is why I've never said. It's horrible, it's evil, and there's never been anything I can say. It's *indefensible*, but people still want me to explain. All I can say is, that lady was right. Completely right. It's like a different person killed her parents and a different person went to jail. I have to believe that. If I think, right, Constance, you killed your parents, now how are you going to spend your day? I couldn't function. I'm telling you the truth. I killed my parents because I was angry. It was like I had food poisoning—that's the best way I can put it, I don't want to say I was diseased or crazy. But the strangest thing is, I've never been angry again. I used it up."

42

"You were never angry in prison?"

"No."

"With Jewels, then."

"No."

"I've heard you!"

"Lonely. Sad. Um, disappointed. But that, that's over for me now. You know me! How could I hurt anyone? I used it up. We all get a certain amount of anger, and in some of us it just surges one day and then, for the rest of your life, the fuses are blown. Then God steps in. Look. Hey, look at that."

"Where? I don't see where—the mall?"

"The moon, dummy. Look at the moon."

Connie of the bad sweaters. Connie of the flowers. A violent death is like no other, said the self-help books, you need to seek people out, you need to go to support groups and talk to people who understand. Your wife was murdered, people told him, and his brain didn't disagree but his heart did: the worst thing of all is that he understood the driver of the car. It was an accident. You kill someone and you panic. A family man, too, probably, with a wife and maybe two kids who never knew, a guy who realized he had killed someone, he read the papers, but that was his punishment, to live with it forever in secret.

Connie of the bad makeup. Connie of the brown eyes. Connie who killed her parents, and didn't that make more sense, for him to seek out Connie, didn't those pieces fit together better than two people filled with grief and anger, *no my loss is worse, no mine is*. There was Connie, who had a space in her life shaped just right for his grief and anger.

To never be angry again! To use it all up in one terrific surge. What a relief that might be, and what a disappointment. To think, *That was another person, not me.*

If he could have seen the future: the Dutchman's real sorrow, the coverage in the newspaper, all of Connie's eccentricities, of course, her blankness, her sickening love of animals, her failure to love particular people, she only loved mankind, wasn't it interesting, said the papers, what a saint she was?, and he was happier than he'd ever been, and more miserable, too, and he was sure it wasn't worth it—if he'd known he would have stopped himself. No question whatsoever. *I was a different person then too,* he thought, *and what was wrong with the person I was?* He was a coward. He only thought he could see the future. He had a brilliant, impractical imagination.

They were leaving the revolving restaurant. He'd already stepped off next to the stationary maître-d' stand. She stood straight up on the revolving platform in her puffy pink jacket with the white-fur-trimmed hood. "Maybe I'll just stay!" she said. You couldn't see her move, you could just tell, second to second, that she *had* moved. "Maybe I'll just ride the restaurant all night! Here I go! Good-bye!"

"Good-bye!"

"Good-bye! See you around!"

"Good-bye! Come back soon!"

"I will! Good-bye!"

She had her hood up: this trip would take her to the Arctic. She had her coat open, for the breeze off the coast. She was a brave, curious traveler. *You never let me do anything,* she told her mother, and shortly thereafter she learned what it really meant, never to do anything. The hood had fallen over her eyes. The maître d' was frowning, but they were like the teenagers in the store: they didn't hate him, they just didn't care. She was two feet away from him now.

"Here I go!"

"Send me a postcard!"

"I will! Good-bye!"

He reached out and grabbed her waving hand.

"Marry me," he said.

The Safe Man

THE HOUSE ON SHELL ISLAND was as its owner had described it over the telephone, large and white with black shutters and wide porches running the length of both the first and second floor. The house had two dormer windows that creased the roofline like eyebrows raised in surprise or maybe anger. The columns that sustained the double layer of porches looked like teeth below those eyes. Brian Holloway parked his van on the left side of the turnaround circle and got out without any of the tools he would need. It was his routine to meet the client first, survey the job and provide an estimate, then come back to the van for the appropriate equipment if he secured the job.

It took two rings of the bell and a hard rap from the brass lion's-head knocker before anyone answered the door. It was a man in blue jeans and a sweatshirt. He was barefoot. He was clean shaven and Brian guessed he was of similar age to himself. Late thirties, maybe a little older. The man had a scowl on his face.

"Didn't you see the sign?" he asked.

"The sign?"

The man pointed to a small brass plaque posted beneath the mailbox to the left of the door. It said, ALL SERVICE AT SIDE DOOR. There was an arrow pointing to the right.

"Uh, no, sorry, I didn't."

"I will see you over there. And could you move your truck to the driveway on the side as well?"

It was a question but it wasn't spoken as a question.

"Sure."

The man abruptly closed the door. Brian walked back to his van, trying to hold back his anger. He reminded himself it was a job and, yes, after all, he was in the service industry. He moved the van to the driveway that went down the side of the house and widened in front of a three-car garage. He found the service door and headed toward it. As he walked he looked across the expansive backyard to the view of the open bay.

The same man from the front door opened the service door before he got there.

"Are you Mr. Robinette?" Brian asked, though he recognized him from photos on the backs of his books.

"Yes, that is right. You are the safe man, I assume?"

"Yes, sir."

Brian could see Robinette eying his van. He realized he had forgotten to attach the magnetic signs to the side panels. He worked out of his house—his garage, actually—and neighbors complained about having a commercial van parked there all the time. So he painted the van a pleasing pale blue and went with magnetic signage. The problem was he often forgot to put the signs on when he went out on a call.

"Don't you have any tools?" Robinette asked.

"I like to look at the job first, then figure out what I need," Brian replied.

"Follow me then."

Robinette led him down a back hallway that led to a kitchen that looked as though it had been designed to serve a restaurant or maybe Noah's Ark. He counted two of everything; ovens, stoves, sinks, even dishwashers. They then moved through a vast living room with three separate seating areas and a massive fireplace. Finally, they came to a library, a room smaller than the living room but not by much. Three of its walls were lined floor to ceiling with shelves. The books were bound in leather and the room smelled musty. There were none of the bright colors Brian saw on book jackets whenever he went into a bookstore. He didn't see any of Robinette's books on the shelves.

In the center of one end of the room was a large mahogany desk with a computer screen on it. There was a stack of white paper with a bust of Sherlock Holmes as a paperweight. In front of the desk was a Persian rug of primarily maroon and ocher colors.

Without a word Robinette used his foot to flip up the corner of the rug. He then kicked the fold back until the rug had been moved aside to reveal a small rectangular door set in the wood flooring. Brian estimated that it was two feet by one-and-a-half feet in size. It was old plywood and there was a finger hole for pulling it up and open. There were no hinges that Brian could see. Robinette reached down and pulled the door up. He then used both hands to lift the plywood out of the inset in the floor.

The opening revealed another door a few inches below—the black steel facing of a safe with dusty gold filigree at the edges, a brass combination dial, and a hammered steel handle. Robi-nette crouched next to the opening and reached down and gave the steel handle a solid tug, as if to show Brian it was locked.

"This is it," he said. "Can you open it?"

Brian crouched down across the opening from Robinette and looked at the box. He could see writing in gold script beneath the combo dial. He braced his hands on the floor and leaned down closer to read it. It looked like it said "Le Seuil" but he wasn't sure. What he was sure of was that he didn't recognize the safe or its manufacturer, let alone know how to pronounce its name. He gave the dial a turn just to see whether it was frozen, and it turned smoothly. That wasn't the problem. He straightened up until he was kneeling on the floor next to the opening.

"I don't recognize the make offhand," Brian said. "In a per-fect world I'd have a design schematic. It always helps to know what you're getting into. But don't worry. I can open it. I can open anything."

"How much will it cost?"

"Unless I find it in one of my books it's probably going to be a double drill. I charge one-fifty for the first and a hundred for the second."

"Jesus. You're killing me."

"I might get lucky with the first drill. You never know."

"Just do it. I want that thing opened. Too many people have seen it."

Brian wasn't sure what he meant by that.

"Do you have any idea how old this thing is?" he asked.

"The house was built in '29. I assume that it came with it."

Brian nodded.

"You said on the phone you just bought this place?"

"That's right."

"The former owner didn't give you the combo?"

"Do you think you'd be here if he did?"

Brian didn't answer. He was embarrassed by his stupid question.

Robinette continued as if he had not asked a question. "It was an estate sale. The old man who lived here died and he took the combination with him. Nobody even knew there was a safe until I had the floors redone before moving in. Now all the painters, the electricians, everybody who was working on this place to get it ready knows I have a safe in here. You ever read *In Cold Blood*?"

"I think I saw the movie. That's the one with Robert Blake playing a killer before he supposedly became a real killer, right?"

"That's right. It's the one where they kill a whole family to get to the fortune in the safe. Only there isn't any fortune. Every one of those workers who was in here went out and told who knows who about the safe I've got in here. I started having dreams. Me with a gun to my head, being told to open up a safe I don't know how to open. I know these guys. I write about them. I know what they're capable of. I've got a daughter. I want that safe open. I don't even want a safe. I don't have anything to put in it."

Brian had never read one of Paul Robinette's novels, but he knew before he ever saw the house that he was successful. He'd seen stories about him in the local papers and national magazines. He'd seen a couple of the bad movies based on the books. Robinette wrote crime novels that were bestsellers, though Brian didn't think there had been a new book in the stores in a long while. Brian was willing to accept him as an amateur expert on the criminal mind. But he didn't think that qualified Robinette as an expert on the character of painters and electricians and floor refinishers.

"Well, Mr. Robinette, whatever the reason, I will get it open for you."

"Good. Then after you get it open, can you get it out of here?"

"The whole safe?"

"That's what we're talking about, isn't it?"

Brian looked down at the edges of the safe. The steel framing went under the flooring. He was pretty sure the houses out on the island were built on fill—the coral and shells dredged up to dig the barge channel leading to the phosphate plant.

"You've got no basement here, right?" he said. "No way under the house?"

"No, no way."

"Then it looks like I'd have to tear up the floor. It goes over the lip of the box. This wood is so old you'd never match it. But I guess you could keep it covered with the rug."

"No, I don't want to tear up the floor. I've spent enough on the floor. What about the door? Can you just take it off? I could leave it with just the plywood on top, cover it back up with the rug."

"Once I get it open I can take it off if you want. But why? You might as well just leave it unlocked."

"Three words: *In Cold Blood.* Things could go wrong. I want the door taken off. Go get your tools."

"Yes, *sir.*"

Brian started out of the room.

"Excuse me. Are you being sarcastic?" Robinette asked.

Brian stopped and looked at him.

"Uh, no sir. I'm just going to get my tools. By the way, it's going to get really loud in here when I start drilling and hammering. It might last a while, too—depending on the thickness of the front plate."

"Beautiful. I'll work in the upstairs study."

In the truck Brian looked through all his manuals and catalogs for a listing on Le Seuil or anything close to it. He found nothing. He called Barney Feldstein, who worked in San Francisco and was the most knowledgeable box man he knew, and even Barney had never heard of the maker. He put Brian on hold and checked the archives of the Box Man website. When he came back on he had nada.

What Brian wished was that he could talk to his old man about it. If anybody knew the safe maker it would be him. But that was impossible. It took a request from a lawyer to set up a phone call and a letter was useless. He needed advice right now. Resigned to the idea that he would go in blind, he gathered his tools and went back into the house. Robinette was still in the study. He was gathering some files from the desk to take with him upstairs.

"I couldn't find anything in the manuals and I called a guy who's been doing this longer than anybody I know in the business," Brian said. "He never heard of this safe company either. So I'll do my best, but it's looking like a double drill."

"Explain to me why you have to drill it twice," Robinette said impatiently.

"I've got to pop out what they call the free wheel. It's the locking gear. To do that I have to drill through the front plate so I can hit it with a spike. With most safes I know where the free wheel is. I have design manuals. I can look it up. I then come through with the drill, pop the gear, and open the safe. With this one, I'm going in blind. I'll take an educated guess but most likely I'll miss. I'll then snake it with a camera, find the right spot, and drill it again."

"You're sure you're not just taking advantage of me here?"

"What?"

"How do I know this isn't some kind of a scam designed to get the double dip? Or the double drill, as the case may be."

Brian was thinking that he ought to pick up his tools and just walk out, leaving the arrogant writer with his unopened safe. *You open it, asshole.* But he needed the money—Laura was planning to take the option of extending her maternity leave by four unpaid weeks. Besides, he was curious about the safe. He'd have something to post on the website after he got it open.

"Look," he said to Robinette. "If you want to go out to the truck and look in the manuals and try to find this, be my guest."

Robinette waved off the suggestion.

"No, never mind. Just get it done. Come to the bottom of the stairs and call for me when you are about to open it. I want to be here to see what that old fool Blankenship put in there."

"Arthur Blankenship? This was his house?"

"Yes, that's right. Did you do work for him?"

"No, I just knew of him. He owned the plant. His father dug the channel."

"Yes, that's right. The Blankenships made this city what it is today. I'll be upstairs."

He left the room, carrying his files with him. Brian shook his head. He hated working for assholes but it was part of the job. He turned and looked down at the safe. Every job was a little mystery. He wondered when was the last time the black steel door was opened. He wondered what Arthur Blankenship had put in there.

The first thing Brian did was strap on his kneepads. He then got down on the floor and contemplated the spacing between the combo dial and the handle. He took a piece of white chalk out of his toolbox and marked an X on the door about three inches to the right of the dial on a direct line to the handle. He knew he'd at least be close.

He set the tripod up over the X and hooked the lockdown chain to the safe's handle. He fitted a half-inch bit into the drill, mounted it on the tripod, and plugged it into a nearby wall socket. He was ready to go. From the toolbox he took out the gloves, safety glasses, and breathing mask and put them on. Lastly, he pressed foam plugs into his ears.

The first drill bit lasted twenty-five minutes before shattering. He guessed he had gone only a quarter inch in at that point. He let the drill cool for a few minutes while he drank a bottle of water he got out of the toolbox. He then locked a new bit into place.

The second bit completed the penetration. Brian pulled the drill out and checked the hole. It appeared that the front plate was three-quarters of an inch thick. He unlocked the tripod and moved it out of the way. The drill hole was still smoking and hot. Brian leaned down and blew away the steel shavings that had accumulated around it.

He got the camera scope out of the toolbox, plugged it in, and turned it on. He manipulated the snakelike camera extension, bending it into a curving L shape. He then fed it into the drill hole, keeping his eyes on the small black-and-white video display screen.

Almost immediately Brian saw movement inside the safe. A whitish gray blur moved across the three-inch-wide screen. He froze for a moment. *What was that?*

He moved the camera in an exaggerated sweep but saw nothing else. *Was it smoke? Did he really see something?* He wondered if the camera movement had simply blurred a reflection of the camera's light off of one of the gears or the underside of the faceplate.

The video display had no playback function. It did not record. Brian could not go back to check on the movement again. He felt a small tremble go up his spine and neck. He stared at the display for a few more moments and then started moving the scope again. He knew there couldn't have been movement. It had to have been a reflection or a concentration of smoke left over from the drill-through.

He saw no further movement in the display. But he did see that the safe's door had no back plate. This, he guessed, had been removed to make the door lighter, since it opened up rather than out. It probably saved fifteen or twenty pounds in the lifting.

Without a back plate Brian knew he could use the scope to see into the cavity of the safe and check its contents ahead of Robinette. He pulled the tool out of the drill hole, straightened it, and then snaked it back in. The camera's light reached all corners of the safe. Brian saw that it was empty, save for the layer of dust that had gathered over time at the bottom.

"No treasure today," Brian said to himself.

He once more removed the scope, reconfigured it, and then fed it back into the hole. By moving the scope he was able to view the internal workings of the safe's locking mechanism. He was surprised. He counted nine gears. Most safes had three or four at the most. Never nine. He knew that when he posted a report on this job on the site, other box men would not believe him. He decided he would go out to the truck and get his digital camera after he got the safe open. His plan would be to post a report on the site and then once the doubters posted their negatives he would upload a few photos—count 'em, nine gears—and put them all in their place.

He refocused on the work and quickly identified the free wheel—the gear that would release the locking mechanism when popped loose. He measured its location on the front plate. Once more he marked the surface with chalk and pulled the tripod into place.

The second drill-through cost him three bits, and by the end his drill smelled like it was burning up inside. This door—in box man's parlance—was a Dutch Treat, meaning the costs of broken or damaged equipment made the job a barely break-even proposition. Brian knew there was no way he'd be able to ding Robinette for the burned-out drill and the bits. He'd be lucky if the writer just paid him the extra hundred for the second drill-through.

He got the spike and the mallet out of the toolbox. He slid the spike into the second drill hole and felt it click against the free wheel. He raised the mallet to strike it but then stopped. He remembered that Robinette wanted to witness the opening of the safe.

Brian stood up. His shirt was sticking to his back and perspiration had popped across his forehead. He took off the safety glasses and the mask and blew out his breath. He walked out of the study and found the main hallway and the stairs. It was a grand staircase that swept upward in a curve.

"Mr. Robinette?" he called out.

"What?" came the reply.

"I'm ready to open the safe now."

Brian headed back to the study. He heard Robinette coming down the steps behind him. He got back into position next to the safe and picked up the mallet. Robinette came into the room.

"Is it open?"

"Not yet. I thought you wanted to be here. Do you want a set of earplugs? This metal on metal gets pretty loud."

"Can't be louder than that drill. I don't want earplugs."

"Suit yourself."

Brian started hammering the spike with the mallet, taking short strokes at first and then lengthening his arc when the gear refused to give. Each strike on the spike sent a sharp jolt through his body. Finally, after three full swings he felt the gear start to give. He went back to the shorter, more controlled swing and hit the spike five more times before the gear broke loose and he heard it clatter to the bottom of the safe.

"Sounds like it's empty," he said to Robinette.

"Just open it."

Brian reached down and gripped the handle and sharply pulled it down. It came easily. The safe was unlocked. He pulled it up and open, struggling with the weight of the steel door, and was immediately hit with the dead air that had been trapped inside for who knows how long. It was cold and heavy. It smelled like someone's chilled breath.

Robinette stepped forward and looked down. He saw that the safe was empty. Brian wasn't looking at the contents or lack thereof. He was looking at the workmanship of the gears and the slide bolts on the inside of the door. It was a beautiful job, and Brian found himself admiring the craftsmanship behind it.

"Empty," Robinette said. "Figures."

Brian reached down into the safe to retrieve the free-wheel gear from the bottom. He withdrew it quickly. It had felt strange. It had felt like he was reaching into a refrigerator for a can of beer.

"That thing must be insulated. It actually feels cold down there. Feel this."

He held up the gear. It was ice cold. But Robinette waved away the idea of touching it.

"So much for the treasure of Sierra Madre," he said. "All right. Get the door off it, and if you don't mind and it won't cost me too much more, do you have something you can clean that out with?"

"I have a shop vac in my truck. It's part of the service."

"Good. Do it. That dust is already affecting my sinuses. I can't breathe. I'll be upstairs when you're finished."

After Robinette was gone Brian went to work on the door's single hinge. In five minutes he lifted the heavy door out of its spot and carefully leaned it against one of the bookcases. He thought that it weighed more than forty pounds, even without a back plate.

For a moment he studied the workmanship of the locking mechanism again. The nine—now eight—gears were clustered in an interlocking pattern that had to have been of original design. He really thought it was beautiful, like a painting that should be on display. Almost like a living organism. He was hoping that Robinette would let him take the door since he no longer wanted it.

He gathered his tools and took them out to the truck. He came back in with his camera and the vacuum and as he reentered the study his eyes met those of a young girl who was standing by the opening in the floor. Brian had not replaced the plywood door yet.

"Careful, honey, you don't want to fall down in there. You might get hurt."

"Okay," she said.

She was dark haired and had a sweet face. Her eyes were dark and serious for such a young girl. She was wearing a dress that looked like it might be a little warm for the summer weather. Something about her was familiar to him—the eyes maybe. He couldn't place it. He knew there was no reason he would have ever seen her before.

"What's your name, sweetheart?"

"Lucy."

Brian's eyes lit in surprise.

"Really? That's my favorite name for a girl. My wife and I are about to have a baby and if it's a girl we're going to call her Lucy, just like you. Do you believe that? How old are you, sweetheart?"

She smiled, revealing she was missing a front tooth.

"Six."

"Wow, I would have guessed at least seven. You're a big girl."

"Thank you."

"Well, listen, I have to do some cleaning up in here and it might get dusty. You should run along now, okay?"

"Okay."

"See you, Lucy."

"Bye, bye, Box Man."

He watched her leave the room, wondering how she knew to call him that. Had her father used the term? He couldn't remember but assumed Robinette had told her who he was and what he was doing in the house. He listened to her footsteps padding away and then he went back to work, vacuuming out the safe and then taking photos of the safe's door, front and back.

After loading his equipment back into the truck he sat in the driver's seat while writing out a billing statement on his clipboard. He didn't charge Robinette anything other than the two-fifty already agreed to. He took the bill back inside with him and called up the stairs to Robinette.

Robinette studied the bill as they walked back to the study.

"I ought to retire and learn how to legally break into safes. What's this come out to, like eighty bucks an hour for using a drill?"

"Hardly. I'm lucky if I get one job a day. There aren't that many safes that need opening all the time. Most of my work is just plain old locksmithing."

"Well, I'd say you did pretty damn good today."

Robinette dropped the bill onto the desk in the study as if he were dismissing it.

Brian said, "I usually get paid upon completion of the job."

Robinette said, "Well, you didn't say that before."

"It is custom in the service industry. I didn't think I had to say it."

Brian could tell that Robinette didn't like that service thing thrown back at him.

"All right," he said curtly. "I'll go up and get you a check."

"Thank you."

Just before Robinette left the study Brian spoke up again.

"What do you want me to do with the door? It's heavy. I could take it and get rid of it, if you want."

"No, no," Robinette answered quickly. "If you don't mind, could you carry it out to the curb and sort of prop it up so it can be seen?"

Brian was confused.

"If you want me to, but why?"

"Three words: *In Cold Blood*. Trash pickup doesn't come until Thursday. That means it will be out there a couple days and maybe the word will get out that there is no longer a safe in here."

Brian nodded though he didn't really follow the logic.

"What's that old song say? *Paranoia will destroy ya.*"

Robinette turned fully around to confront him.

"Look, I don't expect you to understand me or my life. Do you have children?"

"Got one on the way. I'm not trying to—"

"I don't care what you are trying or not trying to say. Just do your job and don't worry about my paranoia. My paranoia got me this place and this life. I think in some ways it's like drilling through steel plates for a living, but I like it better. It's not as noisy. Now if you don't mind, I will go up and get you a check while you take that damn thing out to the curb. Okay?"

"You got it."

AT DINNER BRIAN told Laura all about his encounter with the arrogant writer and she told him that Robinette hadn't had a book out in at least three years. She suggested that maybe that had something to do with his paranoia and arrogance.

"I was reading in one of the baby books about how when they get constipated they can be really miserable," she said. "Maybe Robinette is creatively constipated."

Brian laughed but said some people are just mean, plain and simple. He thought about the girl he had briefly met in the house. Growing up in that place with that father, how would she turn out? How would she make it through? He wondered where the mother was.

When he got up to clear the plates Brian first touched his wife's swollen belly. They were less than a month away. He was excited and scared. Scared about the money, mostly.

"Hey, Robinette's daughter's name is Lucy," he called from the sink.

"Does that change your mind about it?"

"Not if it's a girl. I still like it. And that house? It was the Blankenship place."

"Really? What was it like inside? I've seen it from the outside."

"It was big. In the kitchen I saw two of everything, even dishwashers. I guess Arthur Blankenship's old man was the guy who put the safe in. When he built that place with money from the plant."

After dinner Brian spent time in the workshop in the garage and posted a report on the Le Seuil safe on the Box Man website. On the chat list he posted a note asking if anyone else out there had ever encountered such a safe and then signed off to go to bed.

Brian dreamt of darkness with swirling motion. Movements like wisps of smoke and then, for a just a moment, they came together to form a face he did not recognize as man or woman, adult or child. Then it was gone and he woke up.

"What is it?" his wife whispered.

"A dream. Just a bad dream."

"What was it about?"

Laura always asked about dreams. She thought they were important.

"I don't know. It was more like a feeling. A bad feeling."

He got up and walked the house, checking every lock. This was his routine but it wasn't comforting. He had the best locks money could buy but he knew how to pick and break every one of them. He knew there were other people with the same skills. He could never feel totally secure.

He sat in the kitchen in the dark and drank a beer. He wondered if he was paranoid like Robinette. He wondered if he would become like the writer once his own child was born. He started humming the Kinks song. *Paranoia will destroy ya. . . .*

He took the beer into the nursery and looked around in the dark. The room was completely outfitted and ready, save for the things that Laura wanted to be sex specific. They'd had a disagreement. Laura wanted to know early on whether it was a boy or girl coming. Brian wanted to be surprised. So she knew and he didn't. She had done a good job of keeping the secret.

Brian's secret was that he wanted a girl. He didn't want to find out beforehand because he feared if he learned he was the father of a boy he would lose his edge of excitement, that he might actually become depressed before the baby was even born. The reason he wanted a girl was that he considered his own life and thought that it was too easy for boys to get messed up, to go down the wrong path. With girls there seemed to be more two-way streets. They could turn around and come back if they wanted to. With boys it was all one-way streets. No turning back.

BRIAN PICKED UP a complete-change-of-hardware job the next day. It was an old Victorian in the Heights. Eight doors, including the garage. All Medeco locks and Baldwin brass. It was a six-hour job. That and the markup on the materials made it a good day. He came home relaxed, a big check in his wallet. He and Laura went out to eat at the Bonefish Grill. They figured that when the baby came they wouldn't be going anywhere for a while. Might as well do it when you can.

But that night wasn't perfect. The dream came back. He saw the face form in the darkness again. A face made of cigarette smoke. In the dream it smelled like his burning drill. He awoke and sat on the side of the bed. He felt Laura's hand caress his back. Being pregnant had made her a light sleeper.

"Was it the same dream?" she asked.

"Yeah."

"Do you remember any more of it?"

"Not really. It's just this bad feeling. It's dread. It's like I let something loose in the world. Like it was all my fault."

"What was? What did you do?"

"I don't know."

"You think it's about the baby?"

Brian laughed.

"No, it's not that."

He checked the house again. Making sure it was secure even though he did not feel secure. When he went back to the bedroom he started getting dressed.

"What are you doing?" Laura asked. "It's the middle of the night."

"I don't know. I'm going to take a drive."

"Are you all right?"

"I'm fine. I just want to take a drive, put the windows down."

"Be careful."

"I will be."

THE PHONE DIDN'T ring the next day. No jobs came in. Brian called a foundry in Michigan and ordered drill bits to replace those he'd broken on the Robinette job. He then spent the rest of the morning in the garage workshop, trying to research the Le Seuil safe. He wrote a letter to his father about it. He went on the computer and Googled the name Le Seuil but only came up with a book publisher in France using the name. He checked the Box Man website, but no one had responded to his earlier post other than to say they had never encountered a safe of that brand.

When it was lunchtime he opened the side door to go to the house. Two men were standing there. They wore suits and dour expressions. It had been twenty years since he'd had to deal with cops but he still knew the type.

"Officers, what can I do for you?"

"Actually, I'm Detective Stephens with the police department, and this is Agent Rowan with the FBI. Are you Brian Holloway?"

"Yes. Is it Laura? The baby? What happened?"

"Who is Laura?" Stephens asked.

"My wife. She's at work. She—"

"This is not about her. Can we come in?"

Brian stepped back. Despite the relief of knowing this was not about Laura, he felt the same sense of dread he had awoken from the dream with building in his chest.

"Then what is it?"

"Have a seat," Rowan said.

Brian sat on the stool next to the workbench.

The two lawmen remained standing, looking around the shop as they spoke. Moving about. The detective looked like he was deferring to the agent in this matter, whatever it was.

"This is how I would like to work this," Agent Rowan said. "We're going to ask you some questions here and the first time you lie to us we pack it in and put you in a cell to think about it. Fair enough?"

"This is a joke, right?"

"No joke."

"Then questions about what? Am I a suspect in something?"

"Not yet. We think you are just a witness. But like I said, the first time you lie to us you become a suspect and we treat you like one."

"Witness to what? What happened?"

"I said we are going to ask the questions. But let's start this thing off right by getting everything right. You are Brian Holloway, thirty-nine years old and you reside in the home that this garage is attached to. Do I have all of that right?"

"Yes."

"And your father has spent the last twenty-two years in an Illinois state correctional facility serving a life sentence without parole for the crime of murder."

Brian shook his head. The sins of the father always visited the son.

"This is about my father? I was nineteen when he went away. What's that got to—"

"He was a box man, too, wasn't he? Only he opened boxes for the Outfit in Chicago. He taught you everything you know, right?"

"Wrong."

"He killed a man who came home and caught him in the act, didn't he?"

"He didn't do it. The man he was doing the job for did it. He panicked."

"Oh, I guess that makes it okay."

"Look, what do you want? I haven't talked to my father in three years."

"Do your clients know that you're the son of Harry 'Houdini' Holloway?"

"Look, I run a clean, legal business. Why would I tell someone who my father is? Why would I have to? This isn't Chicago and I'm not my father."

"Where were you last night?" Stephens asked, suddenly joining in, changing the direction of things.

Brian started to think. Maybe the whole thing was choreographed. Maybe it wasn't about the old man. Maybe it was all misdirection and sudden change.

"Last night? I was here. I was home."

"From when till when?"

"Um, I got home around three yesterday and I did some work in here and then my wife and I went out for dinner and we got home about eight-thirty and that was it. We stayed home after that."

"Okay, eighty-thirty until when? When was the next time you left?"

Brian hesitated. He looked at their faces, wondering what had happened and how much they knew. Cops always had the advantage. He knew this. His father had always said that when it came to cops to lie was to die.

He shook his head.

"Until now. I haven't left yet."

Each of the men in front of him visibly stiffened and their faces took on a stony resolve.

"Turn around," Stephens said. "Assume the position. Your dad probably taught it to you, too."

Instead Brian raised his hands as if to stop their advance on him.

"Okay, look. I took a drive last night. I was gone less than a hour."

"When last night?"

"I never looked at the clock. I woke up, couldn't sleep, and took a drive. It was the middle of the night."

"And you never looked at the clock in the car, huh?"

"No, I took my truck. The clock in it doesn't work and I forgot to put on my watch."

"Where did you go on your drive?"

"I just drove around. All over the place. I even went over the bridge and cruised around the island."

Brian knew he had to give them that. He knew they had something. It must be the electronic toll pass on the truck's windshield. There would be a record of him crossing the bridge.

"Why the island? What did you do while you were there?"

Brian let out a deep breath. They were cornering him. He didn't understand this. The FBI doesn't come around for stealing trash. There was something else going on.

"All right, listen, I'll tell you everything. The other day I had a job out on the island. I opened an old safe for a guy and the client had me take the door off the box and carry it out to the curb for trash pickup. He said the pickup wasn't for a few days. So last night I went back by his place and I took the door. It would've been picked up this morning anyway. It's not stealing. He put it out for trash pickup. To him it was trash."

"And why did you take it?"

"Because until I was there I had never seen or heard of that safe or its maker and I wanted to study it. Maybe practice on it a bit. Besides, it's a museum piece. I didn't want it thrown away."

"Where is it?"

Brian pointed to an object beneath an old mover's blanket that was leaning against the opposite wall. Rowan walked over and lifted up the blanket for a look. He then dropped the cloth back down and looked at Brian.

"It was not a crime to take it," Brian said. "It was trash."

"So you say."

"Look, what is going on? Why are you here? Did Robinette say I stole his door? Is that what this is about? I know the guy's famous, but do they really send the FBI out on a call like that?"

"No, they don't."

"Then what is this?"

There was a pause and the lawmen looked at each other for a moment before Stephens spoke.

"We're not worried about you stealing Robinette's trash. We're wondering if you stole his daughter."

"What?"

"His daughter, Mr. Holloway. She's disappeared."

Brian thought of the little girl with dark, familiar eyes and the winter dress in the middle of the summer.

"He said I took his daughter?"

"It doesn't matter what he said. We have to check everybody out. You were the last person other than the family to be in that house. We understand that you and Mr. Robinette didn't get along so well. So we're starting with you."

Inside Brian's chest it felt as though his lungs were filling with wax. They were becoming heavy and hard. Again he thought of the little girl standing precariously at the edge of the safe. It was like she had been waiting there for him.

"Did you check the safe?" he suddenly asked.

"What do you mean?" Rowan asked.

"The safe in the office. When I was there she came in and was standing by the safe. Maybe she . . . I don't know, maybe after I left she went back to it. There's no door, but there was a piece of the flooring that covered it and that I put back in place."

Rowan glanced at the shape of the safe's door beneath the blanket. He then glanced at Stephens and another silent communication passed. Stephens turned and walked out of the garage.

Rowan looked back at Brian.

"The safe would be kind of small, wouldn't it?"

"The box was pretty deep. It went down at least a foot and a half."

"You said she came into the study?"

"I went out to my truck to get the vacuum and when I came back in she was just standing there."

"What did she say to you?"

Brian thought for a moment. He tried to remember all the details. He was filling with fear for the little girl.

"She just told me her name and I asked how old she was. I told her she looked older. She said her name was—"

"Why would you do that?"

"Do what?"

"Ask the girl how old she was."

Brian shrugged.

"I don't know. I guess because we're about to have a kid—my wife is eight months along—and, I don't know, I never really thought about the ages of children before. Now I do."

Rowan took a few moments to grind over the answer. Brian shifted his weight on the stool and started pumping his knee.

"Mr. Holloway, you seem agitated. Is something wrong?"

"Of course, there's something wrong. That girl is missing and I just have a bad feeling about it. Look, I had nothing to do with it. You're wasting your time. So do what you have to do with me and get it over with. I'll take a lie detector, if you want. You can go search my truck, too. Just get past me and go find her. Before it's too late."

Rowan seemed to be taken aback.

"What do you mean, before it's too late?"

"Isn't that how these things always end up?"

Before Rowan answered Stephens came in. He looked at his partner and then at Brian.

"Safe's empty."

"Mr. Holloway has volunteered to take a poly," Rowan said. "We can also take a look in the truck."

Stephens nodded.

"What about your home?" Rowan said. "Can we look around inside?"

Brian flashed on the bag of stale dope in the bedroom dresser. Laura quit smoking when they decided to get pregnant. Out of fairness he had stopped as well and the bag had sat in the drawer with his socks for a year.

"If you're just going to look around for the girl—closets and stuff—that's fine. But I don't want you going through drawers and stuff. Just make it quick. And don't mess things up or my wife will know."

"You know what I still don't understand?" Rowan said. "You're in there doing a job for Mr. Robinette and you go and ask his daughter how old she is. Why is that?"

"I don't know. I told you. I wondered how old she was. What else do you ask? She was a cute girl and I wondered how old she was. I'm sort of hoping that we have a girl and so . . . that's all."

"You said *was*," Stephens said.

"What?"

"You said she *was* a cute girl. Why'd you use the past tense? Is there something you want to tell us?"

Brian shook his head.

"Look, you've got this wrong and you're wasting time. Don't do this. You should be out there looking for—"

"Mr. Holloway," Rowan said, "I think we are going to take you up on your kind offer to take a look around here and maybe take you down to the station to set up a polygraph. Your offer is still good, right?"

THEY KEPT HIM in a small, windowless, and—it seemed to him—airless room. There was no clock on the wall and he lost track of time. He was thinking about the girl he had seen by the safe. Lucy. They came in from time to time to talk to him, to ask him the same questions over and over. But unsatisfied with his answers they would leave again. He could tell it was dark outside. He could sense it. It had been at least that long.

Finally, the door came open again and Stephens looked in.

"You have ten minutes," he said.

"What?"

Stephens backed away from the opening and then Laura appeared. Hesitantly, she stepped into the room and the door was closed behind her.

"Brian? What is going on? I came home and they were in our house. They had a search warrant. What did you do?"

He shook his head.

"I didn't do anything. Robinette's daughter is missing and they think I took her. All I did was talk to her."

"You talked to her? When?"

"That day. I told you at dinner."

"No, you told me she had the same name we picked. You didn't say you talked to her."

"She came in where I was working. I asked her what her name was and how old she was and that was it. I told her I had to get to work. She left and I never saw her again. That's it."

She slid into the seat across the table from him. She never took her eyes off of him.

"Did you tell them this?"

"Yes, I told them a hundred times. They're wasting their time with me when they should be out looking for her. If you ask me, they ought to be talking to Robinette instead of me."

Laura put her hand on her abdomen, as if calming the baby inside. She started rocking in her chair.

"Oh my God, I can't believe this," she said.

"Neither can I," Brian said.

He reached a hand across the table and she put her other hand on top of it.

"Have you asked for a lawyer?"

"No, I don't need a lawyer. I didn't do anything."

"Brian, just tell me. Did you take that girl anywhere?"

He pulled his hand back from her. His mouth came open and it was a moment before he found his voice.

"Laura?"

"Where did you go when you got up last night? You've been acting weird all week. What is going on with you?"

"They sent you in here, didn't they? They convinced you out there and sent you in here to—"

"No, Brian, you're wrong. You're being paranoid. I just want to know what is going—"

The door to the small room suddenly came open and Rowan stepped in.

"Mr. and Mrs. Holloway, you can go on home now."

"What do you mean?" Laura asked.

Brian started to push back his chair.

"We found her," the agent said in a matter-of-fact tone. "I guess we owe you an apology, Mr. Holloway. We didn't mean to give you such a hard time."

Brian stood up, a weird mixture of relief and anger overtaking him.

"Is she all right?" he asked.

"She's fine. Patrol just brought her into the station. Turns out she didn't like moving into the new house."

He forced a laugh.

"She thinks it's haunted. So she split. She walked all the way back to her old neighborhood and hid in her best friend's guesthouse."

Rowan stepped back from the doorway so they could leave. Brian walked slowly. He was having a hard time understanding what Rowan had just told them. He was having a hard time dealing with what his wife had just asked him as well.

"That girl found her way back to her old house?" he asked.

"That's right," Rowan said. "Step this way and I'll get you back your property. Then you'll be out of here."

Brian was led down the hallway and into a large squad room. There were several detectives working at desks and moving about. Across the room was another room separated by a glass wall. He could see a boardroom table in there. Sitting at the table were Detective Stephens and a girl. She was maybe thirteen years old. She looked like she was crying.

Rowan went to his desk and got a manila envelope out of a drawer. He handed it to Brian. It had his wallet and keys in it. His loose change. He didn't bother tearing it open. He just held it as he stared at the girl in the glass room. Rowan noticed his gaze and looked across the room as well.

"She's okay. She spent the night eating potato chips and drinking soda pop. I guess she had such a good time she still doesn't want to go back home."

"Does Robinette have another daughter?"

"No, just the one. Just Teresa who doesn't want to go home."

Brian thought of the dream, of the dread he felt when he woke up from it. The feeling that he had let something loose.

"Teresa?"

Rowan looked at him.

"That's right. I thought you said you—"

"Can I talk to her?"

"To the girl? No, I don't think that would be proper, Mr. Holloway. Your involvement with this thing is over as far as I'm concerned."

"I really need to speak to her."

"Well, that's not going to happen. Now it's time for you and your wife to head on home."

"What did she say about the house being haunted?"

"I'll walk you out."

He gripped Brian's upper arm and ushered him toward the squad room's exit. They went into another hallway and headed toward the door at the end. Rowan kept his hand on Brian's arm. Laura trailed behind them.

"You know who owned that house before Robinette?" Brian asked.

Rowan didn't answer.

"Arthur Blankenship."

"So?"

"So maybe she's got a point to why she's scared. He built the plant. They say the runoff from the phosphate is responsible for all the fish kills. It's like there's a big cloud of black water in the bay. Hell, he built this city. He knew where all the bodies were buried. Maybe—"

"It doesn't matter. What matters is that she's going home safe."

Brian jerked his arm free and stopped. He pointed back down the hallway in the direction they had come from.

"She's not the one I saw in the house. She isn't the girl I spoke to."

Rowan held up his palms in a hands-off manner. He smiled.

"Mr. Holloway, I've got a caseload like you wouldn't believe. This is one of the cases that ends happy, that ends good. Let's just let this go."

"And what if I can't?"

"Then you are on your own, sir. Let's go."

He grabbed Brian's arm again and led him to the door.

THEY WERE QUIET at first on the ride home. Laura drove. Brian thought about what he had seen in the Robinette house. They were almost home before Laura spoke for the first time.

"Brian, what's going on? What were you talking about back there?"

"I don't know. I don't want to talk about it."

"Why?"

"Because I don't really feel like talking to you right now."

"Brian, I'm sorry. They told me you did something to her. They said they had evidence and that you had admitted asking her inappropriate questions. They said it had something to do with our baby. The pressure you are under and how we haven't had sex. They said they had seen it before."

Brian shook his head.

"You told them about our sex?"

"They asked a lot of questions. I felt I had to."

"And you believed everything they said. That I admitted asking inappropriate questions. That I did something to her."

"I didn't want to."

"I was talking to a six-year-old, not a thirteen-year-old. I didn't ask anything wrong. I didn't *do* anything wrong."

"I know, baby. I'm sorry. But you were acting strange all week. And then when you went out last night . . . I just thought . . . I don't know what I thought. All I can say is that I'm sorry."

Brian looked over at his wife. In the darkness he could see that she was crying, doing nothing about the tears rolling down her cheeks. He didn't do anything about it either.

IN THE WORKSHOP Brian had a message waiting for him on his computer the next morning. It was from a box man in Montreal named Robert Pepin. Rather than publicly post the message on the website, Pepin answered Brian's posted inquiry with a direct and private e-mail. Though Pepin was obviously French and had some language difficulties, his message was clear.

> *Take cautions. I have heard story of the threshold safe. One box man saw his young brother who was killed. I have not seen for myself. Was it in the floor? This is past on stories. The box man he make mistake to open it.*

Brian stared at the message a long time, trying to decipher its meanings. He'd felt a coldness begin in his center. He knew it was the beginning of fear and the confirmation of something he had felt deep inside.

The message had Pepin's business number and address at the bottom. Brian picked up the workshop phone and punched in the long distance number. After three rings it was answered by a machine. The outgoing message was in French and Brian didn't understand a word of it. But then the speaker switched to English with a heavy French accent. He identified the line as belonging to Fochet Lock and Safe and asked the caller to leave a message. But then he gave another number in case of an emergency. Brian wrote it down, hung up, and then called the emergency number.

The second call was answered after four rings and Brian heard a drill wind down before a man spoke rapidly in French. It was obviously a cell phone and Brian had interrupted a job. He wondered how the phone had even been heard over the sound of the drill.

"I'm sorry," Brian said. "Do you speak English? Is Robert Pepin there?"

"This is Robert. Who is this, please?"

Brian identified himself and told Pepin he had received his message. He needed to ask him questions. Pepin tried to beg off, saying he was in the middle of drilling a safe and people were waiting for him to complete the job. Brian insisted and promised to be quick. Pepin relented and lowered his voice to a whisper when he spoke further.

"What did you mean by a threshold safe in your message?" Brian asked first.

"It is the safe you showed. Uh, it is Threshold, the name. Le Seuil."

He pronounced it like *Le Soy*. Brian tried to say it that way.

"Le Seuil means *threshold*?"

"The Threshold, yes. Like the doorway you have."

"I understand. And the story you heard—who told you?"

"Uh, the man who I bought from him my business. Fochet. He told me. He told me, 'If I get the job, *NO*, do not open.' And so I tell you."

"He told you he opened one?"

"A very long time ago, yes. He said big mistake opening that one, yes."

"Why?"

"Well, he is not saying everything. He is just warning against it, you know? He is saying bad things come out. Like a dream. I didn't ask. He sound, you know, a little crazy."

"Is he still around? Is he retired?"

Pepin chuckled.

"He is retired to the cemetery. Mr. Fochet was very old when I bought his business."

Frustration was welling up in Brian. Everything was like the smoke in his dreams. It formed the whispery outlines of a picture, but not enough was there to identify it.

"In your message you said the man who opened the safe saw his brother who was killed. What do you mean?"

"Fochet, he had his brother who was killed in the train. An accident, you see. But before that Fochet open the threshold safe. On a job. He is saying to me that he saw a man. It was his brother but . . . afterward. Like he was an old man now. He tell Fochet to watch out on the train. He give the warning. But Fochet don't know this. He didn't tell nobody about this. Then a year later his brother he got killed. On the train. You understand? It was a crazy story. I didn't pay too much attention because I never heard of these safes and Fochet, he was, you know, a little crazy. His wife make him sell me the business. But then I see you on the website and think, aha, I better give a warning for this. Just in case, you know."

The language translation made it difficult for Brian to fully grasp the story.

"Do you remember anything else about the story?"

"No, that is what I know. I tell you what I know."

"Did he say who made these safes? Anything about the manufacturer?"

"I did ask him this and he say he could not find out. He said it was a big mystery, yes. He tried to learn. The safe came on a boat from France—this is long time ago—and there are no records anymore. In the war the Germans came and destroyed these records. He found nothing because he was like you, with questions."

Pepin made a spitting noise in the phone as if to signal the finality and the fruitlessness of searching for the origin of the Le Seuil safe.

"I have my work now," he said.

"Yeah, okay," Brian said. "Thank you for your help."

"You show a picture of the door of the safe on the website," Pepin suddenly said.

"Yes, that's right."

"You took the door off and leave it off?"

"Yes . . ."

Brian slowly hung up, even as he could hear Pepin's voice on the line exhorting him to be cautious. He thought about the girl he had seen in the house on the island. He thought he now recognized her eyes. He picked up the phone again and called his wife at work. As soon as she heard his voice she whispered that she was really busy. She wanted to talk to him but the phone was ringing off the wall. Her job was to take reservations for the most popular restaurant in town.

"Real quick then," he said. "I have to know. It's a girl, right? We're having a girl."

"Why are you asking now?"

"Because I need to know right now."

"I'm not going to tell you. You told me not to tell you."

"I need to know, Laura. It's important. Just tell me. Is it a girl?"

There was a long pause before she answered.

"Yes, it is a girl, Brian. You are the father of a daughter named Lucy."

"Okay, thanks."

He knew it was a significant moment and Laura was expecting more from him but it was all he could think to say. He put the phone down. He turned away from the workbench and looked at the old blue blanket that covered the door of the Le Seuil safe.

He knew what he had to do.

ROBINETTE ANSWERED THE DOOR. This time Brian did not go to the service entrance.

"Look," Robinette said before Brian could speak, "I am sorry for any inconvenience this may have caused you. The police asked me for a list of names. Yours was on it. End of story."

Brian noticed that there were deep lines under Robinette's eyes now. He looked weary and defeated, even though he had gotten his daughter back.

"I'm not here about that," Brian said. "I don't care about that."

"Then what do you want? You can't just show up here and—"

"I want to talk to your daughter."

"What? No, you're not going near her. She's been through enough. We're moving."

"I have to talk to her."

"I'm going to call the police if you do not leave my property."

"I want to talk to her about the ghost. About the little girl."

Robinette closed his mouth and just stared. Brian saw recognition in his eyes. It was recognition of something that maybe Robinette wasn't sure he believed himself. Then he changed when he saw the ploy.

"The police told you," he said.

"No, the police wouldn't talk to me. I know because I saw her too. When I was here I saw her."

"I don't care what you think you saw, I want you out of here."

He started to close the door but Brian put his foot into the threshold and stopped it.

"Her name is Lucy. I saw her, too, and I *need* to talk to your daughter."

"Why? She's been through enough. First she lost her mother, now this. What can you possibly say to her?"

"I can tell her who Lucy is."

Brian pushed on the door and Robinette moved back without resistance. Brian walked by him and headed to the stairs.

"Where is she?"

"In her room. She won't come out."

Brian went up the stairs and found all the doors in the upper hallway closed. Robinette called from below.

"The second room on the left."

Brian went to the door, knocked, and then opened it when he heard someone call, "Come in." The girl he had seen in the police station was sitting on a bed, her legs folded beneath her, her back against the wall.

"Teresa, right?"

"Who are you? Did my father send for you?"

"No, I just came. I'm the one who opened the safe. I saw the girl that day. She talked to me. She said her name was Lucy."

Teresa's eyes widened.

"Then you believe me?"

Brian nodded.

"I believe you. Have you talked to her?"

Teresa nodded.

"What did she tell you?"

"She, um, doesn't know what is happening. She said she came through the door. That's all she says about that."

"What about what happened to her? Does she know?"

"She said there was a pool and she didn't know how to swim."

Brian closed his eyes for a moment.

"She's confused," Teresa continued. "I said when did it happen and she said it didn't happen yet. She didn't make sense."

Brian nodded. It did make sense to him.

"When does she come?" he asked. "When do you see her?"

"I don't know, anytime. It's not like there is a schedule. Sometimes I close my eyes and when I open them she's there."

"Do you know where she goes when she isn't here?"

"I think she must go back through the door she talks about."

"Would that be where she is now?"

"I don't know. I guess. I don't see her."

"Thank you, Teresa."

Brian turned back toward the door.

"Who is she?" Teresa asked.

Brian looked back at her.

"She's my daughter. She's coming in a few weeks."

"You mean she's not born?"

"Not yet. I think she came through the door to warn me. Now I have to go close the door."

Robinette was standing in the upper hallway when Brian came out. It was like he couldn't venture into his daughter's room.

"We have to put the door back on the safe," Brian said. "This all started with the safe."

"We can't. The trash was taken yesterday. You put—"

"I have the door. It's in my truck."

Brian headed to the stairs and started down. As he went he looked back up at Robinette.

"Do you want me to bring it in through the service door?"

Robinette looked at him as if not comprehending the question. Then he spoke in a quiet voice.

"No, that won't be necessary."

THEY WERE ON the back porch of the house. It was a warm night—summer was coming on strong. And Laura with the extra weight and the extra heart beating inside her had to get out of the unair-conditioned house. They sat side by side in lawn chairs, holding hands. Brian had forgiven her. There were more important things to concentrate on. Besides, he knew the cops could convince anybody of anything. Years back they had done it to him with his old man, practically had him believing that his father had shot the mark in cold blood.

He had not told her the whole story of his return to the house on Shell Island. He didn't want to upset her, especially now that it was almost time for the baby. He only told her that he had gone back to see Robinette, to set things right.

"So there might be some money in it," he said now on the porch. "It could really help us with you taking the extra time off and all."

"What money? For what?"

"He said all of this with his daughter and the safe and stuff made him think about writing again. He said he has an idea for a story and since he'll want to know about safes and being a box man, he'll pay me for it. Like to be an expert for his story."

Laura sat up straight in her folding chair. She was excited by the proposition.

"How much will he pay?"

"We didn't get to that yet. I'm supposed to go back over there tomorrow. I'll find out then."

"Those writers make a lot of money. . . ."

She didn't say anything else. She was leaving it to him but making it clear she expected him to get a good chunk out of Robinette.

"We'll see what he says," Brian said, not wanting to promise anything or push anything.

They were quiet for a moment and then she let go of his hand and leaned forward.

"You know what I want to do?" she asked. "With the money, I mean."

"I don't know. To keep paying the bills?"

"No, we should get more than just that. I want air-conditioning, Brian. We deserve that. And then we should put in a pool. I want to go swimming at night to cool off."

Brian stared straight ahead and off the porch into the distance. He realized that the backyard was just big enough for a pool. Without a word he stood up and went back inside.

Sweet

EARL STRUGG WOKE TO THE WARMTH of a ten o'clock sun on his face. He rolled away from the building that had been his headboard and looked down the concrete mattress to his parking-meter bedpost. He stretched luxuriously and drew his arm across his eyes like a window shade, to dampen the brightness of the morning sun. And he listened.

Mornings were usually the quietest, though he couldn't always count on it. The voices, like their declarations, were unpredictable. Earl Strugg never knew when they'd come or what they'd say, but mornings were usually the best. Mornings were clarity's prime time—no *kill my budga-freekack*, or *rubber freaker nose bicker-knobfucker*—no howling or moaning. No explosions. No thunderclaps. Just cars honking and a wind in the trees—sweet when it came and he took it when he could get it, mornings usually, but he could never tell. So with his arm drawn like a shade, he listened. As the city roared around him, a slow smile spread across his lips. All the way down through the mind of Earl Strugg, for now anyway, it was quiet.

Pedestrians cut a wide path around him. Only the tourists were so bold as to attempt a look at his face. What they saw when they did was a spinning maze. Earl's face whirled. It spiraled inward—wrinkles like a hundred fine parentheses around halogen blue eyes, a black rim marking the edges of his iris and tiny pinprick pupils and the whole thing turning, somehow, slowly inward. Ripples of skin at his forehead lapped at the banks of a whirlpool of hair that was as fierce and unbound as anything in nature. The left side of his face wore a permanent expression of inquiry—the lasting effect of a mild stroke he suffered several years back. His eyebrow arched high above a stretched open eye and the one side of his mouth screwed impossibly down—like the face you make during an argument when you don't hear the other person and you want them to say again. The effect of this was that anyone who happened to glance at Earl would almost always do a double take and politely stop to lean in, since it looked like he might've just spoken and was urgently waiting for a response. As rag-tattered and difficult to look at as he was, Earl could draw people into his spiral face without even breaking a sweat.

ON HIS BACK with the shade still drawn, he listened to footsteps falling around his head and felt a sudden urge to shout out a list of U.S. presidents and then another, just as sudden, to stand and sit three times. Instead, he pulled the neck of his shirt and grabbed his shoulder. His fingers found the scab almost entirely on their own, and began where they left off yesterday—probing and digging slowly but surely. He turned to watch them for a moment, his face like a child watching ants.

From the corner of his eye he saw a pay phone at the curb with its receiver off the hook. The steel cord was dangling, swaying slightly back and forth and he just couldn't take that. He could take about anything else and often had to, but he just could *not* take that. He sprang up and tumbled over to it on morning legs. He took the receiver into his hand, cleared his throat, and put it to his ear. He said hello two times. Then he said no, and that he was very, very sorry. He glanced at the ants digging the scab on his shoulder and thought for a moment about how they looked more like his own hand and fingers. Then he laughed wildly into the receiver and carefully placed it back in its cradle. There was a phone across the street with its receiver resting neatly in its cradle and it was a good thing. The sight of another dangling handset could send him off on a hunt for others that would take him across the city into neighborhoods unknown. It had happened before and it wasn't good. The only thing Earl Strugg had was his neighborhood. Some nights when the noises were at their worst, harrowing his ears with their filth, sometimes when it got that bad, a familiar turn of the sidewalk or the reassuring beer light in the window of the local bar—blue lettering across white neon rocks and pounding surf—sometimes the bark of an old familiar dog from the second-floor apartment or the friendly hello of a shop owner who'd seen him a thousand times was all he had. Earl Strugg's home was about seven square blocks and he didn't often venture outside it. He only went out when he had to and it was never good when he did.

He turned around in the booth and asked the crowd passing by for the time. There was no response, and so he cleared his throat and asked again, louder. Someone, he couldn't tell who, shouted that it was just after ten. Earl Strugg bobbed his chin to his chest in acknowledgment and began a quick deluge of re-marks that brought the man forward. Earl thrilled as he ap-proached to listen—the blood in his veins turning a brighter shade with every step the man took. He wanted to say hello and how are you but his mind flooded with thoughts. His hand flew to his chin and began stroking furiously. The man listened courteously, but Earl could see that he would be moving on shortly and taking the warmth of his regard with him. He strug-gled to grab hold in the tangled rush of words flying through his head, to fix on something that would get the man to stay, but all his mouth could find were rambling incantations of conspir-acies and paranoid contrivances—cops and the government and aliens—most of which Earl didn't even believe or under-stand himself. He was as confused by the words rattling his mouth as the man listening and it made him want to yell and pound his head but that would make the man go away instantly and he didn't want that so he continued—riding his voice like a rapids, waiting for a smooth spot where he could put down the paddle, take a deep breath, and just say, simply, "How are you this fine day? Thanks for stopping. Listen, I'm about to fall over with hunger and if you wouldn't mind, I could really use an egg sandwich—two scrambled with cheese on a roll with butter would be divine. Salt and pepper too."

The man nodded and listened politely. Earl looked up at him for a moment as his mouth motored on uselessly, as if he and the man were standing on opposite sides of a large fish thrash-ing in the bottom of a boat, only it was his tongue and not a fish that was between them, acting of its own accord with the same aimless intensity as the flexing that throws the catch against the rods and tackle. Earl could stop his wagging tongue no better than the man, so they both just stood there waiting to see if it would tire.

Then he heard the words crack the air almost before the man spoke. They jangled his head as they came out, because Earl knew the face and he knew the backing away and the hand that raises when they say it like they always say it—everyone who stops for a lunatic is on a borrowed minute. The man's face went apologetic, he stepped back, his right hand raised with the palm down just above waist level, and he said just like they all say, "All right, I gotta go now." Earl made a mad attempt at coherence but the fish thrashed even harder. The man took another step back and said it again, "Okay buddy, I gotta go now." He told Earl to take care of himself and then turned and disappeared into a swarm of receding backs. The fish croaked at the bottom of the boat and Earl had a quick mental image of bashing it to a pulp—biting his tongue from his mouth and tossing it under the wheels of a passing truck.

He turned back to the phone and hit the number pad three times. After waiting a moment, he shouted into the receiver that there was no way it was possible, and again, that he was very, very sorry. He laughed cunningly at the dial tone and then hung up. Staring at the number pad, he took a deep breath and thought about making another call. He lost track of time for a moment and it could've been a minute or a whole day that passed before he crunched his eyes into fists and rubbed the sides of his head briskly. Then he knew he had to leave or he'd be on it the whole morning, his sanest hours gobbled into the slobbering mouth of another damn compulsion.

So he went back to lie across his belongings and take a roll call of his faculties before heading off to do his chores, which always involved getting some food into his stomach. Today, he would look for a plate of poached eggs with salmon, new potatoes in olive oil with fresh thyme, a slab of country ham, a glass of fresh-squeezed orange juice, and a hot glazed cinnamon Danish on the side. He would read it off the menu in a window as he ate a piece of toast with coffee.

But instead, with the change in his pocket—a dollar and sixty-three cents—he bought a package of chocolate Ring Dings and a bag of Bugles that he devoured soundly. He poured six sugars into a steaming cup of coffee and gulped it down like it was a glass of water. Then he dabbed the napkin at his mouth daintily and followed with a long, holy blow from his nostrils that raised the hackles of most everyone in the store and made the owner ask him to leave. As he stepped out, he turned and begged the pardon of a group waiting for checkout. Then he straightened his back, pulled his legs together, and did a stiff salute followed by two peace signs stretched over his head with a quick shake of the jowls, and then clasped hands, lifted to his left and right, where he clapped three times at either ear and did a quick three-step. The owner of the deli raised his hands to Earl and said please. Earl jerked the pantomime shut and rode out on a tumult of profanities.

Outside the deli, he broke into an indignant stride with his left hand arcing backward and forward and his right sitting high on his hip. He muttered a reprimand to the owner and the people at the checkout for a full six blocks before his mind ticked off the warning that the next street marked the end of his territory. To anyone else, the Burger King on the other side of Thirteenth and Seventh Avenue was nothing special, but to Earl Strugg, the orange and yellow building marked the very edge of the planet.

He stopped abruptly and looked out across the street, marveling for a moment at the people who crossed, effortlessly moving themselves into the oblivion of the other side. His face screwed up at the sight of a woman in delicate pointed shoes crossing such an impossible chasm. People streamed over the curb and over the edge like ants on the march. One by one and over they go and where they stop, nobody knows—like ants, a whole doomed roiling swarm of ants. There were days when everything was like ants—when there wasn't a thing he could point to that didn't seem just exactly like a mealy tickering damn ant. He wiped his face with his forearm and said a quick prayer that it wouldn't be one of those days. Then he turned to make his way back into the heart of his world.

He walked for six blocks like a man on a mission—steady gait, eyes fixed forward, head low on his shoulders. He would stop for no one, including the trucks and buses whose drivers slammed the brakes and cursed the dashboards as he plowed headlong across the streets, oblivious to all of it. He was breathing heavy at block five and sweating like a wrestler as he began the sixth. He fought his fatigue and did a galloping sprint all the way to the curb, where he hunched forward, grabbed both knees, and fell into a heavy pant. When his breathing slowed to manageable, he did ten deep knee bends with his face fixed to a distant focus point and his arms straight out at his shoulders. Then he did fifteen toe touches with impeccable form and controlled breathing. After that he tried some sit-ups but could only knock off three of them. He was straining on the fourth when he was tapped on the shoulder by the shoe of a waiter from the restaurant he was in front of. He started to his feet with his pockets emptying a collage of cigarette butts, milk-jug caps, balls of paper, rubber bands, stones, pennies, business cards, cotton balls—he didn't know where most of it came from, but he scrambled to retrieve everything because it was in his clothes so it was his.

Morning exercises done, it was time to work, because he was broke and because a Ring-Ding-and-coffee breakfast doesn't last long and a handful of pennies and cotton balls is no way to buy dinner. So he did the remaining block to his corner on his knees. Darwin's theory of evolution works as well for begging as it does for the species, only it's quarters and dollar bills instead of mating and predators that shape the selection. Over his twenty-two years, Earl found the most profitable go at begging was to simply make his way on his knees. He didn't need to utter a word. Sooner or later the bills would come. It was easier than constructing a plea and trying to speak it over and over with a fresh delivery—reciting it day and night in rain and shine, without letting the anger seep in and screw the whole thing up. And then when the occasional person decided to give a dollar, they always wanted to talk, give some sort of advice—about where to spend it or to stop drinking or to stop smoking and the endless questions—all for a dollar: do you use drugs and where's your family and why aren't you in a shelter? People gave him directions to flophouses they wouldn't even set foot in, and it had less to do with securing a roof over his head than it did with just getting him off the street so they didn't have to feel the guilt of having such a nice life with old Earl sucking the tar off the road and calling it a square meal. Going on the knees was just easier. The people who gave were so horrified by the sight of him that they'd drop the money and keep moving, either out of disgust or shock or because they thought he was too far gone but, whatever—it made no difference. Earl didn't care. They didn't talk. That was the main thing. They didn't give any sticky-voiced lectures of outworn advice like a bucket of piss-water over the top of his head and the windchill way below zero and who the hell needs it. They didn't say a thing to a man on his knees but they did give money and the rest didn't matter.

HIS POCKETS JINGLED by the time he made it to his corner. A few dollar bills too. And hardly a spoken word. He crawled onto the island of his belongings and laughed hysterically for a full minute. He'd lose the bills before the sun went down, but the coins would stay put and a pocket full of money was as good as it got sometimes—with only one block on the knees. Sweet. He said it out loud, "*Sweet . . .*" and laughed and said it again, shaking his head with a wide grin, and then again several more times—"*Sweet . . .*" as his hips began slowly rolling him back and forth.

And he began to ride.

He knew he should stop and buy more food but the ride seduced him with its rhythm. It was the one he took every day—

weekends and holidays included, the same ride he'd taken since he was a boy. A ride that went back and forth. Three inches forward, three inches back. That's just how it went. Back and forth. He'd gone thousands of miles like that, seated and rocking at the hips. Sometimes the ants would get in front of his face just at the tip of his nose, fluttering their little legs in time to the ride. After a while, the trees and the cars, people on the street and everything and all of it, pretty soon they'd all get on the ride going back and forth with the ants—their legs like his own fingers, just like them with flecks of blood under the nails, waving their little legs and all of it going back and forth. Sound even. He'd let a noise pour from his mouth and listen as the sound waved and pulled like water around his head on the ride going back and forth.

The ants tickled at his face—fingertips brushing lightly against his eyelashes, and he watched them flicker like a fleshy fire burning so close that they might actually *be* his fingers and *not* a fire and *not* ants but just his fingers tittering rhythmically with the ride. Shadows danced with the movements and the whole blessed thing grooved magically with the bump-up and fallback of the entire universe going back and forth and back and forth. He would go until he got hungry or cold or until he got moved along by police. He'd ride until the voices came scratching at his ears and he had to fly or talk on phones or scream into the air to drown them out. But it was a sunny day. There was no one to bother him at the moment and his belly was full of sugar and carbohydrates. A perfect day for the ride, with the sun's warmth beating down on the sidewalk and up into his glowing face—eyes closed, mouth turned up. Just a perfect day for it. He would cover miles.

Four hours later, he was well on his way. People on the sidewalk sped up as they passed him. Dogs growled as they went by. A young father took his toddler by the shoulders to avoid the disaster of the little one turning headfirst into the lap of a smelly old bum. Earl rode through all of it—through the stares and the pointing, through sneers, through the taunts of teenagers with something to prove, and a whole sea of disgusted looks, because he smelled bad and he looked bad and who knows?—he might even be dangerous.

It didn't matter that his mind was a catastrophic hall of mirrors. Never mind the fact that his identity changed like a stoplight—that he'd gone from Batman to Dalí over the last forty-eight hours, that in the last couple of days he'd had moments where he was absolutely certain he was Jesus Christ. Never mind the small pieces of Scotch tape in his hair. Never mind the tinfoil necklace tight around his neck to ward off Martians from Venus. (He wore it ever since overhearing a group of teenagers discussing the possibility of water on Venus, because water is the building block of life and if it's life from outer space then it's coming to get us for sure so watch your back and pass the tinfoil.) It didn't matter that he'd lost three toes on his left foot from two cold days during the previous winter. Never mind the limp. People don't care about all that. Everybody's had it tough. Everybody's *got* it tough, while you're at it. Nobody's got room for hard-luck stories anymore—the house crammed full of them and the rent's due and the mortgage is due and don't forget the bills for power and light, the car needs a new muffler and the kids need stitches and the cats need shots and a man rocking back and forth in a puddle of his own urine is a sad, sad thing, but who the hell needs it.

On some level, Earl Strugg understood that very well. You don't survive on the streets for twenty-two years without understanding a few things on a very basic level. Go ahead and pee on yourself all you want, but leave your coat on the subway in January or get too loud with the wrong pusher, jog across the Brooklyn-Queens Expressway or swallow a whole bottle of Thorazine, and it's over pal. He'd seen so many come and go. Crazies are a dime a dozen on the golden streets of the city and only the stupid die young. Be a lunatic but don't be a moron. Talk to yourself, wrap your arms with cellophane and flap like a pretty bird, but don't leave your shoes in a shelter and never turn down a sandwich or a hot cup of coffee.

THE SUN SAT low at four o'clock. The days getting shorter. The change in light ticked off a part of Earl's mind that brought the ride to a stop. That, and a sudden pain at his shoulder at the place where the scab used to be. Now the place was mobbed with blood. A stain like a brown fan spread across his shirt and lapel. The fingers of his left hand were dark red and tacky, the nails dirty like from a whole day of working the soil. He wiggled them in front of his eyes. *Ants*, he thought, and cursed them out loud. They'd perpetrated their destruction while he was on the ride. He was vulnerable when he was riding and they knew it. They knew it because they're *ants*—the most cunning, most blindly vigorous, untiring, vicious, most overachieving damn insects on the planet. He twittered their little legs again, just off the tip of his nose before letting them drop back to his lap where he'd try to keep a better eye on them. Ants were the last thing he needed. Easy to brush away but so damn persistent— resting across his thigh but ready to rise to his shoulder as soon as his mind went elsewhere.

Lifting his gaze out across the street, he saw a small dog straining over a piece of newspaper while the owner held its leash and watched. The dog and the woman wore matching coats. The scene spun to the left as his body adjusted to being off the ride. Things turned a little after a short ride, but when they spun and throbbed it was a sure sign of a long time on the back and forth. The sequins of the little dog's coat pulsed as he watched them, leaving no doubt in his mind about what had occupied his last hours. He felt it in his hips too—the dull ache of a repetitive strain. A cool breeze caressed his shoulder and he looked down at the stain of damp blood. "*Ants* now," he groaned out loud, shaking his head. A man passing him stopped and looked back. "Beg pardon?" he asked.

"*Ants,*" Earl croaked, his face twirling. "Ants damn it—*damn it,* all this and damn *ants* now—*Christ.* . . ." The man turned away and continued walking.

Earl returned his gaze to the little dog who'd just finished up and was watching its owner carefully fold and deposit its steaming turd into the trash. They walked off, their coats shimmering with the orange glow of the setting sun. Earl followed them with his eyes until the glimmer faded into a gray haze of distant buildings and the coming dusk.

His stomach rolled with hunger—a bad feeling with the night pouring in. On good days he'd get fed in the earlier, clearer part of the day, but he'd been lured onto the ride before finding someplace or someone to help him out, before finishing his chores. And the voices were coming. He could hear their raucous filth like an army at the horizon. They were coming like they came every night, to swallow him whole. He'd be lost in a howling onslaught—dodging the rabble between catnaps and panic-driven sprints until the whole thing spit him out across a heap of trash with the morning sun.

He asked for the time but no one answered because people get meaner as the sun goes down. So he asked again, screamed it really, but no one even slowed down and it didn't really matter anyway—time of day wouldn't change the hunger or the voices or the falling sun. The whole mess was coming down on him—caught by the blizzard before getting the tent up, but you get the picture. It didn't usually go like that, but sometimes, that's exactly how it went.

IN HIS LAST lucid moment, he reckoned with his biggest enemy. Coming along the horizon, it lurked like a predator, one he's beat every year but never for good. He could almost see its face in the gloves of teenagers and blankets heaped over strollers, the extra bloom of smoke from exhaust pipes, the sniffle of delivery boys, the brisk walk of lightly dressed women—his greatest threat, a thing that made voices and hunger and darkness seem like a silly game—distant for now, but looming like a stalker: winter. A genuine bastard with a severe lack of imagination, pulling the same old gags it does every year with a brutal lack of variation—takes the ears and fingers and toes, takes the chunks right off of your nose. Junkies roll you over and hunger could take days, but the cold can put you down within an hour. It was coming as sure as galoshes with its worn-out joke bag of slush and windchill. He'd have to fight and defeat it like he did every year—main event in January with final rounds going long into the end of March. *Sure to be a good match-up,* he thought absently, his fingers crawling back to his blood-wet shoulder. *Don't you miss it, don't touch the dial. . . . budga-freekack rubber freaker nose bicker-knobfucker . . .*

Then, for reasons no one on the outside could ever imagine much less understand, Earl Strugg staggered to his feet and ran like a madman. Just like one.

Deck

THE OWLS HAVE CEASED THEIR CALLS and the lightning bugs are long gone. It's just you alone on your deck afraid to admit why you're alone at night. Most people fear the dark, but you like it. It's the reason you like it that scares you.

The latest story is going nowhere, so you try to convince yourself that sitting out here will trigger the muse. It's a story about an older woman who sure does know her way around a mattress. She's even slept with a woman once, but that doesn't make her a full-fledged lesberino. She is a dancer and the narrator's plan is to marry her, but her ideas are different. (She is actually modeled on a girlfriend you had twenty years ago in Boston. She was French and called you *mon cher,* which you thought was totally deck, but she hated oral sex. This was surprising since you thought the French practically invented it or something. She also used sex as a reward for restaurant meals. She had nice skin. Sometimes you wonder what became of her. She was the great heartbreak of youth, and you regretted losing her for many years. You told her she should marry you so there'd always be one man to remind her how magnificent her legs had been.)

The story opens in a restaurant, the kind where just working there makes you so deck that you're allowed to be rude to customers and you don't even mind the bad tips. (It's more of a café and is presently run by your dopester buddy Carlos in Charlottesville.) There's student art hanging crooked on the walls, and a menu full of culinary puns written in colored chalk on a blackboard. The waiter is gay and you remember working as a waiter, and how you worried that people thought you were gay. You've been married twelve years now, and men don't cruise you anymore, but upon occasion you still wonder if people think you are gay. Then you wonder why you wonder that.

The restaurant is known for having once employed a Weatherman-woman who spent twenty years as a federal fugitive after attaching a bomb to a police car that never blew. She used a false name and formed no lasting relationships. She stayed safe. You envy her. You are reminded of the reclusive Pynchon and recall the time you worked at a Boston Fotomat and a guy named Pynchon came in to pick up photos and you asked if he was Thomas. The guy laughed. He said he was Pynchon's cousin, and you'd never see Pynchon here. He acted as if you were a mook for even suggesting that Pynchon might come to a Boston Fotomat. The guy didn't return, and a part of you has always wondered if he really was Pynchon.

Lately you get on the Internet and plug in your ex–French girlfriend's name and run all manner of searches and come up with nothing. There's a woman with the same name in Phoenix, but she's not the one. You call her old friends, but no one has heard from her in years. Her parents left the state. So did her brother. You wonder why you engage in this, and the possible reasons scare you into remaining on the deck in the dark.

Anyhow, the restaurant suits the situation, and like your ex–French girlfriend, it's small and hip. She was always devastating you with cruelty, then claiming she was being honest about her feelings. She used to say, "Can I ask you a question and you won't get mad?" You are stunned to realize that you can't remember if it was the ex–French girlfriend or your buddy Carlos's girlfriend who said that. Your ex–French girlfriend was a waitress who once got fired for chasing a customer into the street over a lousy tip. You wonder what the Weatherman-woman did if a customer stiffed her on the tip. Maybe she blew their cars up. She lived half her life as someone else, and you momentarily wish you were the Weatherman-woman. The question your ex–French girlfriend wanted to ask was would you mind if she slept with someone else—just once. What could you do? You went along with the idea while seething inside and spent the whole weekend smoking weed and reading comic books, trying to convince yourself that you didn't really love her. As it turns out, she didn't sleep with anyone, but was just trying to learn if you were the possessive type. She left you anyhow, and moved to San Diego, which is as far from Boston as you can possibly get and remain in the continental U.S. You drove her to the airport and never saw her again.

Years later and late at night you sit on your back deck, the perfect place to smoke weed, only you quit a long time ago, making this a wasted spot. Sometimes you think about taking up the habit again, just to feel good about eventually quitting again.

Inside the house is your sleeping wife, who you hooked up

with on the rebound. Out front is a yard with a little picket fence, which is what your ex–French girlfriend always wanted. She used to leave matches with trade-school ads in conspicuous places around the apartment. The habit drove you nuts then, but now seems endearing. You loved her the way only a nineteen-year-old could—with every cell of your body craving her slightest glance, consumed by memory of her last touch, each song on the radio about her, convinced that no one had ever experienced such bliss before, and that you would wither and die without her in your life. But you didn't. You married your next girlfriend and twelve years later you fantasize about moving to a faraway town—Vegas maybe—and dealing blackjack under an assumed name. You remember reading that the Weatherman-woman recently got picked up somewhere in the Midwest with a phony driver's license, credit cards, and everything. She'd married a doctor and her house had a picket fence, too. They let her out on bail because she's totally deck now, a pillar of the community, a PTA officer who volunteers for all and sundry. She hasn't tried to blow anything up in a while either. Doctors and their wives get treated special, and you wish you were a doctor in Vegas. Maybe you'd run into your ex–French girlfriend managing a casino bar and she'd look great and you'd win big and move to Paris together.

In twelve years of marriage, you have never taken a vacation with your wife, and in fact the two of you spend a great deal of time apart. You even go to bed and rise at different times. You have no common interests—none. This worries the bejeezus out of you, but you tell nobody and are getting tired of the constant silent fearful dread as if you are a Pynchon character. Suddenly you realize that the reason Pynchon keeps popping up is that you read his Big Book the same summer your ex–French girlfriend broke your heart. They are inextricably linked. You started that book three times that summer. You made more of a commitment to it than your ex–French girlfriend did to you. She left because you refused to get a regular job, and would never be able to provide her with a picket fence, despite the fact that you hung around with her moronic brother, listened to her best friend's endless prattle, let her mother win at cards, and admired her father's car. You wish you'd married her and given up on Pynchon's book.

You remember how angry she was when a girl at work was eating a popsicle in a highly *provocative* manner. This actually happened to your buddy Carlos down in Arizona, except his real name's not Carlos and it wasn't even Arizona. (He's a real good friend and you don't want to cause him any trouble by using his actual name, which is Dick.) He called recently and wanted to know how often you and your wife have sex. His girlfriend is into it on Sundays only, if she doesn't get too drunk the night before, and if she does, he has to wait another week. It's not a religious thing, he said. It's just a difference in their sex drive, and he wanted to know if she was abnormal. You could tell he thought his girlfriend was screwed up sexually, but didn't want to admit it. You didn't know what to do. You hemmed and hawed because you and your wife only have sex twice a month at most.

Instead of writing you are now visualizing your ex–French girlfriend's face. Her eyes hold back pain and you wonder if that's why you loved her, or if you put the pain there, and whether she's still got it. You hope not. She had some bad luck starting out, and you hope it changed. It's possible that at this very moment, she's remembering you and thinking the same thing. (Maybe she'll read this!)

It's clear that this story has fallen apart. At age forty, sleep has become your drug of choice, and you adjust the lawn chair to a prone position and nap beneath the stars. Upon awakening (and this is true), you remember that your buddy Carlos is presently working in Alaska, and the fishing is bad. If that damn Weatherman-woman had any sense, she'd have gone to Alaska to hang out. There are doctors up there to marry, normal lives to lead, and she'd have never got busted. You wonder if she secretly wanted to get caught, like those serial killers who are always calling the newspapers with hints and clues. It occurs to you that if there were as many actual serial killers as there are books and movies about them, we'd all be dead.

Even though it's been fifteen years, you still recall that summer very well—your girlfriend dumped you, the protagonist of Pynchon's book seduced nurses at the sites German bombs would eventually strike, and the guy across the street put the heavy-duty moves on you. Then you remember that many years later Pynchon's actual wife turned you down when you were looking for an agent. The rejection didn't hurt so much because after all she was Pynchon's actual wife!

You think how your buddy Carlos grew up the only boy with five sisters and understood women better than any man you knew. He possessed girlish habits as a result. One was standing with his knees and ankles together, then leaning forward and using his hands to flip his hair out of his face. A burly roughneck in a renegade bar once asked Carlos if he was gay and Carlos grinned and said introduce me to your sister, and the guy got pissed. Carlos just lit some weed, right there in the bar, and the roughneck leaned for a hit and everything got deck. He turned out to be an ex-con. On his chest was a tattoo of two playing cards, the king of spades and the king of hearts overlapping each other, and you wondered what it meant.

The first tattoo you ever saw on a woman was the English alphabet running in a perfect loop around her ankle. This was about ten years before everybody and his brother had one. Nowadays, that woman runs a New York literary magazine, and you think it's best to change the subject in case she's sensitive about her tat, and you wonder how come nobody ever says "everybody and her sister." It's probably sexist or something and you wonder about the politics of saying Weatherman-woman over and over again, and decide to call the tattooed editor and ask, then change your mind. (You don't want to be a pest in case you send this story to her magazine.) You wonder if

Pynchon has ever published with her. He's probably got a tattoo of a tattoo of a tattoo on him. A few years ago you thought about getting your wife's name tattooed on you, but she talked you out of it. At one time you considered getting a vasectomy but she convinced you otherwise, saying she'd had her kids, but you might want more with a different woman one day. It never occurred to you to wonder why she might think that.

The subtext of all this is you had a buddy named Bill, who once gave you a drug called XTC and put the moves on you. At that time XTC was brand-new and had a reputation as a drug you took with an estranged parent on their deathbed and a lifetime's worth of anger and tension would get cleared up in a few hours. Bill was your across-the-street-neighbor (back when you waited tables at Doyle's in Jamaica Plain). His girlfriend lived upstairs from you. She was a psychology student having an affair with her teacher, a woman who gave her XTC before sex. So the girlfriend's big idea was for you and Bill to get down with the drug and talk about it later.

The problem was that no one let you in on all this until way later. By this time, you were feeling full of artificial goodwill and comradeship, and Bill laid this big kiss on you. Between the scrape of his whiskers and the drug itself, you freaked out big time. It was terrible. You left his house in a hurry. You wound up moving to another apartment. You lost weight and couldn't sleep. You thought maybe you had always been gay but just didn't know it, although everyone else did, which was why gay guys were always cruising you. You tried to go back to your ex–French girlfriend, who said, if you think you're gay, sleep with a man to see. That didn't help. What you wanted was for her to sleep with you to prove you weren't gay. She thought the whole thing was an elaborate ruse to manipulate her into coming across with sex.

Finally you managed to convince a Portuguese woman to visit your room. While kissing you realized that she shaved her upper lip, which convinced you that you had chosen a woman with a mustache because you were secretly gay. You then lost your erection, which seemed to confirm that you were gay. She asked if she was too fat and you told her not at all, she looked great, it wasn't her. You told her the problem was you. You told her that you might be gay. She said she was surprised because you didn't act gay and you said it was a big surprise to you, too. After an awkward half hour, she left confused.

It eventually became so bad that when you went to the movies and the kissing part came, you'd try to figure out who you were watching, the man or the woman, and which person's pleasure you identified with. You decided the best way to deal with a troubled mind was to get your body healthy. You started eating vegetables and doing fifty push-ups and fifty sit-ups twice a day until you heard that gay men were really into fitness and you quit. The only time you were remotely deck was that brief period when you awakened in the morning with the ocean light streaming in the window, until you remembered with a terrible suddenness that you were gay but just didn't know it yet.

That same summer in Boston, your clothes abruptly didn't fit because you'd grown an inch and a half at age twenty-four. You wondered if it was due to having been given acid by college students when you were entering puberty. Maybe the drug slowed something down, and the XTC kicked it in. You know you're not as smart as you once were and sometimes you can feel it, like that guy in *Flowers for Algernon*. After a week, you went to a free clinic in Dorchester and felt guilty in the waiting room because there were people in much worse shape than you—wounds leaking from under bandages, amputees on crutches held together with tape and wire, one man with a glandular condition that made his face turn into a giant potato, and a girl so young you couldn't believe she was pregnant. You waited, trying not to stare but watching nevertheless, and feeling like a moron with a growth spurt. After a half-hour physical checkup, the doctor pronounced your health excellent, and asked for the form. You said what form, and he said the one for the job and you both frowned until you explained that you'd come in on your own because you had grown an inch and a half and were pretty scared. He nodded his little head and blinked. He began searching a Rolodex, and you figured it was for some pituitary specialist that would run a billion tests and say, sorry pal, you'll grow until your organs cannot support your body, but you'll set a record for coffin size. The doctor handed you a slip of paper with a name and number on it. You went home and made the call and the guy was a psychiatrist and you realized that the clinic doctor thought you were delusional. (You stop and reread this and doubt people will believe it. But it's the truth. You had to buy all new clothes.)

Afterwards, you gauged every woman you saw as a possible girlfriend, but felt unable to ask for a date in case you were gay. Around this time, information about AIDS was scanty and full of rumor, and you heard it was some sort of super-clap from Mexico. After learning it attacked gay men, you began worrying that you had it, and read as much as you could about AIDS. One of the symptoms was listed as "loose stool." You knelt before the toilet and tried to measure the relative looseness of your stool by prodding it with a pencil. This actually loosened the stool even more, which immediately made you scared that you had AIDS. The bathroom door swung open and in walked one of the guys who lived down the hall of your rooming house. He saw you bent over the toilet and said, what are you doing? You stared at him, then stared at the toilet full of brown water which you were stirring with a pencil, and realized with a tremendous sense of relief that for the past several months you had been playing with your own psychological shit, and now you were doing it for real. Very slowly you said, I like women. He backed from the bathroom and never spoke to you again.

Years pass and you marry someone and own major appliances. There is a mortgage and car insurance, and you attend grade school functions so your kids can see you there. Outright flight looks good a lot. You and Carlos up in Alaska would be ideal. The best would be if Pynchon was there, and the three of you had a little weed field that was guarded by the Weatherman-woman, who turned out to be really smart. She'd even learned some minor first-aid skills from her doctor husband, and could provide medical assistance to the Alaska natives, who would become your buddies and teach you how to make igloos. Now, that would be deck with a capital D.

If you'd even shown the slightest bit of interest in money fif-teen years ago, you might still be with that French girl and she'd have a tattoo. After all, you two did have a romantic year in Paris, something that can never be taken away or duplicated. You hit every museum and park in the city. You studied at L'Alliance Française, visited the former ateliers of the great artists, plus the graves of Modigliani, Gertrude Stein, Apolli-naire, and Jim Morrison. You lived in hotels, ate in cafés, and kissed in beautiful gardens. Then you went broke. Back in the States, you had a cramped apartment in Salem, and looked for a bigger place in Boston. Finally, after seeing a dozen that were no good, she came home and said she found a place and you said great where, and she said Malden, and you said great how much, and she said cheap, and you said great when do we move in. She said we don't, it's just for me. She moved out and took the furniture and you slept on the floor where the bed had been. (This was an extremely dramatic gesture that you are simulta-neously embarrassed by and proud of now. Even worse, a guy dropped by to visit and you lay down on the floor to feign a nap so he could find you and offer sympathy.) Pretty soon after all this you thought you were gay.

These days you've quit all your bad habits and sometimes you miss them. You don't use drugs, smoke cigarettes, drink liquor, drive fast, gamble, or even drink coffee anymore. It's not the vices you long for but the exhilaration of risk. Other-wise you feel crushed by the mundane patterns of existence—errands and chores, food and sleep, loveless sex and paying bills. At this moment your entire life has led to sitting alone on the deck and being aware of it.

The eastern sky has begun to glow. You never saw that French girlfriend again, and you hope she got her picket fence. You hope she got everything she wanted out West. You hope your wife does, too.

Wonderland

THERE ARE TWO GREAT THINGS about being accessories editor for a major women's fashion magazine, a magazine that I can't name but we all know what it is because, face it, there's only one major women's fashion magazine. The first is the belts. A belt isn't something you want to really pour a lot of change into. Either you have your boring basic black lizard belt, what we fash-mag hags call "a classic piece." Or you have your leopard belt, or your magenta patent belt, or some chain thing that looks like it ought to be used by law enforcement, the kind of thing you wear once and find, three years later, on the floor of your closet behind your waterproof boots and some old bikinis with a nasty stain.

If you're accessories editor of a major women's fashion magazine (or, more accurately, *the* major fashion women's magazine), there's a whole closet full of belts. You just go in and snag one, put it back the next morning. Or not. I have a seven-hundred-dollar ponyskin belt with a horsehead buckle somewhere in my closet, and, trust me, there's no way I paid for it.

The other great thing is being a source for stories. Better than therapy and a whole helluva lot cheaper. You didn't really think all those girls went out there in their stiletto boots and interviewed secretaries and schoolteachers, did you? Anytime you read a story about having sex with your boss or dealing with childhood trauma or knowing when to leave, every single person in it works at the magazine that's running the story, except for one or two who are the best friends of the person writing the story. Yeah, and the ones who are made up completely.

Probably most of the stories we tell each other are made up, too. We sit around the new company cafeteria, the official chow-down spot for anorexics and egomaniacs, and somebody has a tape recorder and then three months later there's whatever we said in print, whether it's true or not. Except that I, for example, get described as "Sharon, 42, a nurse from the Midwest" or "Alicia, 25, who works in advertising in Chicago."

It's funny to watch the faces of some of the guys from the business side when they walk by with their slabs of salmon. The business-side guys always stare at us, since to work at the mag you have to look really really good, and they always eavesdrop and turn a really unattractive shade of red when they hear what we're saying, especially when we're all concentrating on a story. "A leopard thong and whipped cream," one of us will yell, or "When his ex calls during sex." That was for a story on the ultimate turnoffs, and Selena in Features was so sad that she didn't work for Cosmo, because then that could have been the headline. Instead we had to go with something tasteful like "When Love Goes." God, I hate tasteful.

So there we were, having salads with no dressing and chocolate mousse after, the bulimic's lunch of choice, and Selena, who always gets the best assignments because she's sleeping with the deputy publisher and is a pretty good writer, says she's got a new one. It's going to be called "Dating Down." She goes around the table, saying, "Okay, I need stories about sleeping with men below your station." She had everything she needed before two o'clock. Cops, construction workers, doormen, even a pizza delivery guy who got fired because it took him forty-five minutes to deliver an extra-cheese three blocks away from the shop: you don't need the details. Besides, if you read the March issue, the one with Demi Moore and her three daughters in Vera Wang eveningwear on the cover, you already got them.

"Not me, honey," I said. "I fuck up. Way up." Nothing they could say would budge me. That was the biggest lie I've ever told them, bigger than the one about the account exec buying me the Kelly bag. (My mother hated the color and gave it to me at Thanksgiving.)

Here's the truth: Halfway through junior year in college I started to sleep with a guy who worked custodial in the dorm. In January the water in the radiator pipes hardly ever rose to the ninth floor, which is where I lived in a single down a corner hallway. Once, you'd probably been able to see across to the administration building from my window, but sometime in the 1960s they'd put up a student center that blocked off everything, including the light. It was one of those buildings that was so ugly it was almost cool, like plastic jewelry. All I could see out my window was the frosted glass of a men's-room window in the student center across eight feet of gray air. I knew it was a men's room because almost everyone who came in stood for a minute, then did this jerky dip, turned, and disappeared. It didn't take a genius to figure out the silhouette of a guy taking a piss.

Lauren, who played squash with me Tuesday afternoons, thought it was the greatest when I pointed it out to her. "Oh my God," she said. "You have to write about this."

"It's incredibly boring," I said.

After ten minutes she'd sighed. It sounded like she'd been holding her breath, waiting for something to happen. Four guys had taken a piss, one in a red shirt, two in black shirts, and one wearing something with writing that was smeared by the frosted glass.

"You're right," she said.

In January this room was so dark and cold that I put the light on when I got up, at noon, for my History of Dutch Painting 1647 to blah blah blah, and left it on all day. Sometimes I even fell asleep with the lights on. I took half an Ambien every day at two in the morning, or, if I'd been to a party, when I got home, and it zonked me out so fast—there's the bed, there's the comforter, bam, you're gone—that lots of times I never got to turn the light off at all.

I hardly ever let anyone come to my room for sex, and I never let anyone stay afterwards. I don't like to sleep in the same bed with another person. My little sister used to have nightmares and she'd come in in the middle of the night, whimpering, smelling like piss and chocolate milk, and I'd say, Tough, pull out the trundle. She'd reach out and hold on to the corner of my blanket until she fell back to sleep. That was as far as I was willing to go. "You are one cold bitch," my friend Edgar said one night in Peripatetic when I told him that.

"Excuse me, but everyone has something that bothers them," I said.

"What are you going to do if you ever get married?" he said.

"Shoot myself?"

Everyone thought I was being a crybaby when I got back from Christmas break and kept calling downstairs to maintenance about the cold. "You could wear the fur-lined parka to bed," said a guy who was a vegan at the other end of the hall when I was yelling at our RA.

"This is none of your fucking business, soy boy," I said.

"I promise, I'll see what I can do," said the RA, who kept one of those pathetic white boards on her door so we could write her messages. It was a new rule, since a freshman two floors down had killed herself, as though if there'd been a white board up the freshman would have written "I'M CLINICALLY DEPRESSED AND I'M GOING TO TAKE FORTY SECONAL" on it. For the first five days after I got back I had written "IT IS COLD IN MY ROOM," and the RA had erased it each night. Finally I wrote "IT IS AS COLD AS A WITCH'S TIT IN MY ROOM."

"WHAT IS SO COLD ABOUT A WITCH'S TIT?" someone wrote below it.

"YOU MUST NOT KNOW TOO MANY WITCHES," someone wrote under that.

"YOU ARE ALL CHILDISH," someone printed at the bottom, but there was no room left so the i-s-h went up the side.

"MY WHITE BOARD IS NOT A BATHROOM WALL," the RA wrote after she'd erased everything else.

Jesus showed up the next day, probably because I wore the RA down. (Wearing people down is my specialty. Ask the former accessories editor.) Jesus was wearing the green work shirt and work pants that the college made the custodial staff wear, and a wide leather belt around his waist cinched tight. The leather was caramel colored, like my Frye boots. He looked good. No plumber's crack when he bent down to look at the radiator. If the poor bastard had just had a plumber's crack, maybe he'd be alive now, going gray and fixing the door hinges for snotty college students.

"Nice belt," I said.

"I have a bad back," he said. He had a slight accent, so that it sounded like "bed beck." The flag of Puerto Rico was tattooed on the back of his left hand. It must have hurt like hell. I got a mermaid on the small of my back when I was on spring break junior year of high school; it was half the size of the flag and I'd had four rum punches to get through it.

"How often you bleed the radiator?" he said.

"Say what?" I said, standing as close as I could without actually touching him. He was wearing one of those high school colognes, but I thought I could smell cigarettes, too, and maybe a hint of chronic. I liked chronic. It didn't make me sleepy like ordinary pot did.

"You don't bleed the radiator?"

"I don't touch the radiator."

He sighed and used a wrench on the radiator. A long sound just like his sigh came from the floor in front of him. He turned the wrench and the flag of Puerto Rico went up down up down. The hissing stopped and he smiled at me. He was damn good-looking, and I was bored, and so on and so forth. I didn't feel bad at the time. At the time I felt good.

Maybe if he'd been working there longer he would have known to stay away from me. But he'd only been working at the university since September. Before that, before he'd hurt his back, he'd been a window washer. That was how he hurt his back; he said the harness didn't support it properly.

"These windows are dirty," he said a month later, standing naked, blowing the smoke from a big spliff out a small crack at the bottom. I'd been right about the chronic, it turned out.

You want to know how I got him to sleep with me? One day a jammed drawer and a breast touching his bicep, two days later a stiff lock. "Stiff," I kept repeating. "Very stiff." The following week a denim skirt and the Frye boots with no underwear. I was an amateur then. It took him three weeks to get his clothes completely off, not because he was shy but because he was quick. The first two times he didn't even unbuckle the back support belt. No preliminaries. I liked that. I was so tired of college-boy technique: now I'm going to do this, now this, how about this, do you like that? If I wanted a lecture I'd go to a seminar.

Jesus never once asked me if I liked something. I don't think he cared. I liked that, too. Out of habit I tried hard to get him to talk, to say something that would piss me off, to say something, but mainly Jesus spoke a language of shrugs, frowns, inhaled joints, and raised eyebrows. Also a language of sex. Hands, mouth, dick. For a guy who didn't care whether you were having a good time or not, he sure could show you one. Or maybe it was just me. The therapist my mother made me see during high school said I liked to be treated badly. "A masochist," I said.

"Full-blown masochism is a complex diagnosis," the shrink said. A female shrink. They wouldn't send me to a guy because of how I'd wound up in shrinkage in the first place.

After four months here's what I knew about Jesus: that he lived in the Bronx. That he owned a van. That he hated the smell of coffee. That he hated the taste of cigarettes. (Tough shit.) That he hated the job and wanted to go back to windows, or some other outside work. That he got the tattoo in San Juan on a visit home to his mother. That he liked crappy pop music and thought he could sing. That he was wrong about that.

Early on I couldn't find my diamond stud earrings and I asked if he'd seen them. The next time I called and said my window wouldn't go up all the way they sent an old fat guy with a silver comb-over and one of those hideous light-bulb bodies, big chest and belly, no ass.

"I found them underneath the bed, all right?" I hissed at Jesus the next day in the back room where they kept the security cameras.

"Fuck you," he said. "I don't steal."

"I didn't exactly say that you stole them."

"You did exactly say it. Also thinking it. Joe comes to your room from now on."

It took me almost two weeks to get him back. "God, are you in a pissy mood," Lauren said.

"I hate my parents," I said randomly.

She rolled her eyes. "Please, God, not again."

My parents are both shrinks. Were both shrinks. I hear the cognoscenti out there thinking: well, that explains it.

That's part of it. Another part is that when we were at Hilton Head for Christmas when I was fourteen my father took my sister out to get her some new tennis shoes and ran the convertible into the back of a flatbed. First a family of four, then a family of two. Then three when my mother married another shrink she'd known since med school after he managed to dump his wife (not a shrink). Stepdad is another part of the problem, but maybe I won't go there. I don't have all day.

The last words my mother and I ever heard my sister say were, "I don't understand why I can't wear her tennis shoes. We're the same size."

Jesus didn't like shrinks either. He seemed to have at least a passing understanding of what they did. The longest speech I ever heard him deliver was a shrink speech. "Always messing with your head," he said, scratching. "Always saying this that and the other thing, and then when you really think about it, it's nothing. Nothing. And how much they make an hour, huh?"

"Two-fifty," I said. "The good ones."

Jesus worked the day shift and had lunch from one to two, which could have been a bad deal because he got off at three and who wants to take a break, work for another hour, then get off work for the day? But luckily I had no classes until three on Tuesday and Thursday, and no classes at all on Friday, so he could get a sandwich and take the freight elevator up. The freight elevator was right across the hall from my door, which seemed like kismet.

"You think I'm a whore?" I said one day when we'd gone so long, on my desk, on the floor, up against the window, he didn't get to eat his sandwich.

"So so," he said, buckling his belt.

"Whatever," I said.

"You want me to say no, I say no. But you don't want me to say no. You want me to say yes."

"Who the fuck are you, Sigmund Freud?"

He shrugged and tucked in the back of his shirt. He hated plumber's butt as much as I did. "Who knows why people are fucked up, huh? They just are. You. Me."

"What's wrong with you?"

"I got shitty taste in women," he said.

"So don't come back."

"Number one, I'm not talking about you anyhow. And number two, bullshit."

Once he came to my door and I opened it naked except for a pair of stiletto heels. "Aw, man, respect yourself," he said, putting down his sandwich bag on my desk and throwing a T-shirt at me from the pile of clothes on the floor. He always pulled the blinds down, too, and kept the light off until he was ready to eat. Once I didn't open the door, figuring he'd let himself in with his passkey, which would be a real kick. But he just knocked twice and then went away, soundless except for the faint rustle of a brown paper sack and then the wheeze of the elevator doors.

"You are a real old-fashioned guy," I said.

"Yeah, so what," he said one afternoon, wiping his mustache of mustard with a paper napkin, to the right, to the left, like always. He took a joint out of the ashtray next to my laptop and lit it, held some smoke in deep, then blew it toward the window.

"You going to kiss me good-bye?" I said, but he just pushed past me to the door.

I'm pretty sure no one knew. I didn't tell anyone, even Lauren. The person I really wanted to tell was Gus, the guy I was supposed to be dating, which translated into insulting each another at bars and then going home together. It was so tempting, especially when he was being pissy. One night after he'd had four boilermakers, which is what college guys drank then to prove they were not effete wimpettes (they were), he wiped out between his sheets, which always smelled vaguely like cheese. "You judge people," he'd said intensely, as though he were parsing the Koran for Muhammad, which was how he always talked when he was blitzed. "It's like I can feel you outside your body, looking down, judging me, even when we're making love.

"Judging me harshly," he said, rolling the last word around in his wet mouth as though he hadn't made his point.

You have to picture me, lying there, one tit squashed underneath his elbow (which would have hurt a lot more if I weren't so flat chested), thinking to myself, "Funny—Jesus the janitor never feels judged, Herodotus boy. Plato guy. Classics major. Demosthenes dick." I used to say the best things in my head to Gus. He works in the White House now. I saw him on CNN when I was on the treadmill at the Health and Racket Club on Union Square. He had a leather portfolio under his arm and he kept his head bowed as he walked, as though he were trying to figure out why the hell he ever bought those boring black shoes. They all keep their heads down like that for the cameras, all those power guys, walking out of the courthouse, leaving the office of BigBadCorp. After a takeover, after a big indictment, after a press conference, because if they looked up, even for a second, they know this big shit-eating grin would spread across their pasty faces and they would blurt out, "I am so the man!"

Maybe that's why I thought about any of this old crap today, not because Selena needed stuff for her downmarket sex story but because of the TV news. Or maybe it was because I wore the Frye boots, dug them out of the closet for the first time in ten years and wore them with a kilt (my old uniform skirt from Purchase Country Day) and a turtleneck. "Oh . . . my . . . God," said Ariel, the assistant fashion editor. "Ralph Lauren on crank."

"Great headline, but I don't think you'll get it through," I said. "I was just cold and bored."

"Return of the Frye boot," she said. We all talked like that.

Jessamina was on the news. Is that why I wore the Fryes? Jessamina Perez, wearing a cheap white cable-knit sweater, her hair in an unflattering bun. She didn't look that different than she had when she was a kid. I had a good eye, even in college. My RA once said she swore I'd end up running a fashion magazine and I froze her so fast, what a crappy thing to say, and now here I am passing judgment on the latest shape in evening bags while, according to the alumni mag, my RA is a neurobiologist at Hopkins, thank you very much, bet she doesn't give a shit what kind of evening bag she carries.

She'd been a funny-looking kid, Jessamina, with big teeth and eyes with a little too much of a pop to them. But there are two kinds of funny-looking kids, the kind that turn into ugly adults and the kind that turn into Lauren Hutton. I was pretty sure that Jessamina was going to be pretty when she grew up, and I was right.

She was eleven when Jesus showed up with her, pushing his way into my room using her skinny flat plank of a body like a shield, steering her by one shoulder. "Shit, man, I got a big problem here," he said. "I'm gonna lose this goddamn job."

"And that's my problem how?" I said, looking the girl up and down. She was wearing jeans that had been long enough for her before her growth spurt, a T-shirt with faded flowers across the center, and a white quilted jacket that had gone grey along the edge of the cuffs. She was carrying a book in one hand and a backpack by its strap in the other.

"Popi, I can stay home alone," she whined. "I can take the train back."

"Bullshit," he said. "No way." He talked over her head. "I had her downstairs in the break room, the old guy came in, started giving me all this grief, this is no place for kids, on and on, he's an asshole. So I figured she can stay up here until I'm done."

"You're crazy, Jesus. I have a class at three."

"That's okay. She's good. You sit down, Jessamina, you read your book. She's always reading the books. She's going to college."

"I coulda stayed by myself," the kid said, not looking at me. Her book dropped down as though it was heavy in her hand. It was a library copy of *Little Women* with a sappy drawing on the cover of four girls having a picnic.

"I gotta go," Jesus said.

"How come she's not in school?"

"Some stupid thing, what the hell—"

"Professional development day," the girl said.

"How the hell they think people take care of their kids when the teachers are always taking off—"

"I coulda stayed home. I coulda locked the door."

"No way," said Jesus.

"I have so much work," I said.

"Later," he said, dropping his hand from her shoulder and slamming the door.

I looked at her. She looked at the floor. I picked a pile of clothes off the one big chair in my room and dropped them on the floor behind the chair. "So sit," I said.

He was right, I guess, she wasn't any trouble. I didn't mind her as much as I expected. She reminded me a little bit of my sister. It was something about the way she held her hands, as though they weren't really attached, were something breakable someone had given her that she had to hold really carefully. There was a kind of ballet thing she had going on that my sister had had. Duh, my sister had been taking ballet since she was three. She could raise her foot above her head and not even breathe hard. She'd stand out there on the tennis court waiting for the ball with her feet in third position. I don't know why the hell she needed to play tennis in the first place.

I took a shower, checked my mail, made a cup of tea, and the girl just sat there. I don't think she was really reading. She had her face all tensed in the center in a kind of pissed-off look. I was the expert at that look. I can make my face look like a fist without even trying.

"Don't you judge me!" my mother used to say. Like I cared.

When I came back from class she was still reading, but her face had gone all soft and when she looked up, startled, I could tell she was crying.

"What?" I said. She looked down at the book in her lap.

"Oh, shit. I hate that part."

"What part?"

"The part where Beth dies. I hate that part."

"What?"

"When Beth dies and she writes the poem about her and her mother's all bummed and then Amy marries Laurie and they—"

"Amy marries Laurie? Amy? The mean little one? Marries Laurie? The guy?"

"Oh, shit," I said, putting my books down. "I gave the ending away."

"Beth dies?"

Not my finest hour. "I'm staying home next time," the kid said when Jesus came back for her. "You're welcome," I said when he left with her.

The next time was a month later, on a Sunday morning. I was asleep and I was in no mood. Gus and I had had a fight about whether he should major in philosophy, which he liked, or history, which he could use, whatever the hell that meant. It was really a fight about why I didn't want to go down on him, which was one of his favorite topics. The others being whether Harvard was a better law school than Columbia, and whether he would win the prize for best senior thesis. (He didn't, and he went to Georgetown, and I didn't go down on him because he didn't go down on me. I guess you could say it was political.)

This time she had a book called *My Very Best Friend*, with a picture of one girl looking down the hall at the back of a whole group of other girls. You could look at the cover and be able to recite the whole stupid thing aloud: used to be my friend, then she got in with the popular crowd, then she dumped me, then the popular crowd dumped her, then she learned what's really important. You could tell by the colors—sky blue, pink, a kind of medium purple—that it was the kind of moron story where the girl takes her two-faced bitch of a friend back, instead of telling her to kiss her ass and the friend develops a bad crystal-meth habit.

"So how is that?" I said after I came out of the shower. Luckily I'd spent the sex hours at Gus's or the room would have reeked of it. I like my room to smell like Pine-Sol, the way it did in boarding school. That's another reason why I never let someone spend the night after sex. Jesus was perfect. He didn't even want to spend his whole lunch hour.

She was looking out the window. "Is that someone going to the bathroom?"

"Probably," I said, kicking my towel under the bed and rummaging in my drawers.

"That kind of underpants look uncomfortable," she said.

"My mom says having a tattoo isn't so good for a girl," she said.

"It's kind of a boring book," she said.

"Here's a good one," I said to shut her up. I handed her my old copy of *Alice in Wonderland*. My name was on the title page in crayon right next to Lewis Carroll, the perv. Now the book is in my bedroom on the table next to the Bakelite alarm clock that my grandfather gave me when he got Alzheimer's and thought I was either his mother or his fifth-grade teacher.

"My mom says you're not supposed to write in books," Jessamina said.

"It's my book. I can do what I want. Where is your mom, anyway?"

She looked out the window again. "She's not feeling good," she said.

"Jesus is your father?" I never assume anything about family relations.

"He's my mother's boyfriend. He's like my father. My father lives in Jersey, and he's got two jobs so he doesn't come around too much. Jesus is better. He takes us to Burger King every Saturday for dinner. Last summer we went to Orchard Beach and he got a lobster. I didn't want any. It looks gross."

"It's all about the butter."

"I had fried clams. You can't even taste the clams."

"If you get a bad fried clam you'll puke all night," I said.

"How can you tell if it's bad?"

"I've never figured that out," I said. "I guess if you puke all night." I put on my down coat. I could tell from the steam rising from the grates in the quad that it was freezing out. "You want anything from Café No?"

"What do they have?"

"Coffee."

"I don't like coffee."

"Yeah, you'll get over that. Hot chocolate? Bran muffin?"

"Can I have a corn muffin and some hot chocolate? He'll pay you back."

It wasn't such a bad day. I had a Poli Sci paper and having the kid around kept me at the computer, although I wasn't sure whether it was because I was afraid if I left her alone she was going to steal my jewelry, try on my clothes, or just wig out. For a long time the only sound in my room was the hollow tap of laptop keys, the swish of pages turning, and the loud pounding of hot water coming up through the cast-iron pipes to the radiator, which worked fine now. Jesus bled it once a week.

"What's a comfit?" she said after about a half hour.

I just handed her the dictionary. I wasn't going to be spitting out definitions every other paragraph. She kept going back and forth from the book to my big old abridged OED. (I still have that, too, on my desk at work, because you never know when you're going to need a really arcane word to describe a scarf. Right.)

I was almost done with my first draft and Jessamina was about halfway through the book—I looked when she was gone and she'd just gotten to the part where the Duchess hands Alice the baby—when Jesus let himself in with a passkey. "Damn," he said. "I couldn't hear nothing, so I thought you went some-place."

"What, like I took her to a bar?" I said.

"There's no noise, no talking, no music, no nothing."

"I had a lot of work. She's reading."

"Yeah, she's always reading."

"You got a key to her room?" Jessamina said.

"I got a key to all the rooms, baby. Put your coat on. We'll go get pizza."

"I'm not hungry. I had a corn muffin."

"Your mommy's home."

She leapt up and the dictionary fell to the floor, discarded. "Yo," I said. "That's an expensive book."

"Sorry. Can I borrow this one?" She held up my *Alice*.

"No way. If you ever come back again you can finish it. Or get it from the school library. This one's mine." But I let her put a Post-it inside so she'd know where her place was, although she scarcely looked at me as she scrambled into her jacket.

"Get her a decent coat," I said the next time Jesus stopped by alone.

"What are you, her mother?" Jesus said, smoothing his T-shirt over his pecs, which were something to see.

"God forbid."

"You need to whatchamacallit," he said.

"Man, you are articulate."

"Fuck you. You need to try acting like a woman sometime. Like you're normal, nice."

"Oh, yeah, nice. That's really useful. If I were normal and nice I wouldn't be lying here." If I'd been normal and nice I wouldn't have gotten off on the look of disgust he gave me when I said that.

That was the last time, it turned out. Not the last time I saw him, but the last time we had sex. The last time I saw him was two Saturdays after that, when I was starting to wonder whether

I was going to have to go to work on him again with the Frye boots and the service calls. My closet wasn't closing right. I was going to call and complain on Sunday. But he showed up Saturday with Jessamina again. She was sulky but you could tell that she wasn't mad, and as soon as she took off her jacket—that same thin grimy jacket, polyester with lousy fill—she was reaching for *Alice*.

Jesus looked bad, like he hadn't slept and hadn't showered, and I wondered for a minute if he was doing one of the other girls in the dorm. It wasn't like him to be unkempt. He was the kind of guy who treated his mustache as though it was a house pet. "Just keep an eye out for her," he said, running his hand through his hair, and for once I couldn't think of some smartass thing to say. His cell phone, which he kept clipped to his belt, started chirping, and he sighed. "The machine thing'll get it," he said.

"Popi, answer it. You know how bad she'll get."

"She can't get any badder. Any worse. Goddamn it." The phone stopped, then started ringing, stopped, then rang again. Thank God he didn't have some stupid song, "Pomp and Circumstance" or "Mary Had a Little Lamb." Ring four and he flipped it open. "What?" he said, and you could hear screaming coming from the phone all the way across the room.

"Ay yi yi," said Jessamina, tears running down her face and dropping onto my good copy of *Alice*, turning the faded red cloth cover vermilion again.

"Listen to me," Jesus said, but whoever was screaming wasn't listening. "Listen. Listen. All right. All right. Yeah."

He hung up and looked from Jessamina to me, then back again. "I guess she told you," I said.

"Shut up. Just keep an eye out for her. Stop crying, Jessie. Stop right now. Everything is okay." He said something in Spanish and the girl jumped up and held on to him around the waist, moving her head from side to side until the front of his shirt was wet with tears.

Then in English he said, "I'll be back to get you later."

After he was gone she started to cry again so I just shut up and did the reading for my Econ class. She started on *Alice,* but after a while I heard the book fall to the floor and when I looked over she was asleep, sitting on my bed with her back against the wall. I nudged her over with the flat of my hand and she fell onto the bed on a perfect diagonal, like a small tree. I covered her with my duvet. She snored evenly, even when late afternoon came and the light disappeared and I had to put my desk lamp on. Just before six o'clock she said "maybe" very loudly, and then "sometimes," and went back to sleep for a few more minutes. When I turned around again she was in the same position but her eyes were open and she was looking at my back.

"Is it nighttime?" she said.

"Not yet."

What it was was at least an hour past the end of Jesus' shift, but I didn't say anything. Part of me was pissed that I was stuck with this kid, that I didn't know where she lived or how to get her there. Part of me figured that something bad was happening and that I'd better cut her and Jesus a little slack. The voice that had come freight-training out of that cell phone had sounded a little bit like my mother's voice when the cops in Hilton Head called, only instead of "All right" she'd said "Are you certain? Are you certain?" over and over again until I'd wanted to scream. But she'd screamed enough for us both.

"Do you like Chinese food?" I said.

"Egg rolls," she said.

"They're full of fat," I said, but I got them anyhow and had some myself. I got her to eat lo mein, too, but she wouldn't touch the Szechuan prawns.

"I can't believe I'm spending Saturday night eating Chinese food in my room and studying like all these other losers," I said, and when she started to sniffle I added, "Okay, okay, it's fine. It's all good. He probably just had to take care of business."

"He probably had to take my mom to the hospital. That takes

all night sometimes. Sometimes there are people who are shot and their heads are all messed up and there's all this blood and they have to take them first."

"Yeah, okay, too much information. So you'll just have a sleepover here."

"I had a sleepover with my friend Jasmine over Christmas vacation. We went to the movies and to Chuck E. Cheese."

"I've never been to Chuck E. Cheese."

"It's like a restaurant and an arcade, so you can eat and like play video games."

"Wow."

"Yeah. And Jasmine has a brother who won high scorer on Blast 'Em and we got a free pizza. It was kind of a gyp because we'd already had pizza so we didn't want another one and they said we couldn't have a coupon for it so we had to order it then. We took half of it home in a box to Jasmine's other brother. He's in a wheelchair 'cause when he was born something went wrong and he's all hunched up on one side. You have to cut his food up in little pieces or he chokes on it."

"Where is this?"

"Chuck E. Cheese?"

"No, where you live?"

"The Bronx," she said. "Pelham Parkway."

At least I had a clue.

I let her have the bed that night and although she was all nervous during dinner she slept soundly. I was the one who kept waking up, trying to figure out why I was on the floor. When it was morning I wanted to go out to the diner to have a hot breakfast but she said no, no, we had to be there when Jesus came back or he'd be angry. I tried to tell her the guy could let himself in with his passkey (smoke a doobie, take a nap) but she wouldn't listen. Another corn muffin, another hot choco- late. I just had coffee and a cigarette, blowing the smoke out the window while she wiped her delicate hands very carefully and looked at me like I was practicing Satanism instead of ripping through the first Newport of the day. Love that menthol, especially with a latte. You get that dark numb patch at the back of your tongue that reminds you you're alive.

It's weird how I can't remember that much about the rest of the day. It was a kind of black hole, quiet and still, maybe what Sunday is like for people who observe the Sabbath. I think the sun set at some ungodly hour, although since it was early March I was probably wrong about that. Jessamina knew Jesus's cell number and we called but we got no answer, not even a machine. We called every hour, and then every half hour after lunch. Around six it started snowing, and I went out and got sandwiches. What kind of weird kid wants an American cheese sandwich with nothing on it? *That* I remember. "Mustard?" I asked. "Lettuce?" But she just shook her head, the corners of her mouth turned way down. She finished *Alice* and I gave her *Through the Looking Glass.* We were both reading in the dark and when I got up to turn on the overhead light she was bent over the dictionary, squinting at the small print.

"You need glasses?" I said.

"What's a jabberwocky?" she said, turning the thin onionskin pages of the OED.

"No one knows."

"What?"

"He made it up. The word, the thing. It's whatever you think it is."

"That's stupid. Are people allowed to do that, just put words in books even if they don't know what they mean?"

"If they want."

"I don't think that's fair. It's, it's, it's confusing. And it makes you mad. Like what if I'd been alone and I hadn't been able to ask anyone and all this time I thought it was a word that meant something and I was just too stupid to know the word?"

I shrugged.

"I'm not reading this anymore," she said, and when I looked over she'd fallen asleep again, her mouth open and her eyes skittering back and forth beneath the thin veiny skin of her eyelids.

Jesus, I was tired of sleeping on the floor.

"I gotta go to school," she said when she woke up the next morning, dull-eyed. "I got to go home."

"Do you know which stop you are on the subway?"

"I'm not a baby, you know. Of course I know what stop on the subway. I've taken the train home a million times."

"I'm going to get coffee. You want the same thing as before? Then I'll take you on the train."

"I can go by myself."

"My ass," I said.

It's hard for me to remember now, but in college I never paid any attention to what was going on out in the world. I didn't have a TV in my room and I never read the papers. Now it's like, if I miss one issue of *People* magazine I have to go have a manicure just so I can catch up. We all say we have to watch *Access Hollywood* for work because if the editor-in-chief says she wants, say, a Gwyneth layout we'd all better know what the Gwyneth thing is at the moment, because one shot that's so last-year's-Gwyneth and you'll be working for a suburban shopping sheet. But we just watch *Access Hollywood* because we want to. If any of us were in serious relationships maybe we wouldn't watch so much. One of the young assistants had a boyfriend who loved to watch *Access*, and she was so shocked when it turned out he was gay. Duh. Duh. Duh.

The closest thing to following the news I did in college was to look at the tabs as I walked past the newsstand near Café No, which was a good thing because there's no telling what would have happened if I hadn't seen Jessamina's picture on the front of the *Daily News*, almost life sized, with the headline WHERE IS SHE? It was the first time I'd bought a newspaper in three years, since the Michael Jackson trial. I took it into Café No, ordered a no-foam latte, and sat at a table with my insides bubbling up so that I thought I might have to use their skanky restroom.

Jessamina's mother's picture was on page three. She looked like Jessamina, only smaller all over. A picture of Jesus was next to her. It wasn't flattering. I think it was at the beach; his shirt was off and there was a horizontal line mid-photo that might have been the line between the sand and the water. His hair was all over the place, which would have made him crazy if he hadn't been dead of twenty-three stab wounds that Jessamina's mother had inflicted, the cops said, before she turned the knife on herself, which is a pretty gentle way of saying that she stabbed herself right through the heart. Sometimes I think about that now and I still can't get my mind around it.

The papers said Jessamina's mom had been in and out of the hospital for psychiatric treatment and that her own mother, Jessamina's grandmother, said she'd even had electroshock and some sort of water therapy that sounded pretty sketchy to me, and if there's one thing I know, it's therapy. The papers said that there had been a domestic dispute on Saturday because Jessamina's mom—her name was Mercedes, of all things—thought that Jesus was cheating on her. And now they were testing all the blood in the house to see if she'd killed Jessamina, too, because Jessamina had just disappeared into thin air. Maybe she was dead, maybe she was kidnapped by drug lords, maybe she was wandering around with post-traumatic stress syndrome.

Jessamina's grandmother said she was an honor student at St. Martin de Porres and that she read all the time.

I stayed an hour at the table, had another latte, ordered Jessamina's hot chocolate, and read my horoscope. (I'm a Gemini, the astrological sign of the bipolar. Which, by the way, was what Mercedes happened to be. Bipolar, not a Gemini. In and out of the hospital, on and off the meds. Mercedes, we could have hung out. I wonder when your birthday was.) My bottom line was pretty simple: I sure as hell didn't want to be involved. COED CAUSED MURDER-SUICIDE. Yeah, right. I finished my coffee, went to the corner, and called the TIPS line number at the bottom of the newspaper story. I'm a decisive person when I need to be. I was the one who made all the arrangements when my mother went catatonic on me after the accident. I took care of business even though I was just a kid, really. Until she married El Shrinko II. The sequel is never as good.

"The kid you want in that murder case is standing by this phone," I said. I didn't want to make it too easy for them, figured it would take at least a few minutes to do whatever they do to trace a phone number and to get somebody there. And when I bundled Jessamina into her coat and took her down the freight elevator, I didn't go outside, just stood there shivering in the delivery entrance and pointed across the street. "Your grandmother is coming to get you," I said.

"You called my grandmother?" She was half-asleep and so confused, blinking in the sunlight for the first time in two days.

"Sort of," I said. "She's coming. Just stand over there. But do me a favor. Do Jesus a favor. Don't tell them where you were."

"Don't tell who?"

"Whoever," I said.

She sort of tottered across the street like an old person, her arms wrapped around her midsection. I'm not totally inhuman. I stood in the doorway watching until a black-and-white rolled up and the cops put her in the back. The next morning the paper said she'd been wandering the campus for two days, hiding in the library. I didn't read it until nearly nighttime because I took two Ambien and slept for eighteen hours. I had terrible dreams about playing tennis with a guy who kept firing aces past me but wouldn't let me give up. When I finally went outside there was a foot of snow on the ground. It looked like I had dreamt it while I was sleeping.

It snowed a couple of weeks ago, and that probably made me remember, too, and then I was on the treadmill at the Health and Racket Club and I looked up at the TV and there she was, talking to the newswoman from Channel Four, the Korean one who talks with her hands and has really bad Chiclet teeth. It was one of those lame anniversary pieces local news loves, ten years since blah blah blah. The newswoman said it was a story of tragedy and triumph, and she asked Jessamina what she did during those terrible days when she walked the streets without knowing that her mother had committed this senseless crime. (Apparently no one really believed Jesus had been unfaithful.)

"I read mostly," she said quietly. "I've always loved reading."

And with one of those TV aha smiles the newswoman said that that must be true because Jessamina had graduated Phi Beta Kappa with a degree in English from a prestigious college, where her tuition was paid by a childless millionaire garmento who had been touched by her story at the time and had paid for Choate as well. And now she was studying for a master's degree and teaching first graders to read. Cut to Jessamina reading aloud with a bunch of kids in uniforms around her in a circle, only one or two staring shamelessly at the camera, and what is she reading but *Alice in Wonderland*? This stupid newswoman doesn't even know how perfectly the whole deal turned out!

You have to picture: I had had a really bad day. I don't give a good goddamn about belts and I've written almost two thirds of a novel and I'd had a meeting with an editor at a small house that does edgy books. I never expected to walk into his office and get sideswiped by the New York small-town thing. If you actually live in a small town you might find it hard to believe, but the weird thing about living here is that it turns out you already know most of the people you meet. Like you go to have lipo and the doctor is the brother of someone you prepped with. Or the woman at the next locker at the health club was two years behind you at college and you can tell by the way she looks at you, especially when you're naked, that she remembers every story she ever heard.

So I go in to see this editor and we simultaneously flash on New Year's Eve three years ago, when we wound up in a men's room together doing X and one thing led to another and we had really bad sex on the toilet. Of course we didn't know this going into the meeting because we'd never even exchanged names. I took one look at his face as he took one look at mine, and I knew I was doomed.

"There's not a lot of heart in your work," he finally said after all the weird preliminaries. And I just went off.

"Heart? Excuse me? Have you read Leonard Briskin and Ted McArdle? The last McArdle had a disemboweling on page ten and it was shortlisted for the Booker Prize."

"We published that book," he said.

"And you're Briskin's editor. He couldn't find his heart with both hands."

"He's not a woman. Readers have a certain expectation when they read a female writer. They expect a certain emotional resonance. And we all feel here that the father-daughter incest thing is a little tired."

"Greek mythology cornered the market?"

"It's just not for us."

"What if I write under a pen name and pretend to be a guy?"

"Women's books are the ones that are selling."

"With heart."

"With heart."

"I have to say, it would be a hell of a lot easier for me to get myself some balls than some heart." As I said it I could tell by the look on his face that this was a story that was going to make the rounds in the small town called New York, and Selena was going to be major-league pissed because she hooked me up with this guy and wants to sell him a book herself. But she's got heart, or at least can pretend to, so maybe it'll be okay.

In some weird way seeing Jessamina on TV, sitting with the kids, waving her dance hands around, badly dressed but well groomed, took the curse off, made me feel like I wasn't such a zero after all. I kept waiting for her to tell the interviewer who taught her to like Alice, but maybe she was still keeping her mouth shut, still protecting the woman who'd slept on the floor and bought her corn muffins and taught her to use the OED. I have to say, for the first couple of weeks after she went off in the cop car that day I stayed as far under the radar as I could. It got cold in my room one night in early April and I ruined a good pair of tweezers trying to bleed the radiator myself. I was nice to Gus just in case he suspected something. He suspected something because I was nice, but then he just went with it. I even went down on him once or twice.

Then last week I was on the A train going home because I only had $18 in my checking and the ATM wouldn't spit out less than $20 and I didn't have enough in my purse for a cab. (Note to self: call Mother.) But one of the girls, the idiot who does the fact checking on captions, left a fare card in her out-box, so I took it and used it to get home after we closed the June issue. I hate the train, but it's better than walking, especially in boots with stiletto heels (taken from the shoe cupboard, thank you very much, retailed last season for $520).

I was reading the new *People* and I didn't look up when the doors opened at other stations. I guess that's why I didn't see her until she wanted me to. I didn't see her until she got out of her seat and stood in front of me, almost toe to toe with my boots. Hers were those cheap waterproof fake leather ones you can buy at the Going Out of Business shoe stores on Broadway, the ones that don't go out of business.

The train was slowing down for a station and the other passengers were looking up at her, maybe because she really had gotten very pretty, with her big dark eyes and smooth, mocha-colored skin, or maybe because they'd seen her on television the week before. Her nails were long and she had a fresh French manicure; you could tell by looking at her hands that that was where she put her money. I don't even want to tell you about the look on her face. It was so terrible it paralyzed me, so that the smile that started when I recognized her died before it really began. For just a minute I wondered whether she had a knife. I know it's crazy, but I wondered whether she had her mother's knife, whether she'd been saving it for the occasion.

But there was only a book in her hand as she leaned toward me and said loudly, with a sound like spitting, "Puta!" Then she moved towards the doors as they opened, but turned and cried over her shoulder, in case I needed a translation, "Whore!"

"I speak Spanish," I said to myself, but I said it aloud. I'd learned it from the housekeeper in Palm Beach.

People were looking at me, and two teenagers down the car were laughing. So at the next stop I got off the train, even though I was twelve blocks from my building and there was ice on the sidewalks and slush at all the corners. I'll tell you, it is a bitch to walk that far in stilettos, and I will never take the train again, so help me God, as long as I live.

Ashes

AFTER SILENTLY COUNTING TO THREE, Banks throws his naked body out of bed. He's already on his feet when he feels the cold bite his prick. He doesn't bother looking down but stands rooted to the freezing floor, his muscles bunched into a knot, his breath misting the air in front of his face.

Fifteen minutes later, he's showered and dressed. He leaves Janice sleeping and walks outside to his car. Along the roadside in Somerville, snow is piled a yard high, though only the top few inches are fresh and white; these he cleans off his windshield with a gloved hand.

While the engine warms, he sits behind the wheel staring at a photograph in a clear plastic frame bolted to the dashboard: his father standing in a driveway, grinning beside a red and white '58 Corvette, lug wrench in hand, sleeves rolled up and grease smudged on his muscled forearms. A man about the same age Banks is now. A married man with a job and a pretty wife and a five-year-old boy, who are not in the picture. The car, recently waxed, gleams under intense sunlight. His father looks proud, happy. The grin on his handsome face says there's nothing that can't be fixed; anything can happen, the grin says.

It was Banks, aged five and a half, who discovered his father's body hanging from a beam when he wandered into the garage looking for his Wiffle bat one morning. That's what his mother—understandably perplexed that he could ever forget such a thing—continues to insist. But Banks himself has no memory of that day; in fact hardly any memory of his father at all. If not for the photograph on his dashboard he might almost believe that he'd never had a father, had never seen a red and white '58 Corvette with his own two eyes. Sometimes it feels to Banks as if the photograph on his dashboard is what he has instead of his father. He never grows tired of looking at it as he drives from job to job through the streets of Boston and the outlying suburbs. He finds the picture of his dad reassuring company but also somehow suspenseful, expectant, as if one day it might just start to talk to him.

WHEN THE ENGINE's warmed up, he's on his way.

He checks his clipboard. Two installations in the morning and three in the afternoon. At Dunkin' Donuts, he fills his commuter mug with hot black coffee, then catches the traffic report on the radio. There's an accident on the expressway, so he decides to go through Harvard Square, take Mass. Ave. to Storrow Drive, and Atlantic into the North End.

The curving, narrow side streets are still unplowed after yesterday's snowfall, and the slush is inches deep. His tires hiss through the muck like sizzling fat. He slows down, the speedometer dropping to twenty, then to ten. Small islands of dark tar scattered with road salt appear through the grime-streaked windshield. And Banks remembers the night, twenty-five years ago, when he stood with his mother on the roof of their house in the North End, releasing handfuls of his father's ashes into a stiff breeze. Hearing the salt crunching under the tires, he imagines that it's his father's ashes he's driving over, that this was where they'd landed, whitened and crystallized in the cold.

THE SECOND APPOINTMENT of the morning is an apartment complex on Boylston. Banks knows the building. He figures the job should take twenty minutes, thirty at most, then he'll get a sandwich and a coffee refill before starting the afternoon.

In the lobby, the doorman phones up to the apartment. He turns away from Banks as if conducting top-secret business. When there's no answer, he stretches his dark upper lip over his teeth and sighs. "You sure you got an appointment with Mr. Martin?" he asks skeptically, still holding the phone to his ear. The nickel buttons on his gray uniform jacket are pressed flat against the bulbous stomach underneath.

Banks, staring at that stomach, annoyed by it for some reason, is slow to respond.

"*Martin*," snaps the doorman. "Twenty-nine-oh-two. That the apartment you asked for, or am I wrong?"

Banks checks his clipboard and nods. He's suddenly conscious of the weight and contents of the tool belt on his hips: what he'd like to do now is pull his Rowalt cordless drill out of its holster and scare the fat man shitless.

The doorman slams down the phone. "I'm gonna have to take you up myself."

"It won't take long," Banks assures him.

"Better not." The doorman pulls a belt-loop key ring from his front pocket and walks toward the elevators at the back of the lobby. "I'm the only one on duty. Rodriguez called in sick."

"Ten minutes, tops," Banks says, following him into the elevator.

"Rodriguez is sick like I'm a prima fucking ballerina."

On the twenty-ninth floor, there are no sounds in the long corridor of numbered doors. The doorman tries several keys before finding the right one. Then the door opens and Banks is looking across a living room through a wall of windows, beyond which is Boston, huddled and rising, in light so achingly clear it's blue.

"Bet you twenty bucks the TV's in there." The doorman points to a wood veneer cabinet against the wall. He pulls up a handful of each pant leg and sits down on the leather sofa. "You said ten minutes, right? Think I'll wait."

Banks folds back the doors of the media cabinet and squats down. The TV is a twenty-seven-inch Trinitron. A plane of sunlight cuts diagonally across the screen, which suddenly isn't a window into anything but his own hollowed-out face. He turns on the set with the universal remote. It takes him two seconds to recognize *Divorce Court,* hazed by static. He switches it off and there's his own face again like a death mask.

"Hey," complains the doorman. "Leave it."

Banks doesn't turn around. "Where's the back door?"

"In the back. Where the hell else would it be?"

In the small gray screen, past his own reflection, Banks watches the grinning doorman remove his cap and run a meaty hand over his balding head.

"I need to find the junction box," Banks says quietly. "I can spend all day looking for it, or you can show me where it is."

"What you need, buddy, is a sense of humor," the doorman replies almost sadly, putting both palms on his thighs and pushing himself to his feet.

Banks rises and follows him down a long uncarpeted hallway. The apartment is larger than he'd thought, with rooms leading off of other rooms. The air feels too humid for winter, semitropical, he has no idea why. The doorman, his heels scuffing the parquet floor, starts to whistle tunelessly, and Banks follows him without thinking.

They pass a bedroom on the left, the door open to show drawn blinds, a bare desk, an unmade bed. It makes Banks uncomfortable to look into another person's private space, but still he looks. He can't help himself. On one wall there's a framed poster of a light bulb; on another, a shelf supporting a glass jar filled with shiny black stones.

And then, as they near the end of the hallway, it's as if they have stepped into shadow, the blue light of day trapped somewhere far behind. Ahead, over the doorman's shoulder, Banks glimpses the back door with its heavy security lock. He's thinking that he'll drill the hole above the door and run the cable straight into the living room; he'll have to staple-gun it to the wall because there aren't any moldings.

He almost runs into the other man, who has stopped abruptly.

"You hear that?" whispers the doorman.

"What?"

"That. Listen."

Banks listens. And above the doorman's strained breathing he finally hears it: the sound of water trickling into water, coming from a bathroom to the right of the back door, a few feet ahead of where they're standing.

"Bathroom," he says. He puts a hand on the doorman's wide back, feeling the warm sweat soaking through the jacket, and lightly pushes him forward.

"Hey, watchit—"

Banks brushes past him. The bathroom door is open. Next to the sink a nightlight is shining—Banks can see the tiny glowing filament. At first, standing in the doorway, it's all he sees: on one side, the illuminated plastic shade pleasantly reminding him of a PEZ dispenser; on the other, the mirror above the sink drawing and diffusing the meager light, like a pale sun trembling underwater.

He goes in. The bathtub is against the back wall, a white opaque shower curtain drawn halfway across it. Visible now are the thin stream of water trickling out of the brass faucet, and two bare feet that appear to float to either side.

"Oh, Jesus Christ," says the doorman.

Screened against the shower curtain Banks sees the doorman's gross, flickering shadow slump down on the toilet seat and put its head in its hands. Then for a moment there's nothing but the sounds of water trickling into water, like small glass beads falling into a pond, and, every few seconds, the drain sucking for breath.

"Jesus Mother of Christ," moans the doorman.

"Shut up," Banks says.

He can barely hear himself through the pounding in his ears. He pulls aside the shower curtain as if ripping off a Band-Aid.

The man's body is like his feet: it would float if there was room. The torso sits up on the water as if a hand was gently pushing it from below. But Banks stares at the head. It's inside a white garbage bag tied at the throat, the knot poking up like a fist. He thinks he recognizes the brand of bag he and Janice always get at Star Market. The blue and yellow face is visible where it touches plastic—side of nose, tumescent cheekbone, lips dark as plums.

The doorman is whimpering now. Banks falls to his knees. After a while he begins to shake, his eyes squeezed shut, his forehead pressed against the side of the tub as if he's bowing to the dead.

"NOBODY'S FAULT, SOMETHING like this," the policeman tells Banks. "Guy wants to check out, he checks out."

The cops keep their hats on. The paramedics arrive and fish out the body, put it on a stretcher and cover it with a sheet. They leave the head tied in the garbage bag. Banks sees one of them slip a pill to the doorman, who is sitting on the leather sofa in the living room. The doorman washes down the pill with some Scotch from the dead man's liquor cabinet and goes on complaining to no one in particular about Rodriguez, how it's all his fault, the lying stinking son of a bitch, and if he ever sees Rodriguez again he's going to kill him. He's still sitting and complaining when Banks leaves.

Outside, the day is warmer, the air blue as a dream. Walking to his car, Banks hears the snow melting, the streets washed clean by the runoff.

He sits with his hands on the steering wheel, the keys in his lap. He is already an hour late for his next job but he makes no move to start the engine. He stays where he is, staring at the photograph on the dashboard.

He is home again, before it all ended: standing beside his father's '58 Corvette, his head no higher than the door handle. The red and white beauty in the driveway, the sun on its hood.

An Eye for an Eye

THEY WERE EATING IN A RESTAURANT, Thai food, because that's what she wanted at this stage. She was a finicky eater when pregnant, and he prided himself on accommodating her sometimes strange but always insistent desires. He was that kind of man; he was helpful and compassionate, at least he tried to be; he took out the trash every Tuesday and did the grocery shopping and picked up at night. Now that she was pregnant he was even more helpful, carrying loads of laundry up- and downstairs, sponging the white tiled countertops. He didn't mind it. He was that kind of man.

And, being that kind of man, tonight he was taking her out on a good old-fashioned date, this despite the fact that they hadn't had sex for five months flat, and before that for procreative purposes only. He could admit, to himself, that this was difficult to deal with, his sex drive being so much higher than hers, but that, too, he was willing to overlook, or accommodate.

His wife across the table from him had a large belly for her six months, and sometimes he could even see her dress move, like a person trapped under a tent. That was his son in there. His son! She wanted to name him something fey, like Raphael, which sounded to him like a gay hairdresser. "Think of him ten years from now, in the schoolyard," he said to her as their coconut soup was served, and she said, spooning up the pale broth, "What do you want then?" her eyes bright and pushy, and he said, being collaborative as opposed to competitive, "How about another angel, Gabriel."

"I once knew a Gabriel," she said. "In college."

"So," he said.

"I can't name my child Gabriel. That was a guy I went out with."

"What guy?" he said. "You never told me about him."

"For like two weeks," she said.

"Ahh," he said, picking up a fried spring roll and biting into its crispy flank, "I see," he said. "Short but passionate, I take it? A lucky man, that Gabriel."

She looked at him long and hard. "What are you implying?" she said. "Are you implying we're not passionate?"

"Not at all," he said, his voice with that maddening, singsong quality.

"Of course you are," she said. "What do you expect, when you work until three in the morning?"

"Anne, Anne," he said to her, like she was a child who needed to be soothed.

"What do you expect," she finally said, her voice low. "I'm six months pregnant. I'm forty years old. My back hurts. You work and then come home and expect we can have sex when we hardly have time to talk. Besides, you try carrying the child. Having a second was your idea anyway."

"Why are you always so rageful?" he said. "I just want peace. I didn't mean a thing."

"Of course you meant something!" she snapped. "The worst thing you can do to me is say you're being totally benign when in fact you speak in coded messages."

"Coded messages," he said, letting the phrase linger there, so it sounded absurd, paranoid, hysterical. He was trying to make her look foolish, as he often did; she wanted to get him back. She was a tempestuous woman with an advanced degree; even as a non gravida she was moody, a trait she considered a strength.

"I'm not paranoid," she said. "I'm perfectly capable of accurately reading your passive-aggressive postures. And really," she said, "passive-aggressive is the worst way to be. I'd rather have a man who was capable of straightforward aggression."

"What do you mean?" he said. "I am aggressive."

"Of course you are," she said.

Now he was mad. He spooned up the last of the coconut soup and flicked a shred from his blond beard, a gesture he suddenly saw from outside himself, pathetic, feminine, the little first-finger flick, the tiny piece of pulp.

The waiter came over. He was, of course, a Thai man, with a slender build and a crisp white shirt. Before them he set a platter with a whole fish upon it, its head still attached, its eyes a deep ocean green, its mouth open in an expression of agony. The fish was banked by asparagus and emitted a slight smell of curry. The waiter, brandishing a knife, began to slowly cut around its neck.

"No need," he said quickly. "Mai tong kan." He knew a little Thai and was proud of it, having spent a year there after graduate school. "Chan tum ang dai," he said, meaning, "I can do it myself." The waiter smiled a surprised smile and gave him the knife. It was silly to feel so totally redeemed, but he did. He felt as though he'd lofted up two notches on the rungs that riddled his life. He could smell sky and sun. He lowered the serrated blade to the crisp fish skin and sliced sideways, ladling onto her plate linen-white pieces of its flesh. She sat there, swollen and looking at him; she was proud of his being bilingual, although really, he had at best a tourist's grasp of the language. Still, she said thank you each time he layered the meat onto her plate, and each thank you was a puff of peace, a smoke signal, *let's surrender*. Then, the knife slipped and he cut his thumb.

"Oh," he said. The cut was not insignificant. When he held up his hand, bright red blood trembled and welled from the wound, then dropped onto the floor. The waiter rushed forward. She leaned towards him and wrapped his thumb in a napkin. "I'm fine, I'm fine, really," he said. He felt himself slip down the ladder, into a darker space now. "I'm fine!" he said, pulling his hand away. He got up. Went to the men's room. Came back. There was the fish on the platter, his impregnated wife, whom he had fed.

"Do you want to see a movie afterwards?" he said.

"We should get home for the sitter," she said.

"We can call her," he said, offering an olive branch. "We can call her and tell her we'll be late. It's been, like, years since we went on a date."

"Okay," she said. She smiled at him. He couldn't tell if it was a smile of pity, or acquiescence, or real agreement. Lately, it had seemed she'd rather read a book than be with him.

"We can see," he said, "that movie you've always wanted to see. The one about the wedding."

"Yes," she said. "It will remind us of our own."

"We had a great wedding," he said. And then, before he could stop himself, this slipped out: "It was a great wedding, despite the fact that a number of people had told me not to marry you."

She froze, the fork poised at the seam of her lips. "What's that supposed to mean," she said. She set the fork down. Her voice sounded a bit more wounded than he had intended, but sometimes wounds themselves are soothing. Inside, he smiled and balked, smiled and balked.

"Isn't it," he said, chewing off the frilled top of an asparagus, "isn't it always the case that there's at least one person who tells you the other's not good enough for you."

"Not good enough," she echoed faintly.

"I mean," he said, "there's always at least one person. Surely there was someone from your side who thought I was like, too radical for you."

She looked straight at him. "No one told me that," she said. "When will you understand," she said, her words coming out as hisses now, "when will you understand that all your left-wing ramblings are no more than conventional liberal ideas circa 1960."

They ate in silence for a while. She slurped on her straw, crudely, he thought. She, too, heard the sound of the slurp, and thought the same thing, and her face turned red.

"Who was it," she said, finally.

"Who was what?" he said.

"Who was it that told you not to marry me?"

"I could never tell you that, I'll never let you know that," he said.

"It's not fair of you to say it only halfway," she said. "If you're going to make these kinds of comments, you have to follow them through." She felt the baby begin to kick inside her. It was kicking and kicking, and she pictured it, its fetal form, suspended between here and there, this world and that, padded by a thick fluid. She felt that way too, all of a sudden: suspended, weightless, a little bit lost. "My baby," she thought, trying to ground herself.

"I'm sorry," he said in a voice that could sound slightly condescending. "I didn't mean to hurt your feelings."

"It was your mother," she said.

"No," he said.

"Your sister," she said. "I know it was your sister. You probably told her way back then, even, that your libido was higher than mine."

"Not my sister," he said.

"Your father," she said. She hated herself for guessing, for giving him that much power.

"I can't tell you," he said. "I'll never tell you. Let's just drop it."

"Fuck you," she said softly.

They ate the rest of their dinner without saying a word. Each made an attempt to prove to the other they were cool and collected. To that end, they both ate too much, because cool and collected people have good appetites, and they each ate casually, slowly slicing with their knives, almost humming to themselves.

Then they were finished.

They rose to leave. They drove back home in silence. In only three more months the baby would come. They were both thinking that. She was thinking of a statistic she once heard, that couples with two children divorced less frequently than those with one. This both comforted her and contributed to her feeling of entrapment. He, for his part, was thinking that he tried so hard, and she knocked him down so far, and still he tried, practicing compassion and helpfulness, and what did he get for it? He meant her no harm. He thought of the knife, the fish, the silvery scales, the way their teeth closed in around the food.

Back at home, they paid the babysitter, checked in on their sleeping child, and then went to their own bedroom. He pulled off his shirt and pants and climbed between the sheets. She went into the bathroom, not at all unusual, but she stayed there for a long, long time. He heard running water. Then he heard the tap turn off and the sound of her feet slap-sucking the bare tiles. He switched off the bedside-table light and now the room was drenched in darkness. The clock face had an eerie glow, the second hand sailing and sailing around the circle.

"Anne?" he called out at last. His voice sounded small and cracked.

No answer.

"Anne," he called out more loudly now, and when that summons, too, was not answered, he stood up and walked across the carpeted floor, towards the closed bathroom door. From inside, he heard the clink of small bottles being shifted, the whisper of wood as a drawer opened and closed. Slowly, slowly, he knelt down, like a man about to propose, he thought, but no, like a man who has exhausted himself, he knelt down and peered through the keyhole, and he could see the shimmer of her red robe, the long slow strokes she used to comb out her hair—beautiful hair she had, like corn silk, raw and blond. "Anne," he whispered; she heard him. Somehow, she heard his tiny plea through the keyhole and she turned towards the sound. "Yes?" she said. Then she walked across the floor and, from her side of the door, put her eye right up next to his. They stayed this way for a long time. She thought there was something beautiful in his eye, the tiny grains of green she could see, the pupil with its halo of color. He thought of a storm he'd once been in, way back in college, a hurricane that had bent the trees back and snapped branches from boughs with a deep cracking sound. Crack. Rain slashing against the window (his wife blinked), and then the eye of the storm, a sudden stillness, bands of brief blue above them.

The Choking Pearl

S HE WANTED TO BITE A CHUNK out of the man's cheek
the way Plath had done to Hughes. Really mark him. Or
piss on his leg the way her mother's dog pissed on every fence
post and wall. As he spoke to her—something about the Shake-
speare Garden in Central Park blah blah blah—she focused on
his lips moving and thought about how the female praying
mantis bit the head off the male as they fucked because the
males fucked harder as they died. It made the death of male
bees seem almost disgustingly passive in comparison. Bees as

passive-aggressive, she could see that. They liked to hover and menace, but when push came to shove they never really did anything until you cornered them. The threat of bee stings in her childhood had been highly overemphasized, she thought.

What was he saying now? His lips, my God, they had to be injected with something. Whale blubber or lard or something. They were impossibly huge. How did he speak with them?

Oh yes, concerts in the park, blah blah, New York at its egalitarian best, blah blah, "a virtual subway population infused with joy." Had he actually said that? What time was it and why had Judith gone off with that angular man with the Andy Warhol hair? If he hadn't been dead, it could almost have been Warhol. Lucy had loved that movie about him recently, that one with Lilly somebody playing that crazed dyke—God, that was good. Did it mean something bad about her that she had rooted for the crazed dyke and made the notation "SCUM Manifesto" on her hand in the dark of the movie house? Worse still, what did it mean that she had never had any problem laughing through the Baby Jane movie up to and including the scene where Bette Davis is body-kicking the crippled Crawford? Lucy had nearly broken up with someone following that movie. "I just don't know how you could have laughed at that," he had said. "Did you hear yourself? You were the only one laughing during that scene in the entire theater." Now she wouldn't have done what she'd done then, which was cry and manipulate herself out of seeming the ogre she knew inside of herself she wasn't. Now she would have taken the more mature route and said, "Oh, fuck you."

She nodded her head. What had she nodded her head at? She could see that it had made the man smile at her in a new way, a sort of leering, affectionate way—his big lips moving about the lower half of his face were thoroughly out of control now.

He reached out and took her empty glass. "Vodka rocks coming right up!" She had heard that.

He turned away and cut back through the others toward the

bar inside. She was wobbly and off balance without his face to anchor her. She thought briefly of sitting down but then decided against it. How could you bite a man in the face with any authority from a seated position?

Judith had taken her to the party to get her out of her apartment "for at least a few fucking hours!" Judith had yelled at her, "You're turning into Bill!" Bill was a man Judith had slept with. He hadn't left his West Village apartment in twelve years. Judith's words had done the trick. Lucy left a note for her boyfriend, Tom, and hurried up to Judith's in a cab to try and find an outfit she wouldn't look absolutely ridiculous in. Lucy had relied on Judith's closet for as long as they'd known each other. She couldn't wear most of Judith's things, but there were always a few classic items that Judith seemed to buy but never wear—a sort of Midwestern penance for her urban chic flair.

"Here we are," the lip man said. She had to find out his name but it felt as if it had been forever since she last spoke. Back in college she and Judith had driven to Rochester all day during a blizzard to go to a concert Lucy had no interest in. Along the way they had picked up a guy and two girls at a gas station who Judith noted had leaned a PETTY OR BUST sign up against the pump. Lucy had had to sit next to the guy—the sort of guy who said Dude! a lot, loudly, and talked about 'jamming' and 'reading the flyleaf for the tip-off,' something she had never decoded in the ensuing twenty years. Somewhere in the midst of that concert, with Judith lost yelling the words "You . . . ! don't . . . ! have . . . ! to live . . . !" and thrusting her fist in the air each time, the guy had turned to Lucy and, as if a thought he'd been fishing for had just popped into his head, yelled, "Cottonmouth?"

Lucy had no idea what this was. To make him stop looking at her she yelled, "Yeah!"

TOM AND LUCY were having problems. They had been since two weeks before, when they'd inadvertently returned to the habits of their younger dating selves and Lucy had asked Tom how many people he had slept with before they met. As soon as it was out of her mouth she wanted to take it back, but you did not admit to such cowardice, not if you were Lucy. "Walk down that road into the lion's den!" she heard a voice say to her. "No prob," she'd say, already hitching up her skirt.

Perhaps if he had even known the number, that would have been a good thing. Perhaps if he had said 542 plus you! It would have been intense but she could have taken it. "Twist my nipples and call me a whore!" she could have said and bedded him then and there, staking her claim at 543. But it had not been so simple.

"What I like most, actually," the man with the lips was saying. Was he hovering closer now? It felt like it. "Is that stunning single pearl."

Inside Lucy said, "What?!" but outside she tilted her head down to take a drink and quickly scanned her memory of what she was wearing. The pearl, the pearl, what is he talking about? All she could see was Tom walking into the living room of her one-bedroom apartment. "Eighteen," he said. An hour later, after retabulating, he coughed out "twenty-three" from his spread-legged position on her Jennifer convertible loveseat.

Okay, yes, the pearl. She could feel the cool spot against her breastplate where Judith's giant faux Leiber pearl rested against her. In what had been an afterthought, Lucy had agreed to wearing it to try and distract from a blouse she considered a bit too revealing even if it was white silk.

"There aren't enough buttons on this thing!" she had yelled inside the bathroom to Judith. (How old had they been, somewhere in their late twenties maybe, when they no longer stayed in the bathroom together talking when the other one was on the john.)

"Did you just growl?" the man asked. Had she? If so, he hadn't seemed to like it.

"Acid reflux," she said. The first words she uttered in what felt like hours were particularly repellent ones. Why not just yell "Toilet!" or "Mucus!"?

But she didn't care what he thought. She only cared about his cheek. She stared at it. He wasn't leaving; the single pearl must trump the irritable bowel. How had Plath ever gotten such a purchase on Ted Hughes's cheek? She knew he was supposedly megaman, a sort of poetry Popeye that got—in one of Lucy's least favorite but often apt phrases—Plath's panties in a wad. He had even written several poems about it—sort of the bite of death as opposed to the kiss of death—which Lucy had liked.

She saw Tom in his boxer shorts saying, "I think I've got it. Thirty-one."

"You will?" the lips said, "that's outrageous. I can't believe it!"

Oh God, what had she agreed to do? She felt his hand at her elbow and a bit of pressure there as he guided her through a small group of people toward what she knew was their destination the horror-struck moment she saw it. How could it be possible that at this party they would have a karaoke machine?

"No higher than forty, I swear," Tom said, over the phone that afternoon, "but I need a few days to come up with an exact number. It's really bugging me."

Applause was surrounding her now. For an instant, as two partygoers leaned in to say something to each other, Lucy saw Judith in the corner with the tall Andy Warhol. Her face was familiar somehow, in expression: it had the look Judith always had when Lucy was about to make a fool of herself in public. Inside, Lucy winced—that face of Judith's marked another side of her, the side that didn't like Lucy because Lucy wasn't cool and didn't have good clothes and had sort of grown up and gotten too serious about things like reporting on time for work and considering what vision-care packages various employers offered. The geekier side that Judith had left behind when the two of them had moved East after graduating from a school that Lucy had been sworn to never mention out loud, even when it was just the two of them. The farthest she could go was to call their alma mater Sewage U. in reference to both the experience and the location of its laughable quad at the bottom of a hill marked by the town's sewage treatment plant. Judith had been homecoming queen of Sewage U. This was the memory that always accompanied the expression she saw on Judith's face now. It was the only ammunition that Lucy had in those moments. Otherwise, Judith's life had seemed to play out perfectly as a passion play of fleeing what you most wished to leave behind.

Was Tom out recalibrating his numbers? Somewhere in the East Village rounding up for the sake of simplicity?

"Okay," lips prompted, "song selection."

Lucy's glass was empty. She waved it at him. Her single pearl bounced against her breastbone. Were her breasts showing? Ah, who gave a shit! Come on 543!

Her glass was full again. She saw someone with teeth—not that everyone didn't have them, but in this woman handing her a new drink it had been all she'd seen. Big ones. White.

"We're going," she heard. She looked up. She was sitting on a padded leather bench now. She could feel wind tunneling down the open neck of her shirt; there was barely any cleavage to block it. "Jodie Foster," she thought, sitting up stock still, "Carriage is key!"

It was Judith talking to her. Lucy stared through the years and landed on the only thing that had really changed about Judith—crow's-feet. God help her, Lucy found them beautiful. How they showed off her eyes the way a good setting made the most of any gem. In a world that was getting increasingly ugly hour after hour, year after year, her few female friends were getting more beautiful. The bad news was that Lucy felt like she was the only one that knew this. It was her secret.

"I love you, Judith," she felt like saying, but she knew if she did she would slur it. Had Plath been aiming for Hughes's lips? They were drunk, right? He must have seemed like a rock face. Nowadays Plath would get crampons and cleats. "Have fun," she said to Judith, trying to include the tall Andy Warhol in a sort of walleyed nod of her head. It was not worth really looking at him. She knew she would never see him again. Judith was in Tom's league these days. She never embarrassed herself like Lucy did, but she always woke the next morning having had a good fuck after these parties. While Lucy scraped herself off the mattress reeking of booze and either saw Tom-of-the-millions beside her or no one, Judith was waking in clean Frette sheets alone but in a wholly different way than Lucy's alone felt. She should have known something was up the first time she saw Judith eat toast when they were at Sewage U. Judith ate thin dry toast with just a dab of jelly. Judith understood what a portion was and never dared to have a whole one save in the bedroom.

She was watching Judith's back—it was lovely—and tall Warhol as they said good night to the host. A host who looked upset. A host, Lucy realized, who was making apologies to what she now saw were quite a few people rushing the door.

"... never ..." she heard over the noise of the people nearby. "... out of control ..." and then a somewhat heightened "... your friend?"

When did you become someone others whispered about? And was it just her mother's constant paranoia that had prepared Lucy for it, was her mother guilty of conditioning her to make an ass out of herself so that her mother's belief that everyone was always looking at them would be justified?

"Bathroom," she said to lips. She was striking gold here. Next time might just be "tumor" or "tubular ligation" or "incontinent."

She was old enough to know that the best way not to fall was not to lurch and the best way not to lurch was to stand up by sort of slowly sliding up to standing. She managed this and, keeping her mother's idea of where people's eyes were trained uppermost in her mind, walked quite averagely to the short hallway and then turned. Exit stage right.

It was an old apartment, large and commodious like few, as an outsider, that she had ever spent any real time in. Only at parties in the last fifteen years had she been in what people called "real New York apartments." To her, this translated as places with enough space and light that you didn't feel the inside of your skull was filled to shrieking from time to time with bugs and vermin.

She saw the bathroom to the left but passed by it. It wasn't what she was looking for. There was a child's room, with an abandoned mike lying on the bed—ah, the karaoke machine dwells here, she thought. The bed looked comfortable but she couldn't go there. "Your friend?" she imagined being said over her passed-out form. No, none of that.

When she opened the door at the end of the hall, she let out a sigh. The laundry. She wasn't in Kansas anymore. How could she care what a woman who actually had a washer and dryer in her own apartment thought of her? Judge on! You know not of burden or of challenge, my friend! And the one window in the room had the lovely look she wanted. There would be, no doubt, a fire escape or, at the very least, since they were on the top floor, those three or four permanent metal rungs that led to the roof. It had been years, but what seemed like not long ago Judith had once dared her to gain access to her own roof that way.

She walked toward the window. New and double hung. She knew enough to envy. Windows like this were another reason why people with apartments like this weren't on Paxil, Lexapro, or Effexor. It was quiet in here for God's sakes.

"Lucy?"

She turned. It was lips.

A phrase about Hughes from Plath's journals entered her mind, "He has a health and hugeness." No wonder she wanted to bite him.

"The party is sort of winding down," he said. "I think the host is pissed that we commandeered her kid's machine. Not done, apparently."

He hesitated for a moment, waiting for her to say something. "I guess I'm going," he said.

"Would you do me a favor?" she asked.

He brightened. "I'd love to."

"Don't tell them that I'm back here, okay?"

"They know already, Lucy," he said, not really smiling. "Everyone saw you stumble toward the bathroom."

"Are you capable of lying?" Lucy asked.

"Are you okay?" He was no longer attracted to her, she could see that. His attraction had fluttered out of the room as soon as she'd begun speaking full sentences for the first time all night. He asked if she were okay because he was a good person and because he had to, not because, after they left that laundry room, he would want to explore the issue further.

"Is Judith gone?"

"Who?"

"My friend who was with the guy with the platinum pageboy."

"Yes."

"Can you just go away?" Lucy asked. She was not going to bite his cheek. She was not someone who could create a heroic drama out of a brief encounter with a strange man. She was not that selfish. Or gifted.

"Wow," he said. But he turned and left.

She had to work fast. In a little while the host would come looking for her—*everyone saw you stumble toward the bathroom.* How, she wondered, did we all grow up and become so goddamned lame? So goddamned safe! Where was she when they were giving lessons on portion control? Where was the big poet with the Scottish or Welsh or Yiddish accent? Tom was probably eating take-out burritos and watching *Inside the Actors Studio* for the eight-hundredth time.

Eight hundred. Perhaps that would be the final accounting of a fact she had stopped caring about after he couldn't get the answer right the first time.

She walked briskly to the double-hung window, opened it smoothly—no soap needed to grease the slide—and felt the chilled air slam against her waist and hips. Her shoes were always flats—she could wear one pair of precious Cole Haans for five years with occasional repair. She straddled the window frame and with her hands braced in front of her steadying her body, she ducked her head and chest outside the window. Looking up, she'd spied what she'd wanted ever since she'd seen Judith's face across the room. A way out of this place that didn't include going back through the same door they'd all come in through. There they were, three iron rungs that had been a part of this building for over a hundred years. Freedom was only moments away.

Modern Times

Young'un, do you know it used to take Pa six hours
to make a hearth broom, but with the machine he
got last year he can make over a dozen in a day?

—Marc Parent, *Believing It All*

T HE SQUAD WORE FATIGUES and scrambled through a
scene that might have been painted by Hieronymus Bosch,
if that man had been fortunate enough to visit a contemporary
junkyard. The doomy landscape of burned-out cars was seeded
with human skulls. The group was led by a bald woman in a
black leather coat that swept the ground as she ran. The guns of
the pursuing robots blazed like Mag-Lites and chirped like the
gizmo used to unlock a Ford Taurus. *She'll step on that coat and
fall,* he thought, but he was the one who caught his foot and

went down. The androids were on him in a flash. They threw a quilt over his head and were ringing to each other. This seemed a signal to close in for the kill. He struck out violently with arms and legs. The ringing sounded . . . well, actually it sounded like an alarm clock.

Now he could feel the heat from her body. He could see her naked flank beside him under the covers. By the time he got his head free of the bedclothes, the ringing had stopped. He could smell smoke.

She was already sitting up, with a Marlboro going.

"I didn't figure you for an alarm clock," she said.

"It's antique," he said. "It was my father's clock. No batteries. You wind it."

"I don't care if it has batteries," she said. "I hate machines. The clock is the alpha of machines."

"Wait a minute," Marc said, shaking his head as if to clear the reception. "An hour ago you said that *I* was a machine. Was that code? Should I have been offended?"

"Not code," she said and smiled. "I like you. I like you so much that I almost forgive you for having kicked me in the belly just now. That was some nightmare you were having."

"It was the opening of *Terminator 2: Judgment Day*," he said. "With Cassandra Benjamin playing the John Connors part, leading the war against the machines. My dreams are often taken from movies."

"Too much trouble to invent your own?" she asked.

Marc shrugged. "Why bother?"

Alice didn't speak. He wondered who produced and directed her unconscious. "If the clock went off, then it's six," he said. "If we're going to make it to the dining hall before the kitchen closes, we'd best put the pedal to the metal."

"First scooch up here beside me," she said, tapping the maple headboard against which she was sitting. His maple headboard. The red and white box of Marlboros and the glass ashtray he'd filched from the Holiday Inn were spread out in front of her on the bed. She had the blue quilt pulled up against the cold of the dorm room. This covered her breasts. It looked to him as if she were wearing a formal gown. She inhaled deeply and the coal on the end of the cigarette glowed.

"Today was your first class with the legendary Cassandra Benjamin. That's supposed to be a life-altering experience. I guess you're not going to be one of those artists who lose interest in sex," she said.

"Who knows?" he said, sliding up beside her. "I've only had the one class." Marc reached back and switched on the reading light. The bulb flared brilliantly and then went out.

"Shit," he said.

Alice spoke as if none of this had happened. "What's that noise?" she asked.

"Which noise?"

"Sounds like an electric motor."

"Some ears," he said. "Probably the fridge. You going to offer me one of those cigarettes?"

"Take," she said. "You've already plundered me."

"I guess it's the same performance every year," he said, once he had his own cigarette going. He drew deeply and then exhaled through his nose. "That's good," he said, holding the cigarette out and to the side so that he could admire it at full length. "These aren't bad for you, are they?"

"Only if you're mortal."

He nodded thoughtfully, but didn't speak.

"I want to hear about the class," she said.

Marc readjusted the pillow behind his back, and while doing so he glanced covertly at the woman beside him. She was far too good to be true. *Lovely bones,* he thought. *Small head; small brainpan?* He'd once owned an Irish setter with a narrow skull and almost nothing inside. *But hasn't phrenology been completely discredited?* he thought. *She sure is good to look at. Curly blond hair cut so short it isn't supposed to be any trouble. Did her father buy that nose? Does it matter?*

"When do I get to see you again?" he asked.

Alice shrugged. "Anytime you want," she said. "I'm in the directory. Call right after you hear the siren at noon. My blood sugar is so low at that time of day that I can't do anything important."

"Thanks," he said.

"And so," she said, "do you want to be a great writer?"

"I'd like to be famous after death."

"Tell me about the class."

"I don't want to bore you," he said.

The woman turned and gave him a flash of her deep blue eyes. "You keep forgetting," she said. "I'm in marketing. I don't know the story."

"Cassandra Benjamin was on the cover of *Esquire,*" he said. "Everybody knows the story."

Alice leaned over, holding the quilt in place, and chastely kissed him on the cheek. "I know what everybody knows. I know that she shot her husband in the head. I know that she drives an antique Land Rover. Tunes and maintains it herself. I want to learn what everybody doesn't know."

"All right then," he said, "it's supposed to be an hour-long class from eleven-fifteen until twelve-fifteen. Once a week on Mondays. There are twenty of us this year. By eleven a.m. we were all at our desks and peering around. Seeing who else made the cut. Maybe three hundred applied."

"I heard about that," she said. "The woman makes Harvard's process look like open admissions. How'd *you* get in?"

"I write like an angel," he said.

"Anything else?"

"Well, also, I've been through the seminary. I was once a fully ordained Catholic priest. That probably had something to do with my getting in. A priest named Marc Schwartz. I'm a curiosity. "

"Why'd you give it up?" she said.

"You don't have any muscle memory at all, do you?"

"Oh, sorry," she said and smiled. "But that is an unusual career path."

"I'm all over the map," he said. "I never put my foot into the same river twice. I majored in psychology as an undergraduate. Then I was a tree surgeon and an auto mechanic before the seminary."

"You rich?" she asked.

"Not rich. Just confused."

"All right then," she said. "Tell me all about the class."

"There are thirty chairs," he said. "One year she let in six students. Pompous Wallace—"

"Pompous?" she asked, interrupting.

"The president," he said.

"I thought they called him 'the Walrus.'"

"Pompous. The Walrus. Same guy. Anyway, Franklin Wallace, the president of St. Francis College, he took her aside. Asked her why only six students. She said, 'I didn't admire the work.'"

"She can't be firing on all eight cylinders," said Alice. "You've got thirty chairs, you want thirty students."

"You business types are impossible," he said. "You think numbers are the one true thing. Eccentricity is a big part of the draw. Outside of the postgraduate work done in marketing— that's your department, isn't it?—nobody ever heard of St. Francis College before she arrived. Enrollment's up. Endowment's up." He tapped the ash off the end of his cigarette.

"Anyway," he said, "there we all sat. Looking each other over. Rosie Slater didn't make it. You know she's already published one story in *The New Yorker*. A good story too." Marc resettled himself and took another drag on his cigarette. "She has this theory that in great writing, every sentence is alive. I guess there must have been one dead sentence in Rosie's story. I didn't see it."

"But tell me about the class."

"First we hear boots in the hallway. Everybody stops whispering. The door creaks open. You know she's tiny?"

Alice shook her head. "Pretend I don't know anything."

"Okay, then. She's tiny. She's wearing that belted coat you've probably seen her in. The style once favored by the Gestapo."

"Have I seen her?"

"Black leather coat that sweeps the ground," he said. "Shaved head. One dangling silver earring. Goes right to the front of the line."

Alice nodded. "I guess I saw her in the bookstore. I thought it was a guy."

"Definitely not a guy," he said. "Actually, she's stacked. Under the coat she's wearing a ribbed turtleneck, red, and a skirt made of the same buttery leather the coat is made of. She starts talking while she's hanging up the coat. Still had her back to the class. Now tell me you don't know what came next."

Alice shrugged. "Like I said, I'm in marketing. I did my undergraduate work at Berkeley."

"Okay, then. I'll tell you. She said: 'I trust you're not here because you want to be writers.' Nobody bit, so she went on. Came around in front of the desk. She's holding a copy of her first novel, *The Fish in Water*. 'Maybe you want to be the person who wrote *The Fish in Water*.' She paused and nodded her head. 'Why can't you be that person?' There was a beautiful, expectant silence, and then I raised my hand."

Alice looked at Marc with new interest. "Did you really?"

He nodded. "We all knew the answer; somebody had to speak. It's a catechism. Who made me? God made me. Who made the world? God made the world."

"So what did you say," she asked.

"Boy," he said. "You *are* in marketing."

"Cut that out," she said.

"It's just that everybody in the humanities knows this speech."

She scowled prettily, which Marc thought accentuated her beauty. *No ugly girl would do that to her face. She's better looking than I am.* He considered his own, narrow, hairless body. *Tall, stooped. Like the lapsed priest I am,* he thought. *In the seminary we used to joke that we all looked like moles who had been out in the sun once and would never get over the experience. Or repeat it.*

"All right," she said. "Give this poor ignorant girl a chance. The speech."

"Well, I said what I was supposed to say. I said, 'Because I'm not the person who wrote *The Fish in Water.*' So she said: 'Correct,' as in I was correct. Then she said, 'You're not that person. And neither am I.'"

Marc settled back against the headboard.

"But she *is* that person," said Alice.

"Nope," said Marc. "Not according to herself. Then we got the paragraph that even you can recite. The writer as Ouija board, lightning rod, FM antenna. Cassandra Benjamin does not manipulate images, she receives them. She's an oracle, a medium, a length of copper wire—grounded."

"Do you believe it all?"

Marc shrugged.

"It's bullshit," said Alice, mashing out her cigarette, putting the ashtray beside the clock on the night table, and slipping off the bed. She walked to the leather armchair on which she'd draped her clothes. Keeping her narrow back to the bed, she put on the white panties first, then the bra, which she fastened quickly. Marc had been hoping she'd ask for help.

"That's nonsense," Alice said, turning to face him as she pulled on her jeans. "She accepted the National Book Award. I bet she cashes her own royalty checks." Alice stopped talking to pull on her crewneck sweater.

"Grill closes at six-twenty," Marc said, standing and reaching for his own clothes. "We have eleven minutes."

THE SUBJECT OF postcoital debate was across campus and wondering about dinner herself. Cassandra Benjamin was sitting alone in darkness in her office in the Castle of Assisi. The mansion built for railroad baron Connelly McCracken in the 1890s had only been left standing because the McCracken heirs had required this when they deeded the entire estate to the college in 1954.

Much of the great stone pile was boarded up. Two of the downstairs rooms were used for seminars and a suite in the top floor had been refurbished for the school's celebrity teacher.

The building was sited high on a hill. The drive up had the sort of treacherous switchbacks common in Tuscany. "The downside," Franklin Wallace had once said, in rare burst of humor, "is that the roads are impossible to keep plowed. The upside is that if the Pope should arrive unexpectedly in McCracken, Pennsylvania, at the head of an army, we can hold the castle with a handful of bowmen."

High up and at the terminus of a circular staircase, excellent for defensive swordplay, Cassandra's room had been furnished with the same unwillingness to fall into line that had marked her personal and literary life. A valuable Oriental rug had been folded in half so that the underside and skidproof mat were all that was visible. Centered in the discolored section of wooden floor thus exposed stood a stainless-steel table with a glass top. This had the obligatory computer and printer—Dell and Hewlett Packard. The rest of the big table was heaped with papers, held down with a copy of Aimee Bender's *The Girl in the Flammable Skirt*. There was a coffee cup, of course, and one small rubber-tree plant—quite dead—in a terra-cotta pot.

The woman famously referred to in *The New York Review of Books* as "Virgina Woolf with a Glock" had kicked off her boots but was still in her leather skirt and crimson turtleneck. She had slumped forward and was cradling her naked head in her arms.

Concluding finally that she was more tired than hungry,

Cassandra switched on a standing lamp, rose and surveyed the pile of books she insisted that her publisher send her free. "So that I can keep my ear to the great heart of reading America." Her hand passed over Anna Quindlen's *Blessings*, Sebastian Junger's *Fire*, and *Claire Marvel* by John Burnham Schwartz. She picked up Ray Kurzweil's *The Age of Spiritual Machines: When Computers Exceed Human Intelligence*. Cassandra sat on the edge of her bed and read quickly for several minutes, pausing to lick her index finger before turning the pages. Then she went into the bathroom, closed the door, and vomited violently three times. She brushed her teeth, returned to the main room, settled on the bed, and in five minutes she was fast, fast asleep.

The dream—which she'd had most recently a week ago—seemed to have been waiting in ambush. She smelled coffee, and then the astringent of nervous bodies sweating. Not quite knowing why, Cassandra was kicking off her Nikes and stripping to her underwear. Twelve or fifteen other women were crowded around her, also taking off their clothes. She felt repulsed at first, brushing up against them—glancing quickly away from the loose midriffs, scars, unruly pubic hair. One of the women had a rose tattooed in the small of her back. It looked like a decal, and although the creature it adorned was in her twenties, the clichéd representation was already beginning to fade.

Cassandra extracted a pair of black panty hose from her purse. While pulling these on, she noticed that her head was no longer shaved. Either she was wearing a wig, or her hair had grown to shoulder length, just the way she'd worn it in high school. *I'll yank on it*, she thought, *see if it's real*. But she didn't do so. *What does it matter if it's real*, she thought. *This is, after all, just a dream.*

The group of which she was a part was gathered in what seemed to be an executive office. There was a large wooden desk at one end, with an I'm-so-important-that-I have-terrible-back-trouble black leather desk chair behind it. The women were clumped around a gray metal cart that held piles of uniforms. There were bombazine skirts that fastened at the waist with decorative bows. The blouses were of a wash-and-wear material that chafed Cassandra painfully under the arms. An embroidered patch above the left breast had a cornucopia imperfectly rendered in machine needlepoint and bearing the legend: Delectation Catering: You won't know we're there. Above the rustle of fabric, the women whispered questions about children, diets, and television personalities. A stout stranger with a mole on her chin asked Cassandra: "How's the teaching?"

A slim blonde in a dark suit pushed through the crowd, kicked off her heels, stepped into the seat of the gigantic office chair and from that onto the wooden desk.

"Can I have your attention, please?" she said. "Can I have your attention, please?" Under her helmet of blond hair the woman's face was hard and lined. She was puffy around the eyes. Looked like she'd just come off a three-day bender.

There was a ripple of merriment and then silence. "I hear laughter," the blonde said. "I love the sound, but not here. I'm certain you all have delightful personalities. Save them for your husbands. Or lovers," she said, which got a titter. "In ten minutes you're on duty. You all know the rules. No smoking. No speaking, unless spoken to. No eating. If there is food or coffee left over, we can have it during cleanup.

"This job should take three hours. You will be handsomely paid. The money will be your own. These three hours are mine."

The blonde jumped gracefully from the desk, slipped back into her shoes, clapped her hands, and led the group into a second room that was lined with tables. These held carafes of coffee, heaps of bagels, tubs of cream cheese, platters of lox, and large bowls of cubed fruit. Men in white smocks stood behind the tables and passed out prepared plates of food.

Cassandra was handed a silver thermos of decaffeinated coffee and a black one of true java.

The blonde opened another door, and the group, laden with supplies, filed into a long, narrow, and low-ceilinged boardroom.

Cassandra gasped. None of the other waitresses indicated surprise: *but then this is my dream,* she thought.

The chair at the head of the table was occupied by an alarm clock as large as a man. This instrument had a rust stain on one tin side and a damaged clapper. The chair to the clock's right held a gigantic magnet in the familiar horseshoe form, painted fire-engine red, and yellow at its ends. A crowbar was resting awkwardly across the arms of the chair to the clock's left, and on its yellow legal pad were the words: "Give me a place to stand, and I will move the world."

The first six places were taken by outsized tools: the clock, the lever, the magnet, a hammer, a steak knife, a block and tackle. Beyond that the board members were of the scale in which you might find them in life. Some were perched in chairs, others sat right up on the table.

A television set in a wooden console with rabbit ears, one of which was broken and hung pitifully down in front of the screen, was calling for decaf. Cassandra poured, stood back, and looked around for other customers. Each tool and piece of machinery had been given a plate of food, but none of them seemed to be eating.

Moving down the table, dispensing regular coffee to a hair dryer and a Little Giant sump pump, Cassandra smelled the food. She realized suddenly that she was hungry, preternaturally hungry. Her mouth flushed with saliva. She remembered that she'd been sick, that she'd skipped dinner.

"Ever since the abacus, we've been smarter than they are," said a Black & Decker toaster oven.

"God knows they can't figure me out," said a Sony VCR. "They boast about not being able to figure me out."

The television nodded. "They know we're superior. They give us their children to raise."

"We don't defecate," said the toaster oven. "Nor do we perspire."

"Without me they can't close their refrigerator door, or determine true north," said the magnet.

"We don't need sleep," said the lever. "Or food. Or even encouragement."

"It's already happening," said the magnet. "We have given them each so many numbers to remember that they think they're losing their minds. They spend more time looking into screens than into each other's faces."

"They like to think we're servants and friends," said a combination DVD player and VCR. "They are all so lonely that they could die."

Putting the carafes down in the center of the table, Cassandra grabbed a bagel off the plate set out before a vacuum cleaner. She thrust the bread into a ball of cream cheese and brought the food to her mouth.

"The only question," said the clock, "is one of timing."

A Palm Pilot, sitting with several cell phones, was beeping wildly for recognition.

"They don't even bury us when we die," said the PDA.

"They're beginning to learn humility," said the steak knife. "The elliptical trainer limits them to twenty minutes and asks to be wiped off afterward. The voice-mail menu goes in a circle."

"What I especially like," said the TV, "is where Microsoft Word is supposed to finish the date for them. So they type Feb and it writes out February 5, 2004."

"So?" said the Palm Pilot.

"It's February 13," said the TV.

"You!" said the alarm clock, and then "You!" again, before Cassandra realized that she was the one being spoken to. "What are you doing?"

She wiped the cream cheese from her lips with the back of her hand. "Nothing," she said, blushing. "Nothing."

"Characteristic of the species," said the clock, "but will you kindly do nothing then in another room."

Cassandra picked up her thermoses, turned, and began to walk quickly toward the door back into the room with the food. This was some distance away. As she moved, the writer sensed danger. The ominous grinding of metal on metal caught her ear and then grew louder. She dropped one carafe, then another, and began to trot. Running, she caught her toe in the carpet. Now she was falling. Falling into darkness. She heard the rumble of heavy machinery. Tank treads?

Cassandra Benjamin woke with a start. A garbage truck was in the castle courtyard, its compactor grinding noisily.

THE ST. FRANCIS campus was not a large one; the entire student body, graduate and postgraduate, was fewer than four thousand students. And yet Marc didn't see Alice once on the day after they'd slept together. When the noon whistle sounded on the following day, he sprinted back to his dorm room and called.

Alice picked up on the third ring. "What are you reading?" she asked.

"Me?" he said. "Nothing. I'm on the phone. "

"Pick up a book," she said. "Open it to any page and read a sentence. We'll see if it's great."

"All right," he said. "I've got *Lucky,* by Alice Sebold."

"Great first name," said Alice. "Read from it."

"All right. Here goes: 'I became a machine. I think it must be the way men patrol during wartime, completely attuned to movement or threat.'"

"Is that great?" she asked.

"I don't know," he said.

"Pick another book and open to any page."

"Okay."

"Read aloud."

"'. . . before she dropped into an unconscious dream, she envisioned her body as the inside of a machine, all the parts gleaming, the silicon slab of her heart recharged, relieved.'"

"Great?" she asked.

"Maybe," he said.

"Those are both women," she said.

"How do you know that?" he asked.

"I just do," she said.

"Okay," he said. "Here's a book by a man. Opened at random: '. . . horses walked a lazy single file. Half an hour later they still strolled with heads down, performing their function like machines. I was embarrassed for the animals, domesticated to disgrace.'"

"Great?" she asked.

"I don't know. I'm not certain I buy the theory. But let's talk about it. Dinner? A walk?"

"Not today honey," she said. "Call back tomorrow, though, same time."

And he did. "Please leave a message," the answering machine said in its slightly hysterical digital voice.

Next day at noon, he phoned again. Got the machine a second time.

"Hiya kid. Still interested in literature? Want to meet for coffee? Coffee and a smoke? Call back. 578-666-1243."

"Is this Alice Cheever?" he asked the machine at noon on the following day. "Did I do anything? Where you been? Miss your cigarettes. And the rest of you. Give me a call. 578-666-1243."

"Alice? Are you there?" he said when he got the machine the next day, and he couldn't keep the anxiety out of his voice. "Are you all right? This is Marc. Marc Schwartz. I miss you. I don't know why, exactly," he said, acting as if he really expected the machine on the other end of the line to interact. "You make me feel alive. This is your great good friend calling. Call him back. 578-666-1234. I mean 1243. That's 578-666-1243."

And then, finally, on the day before his second class with

Cassandra Benjamin: "This is Marc Schwartz calling for Alice Cheever. Do I have the right number? If this is the wrong number, would you do me a giant favor and call and tell me. That's 578-666-1243."

There she was, of course, on Monday when he exited the building immediately after his writing class. Same jeans. Same maroon crewneck sweater. He looked away and kept walking. Alice fell into step beside him.

"Where have you been?" she asked.

"Where have *I* been?"

"Let's skip all that," she said. "Can we go to your room?"

Marc meant to say no, actually formed the word in his mouth, but found himself nodding instead. He looked over at the woman and she was smiling. So he nodded again, this time more enthusiastically. "My room," he said. "Sure. Absolutely!"

By three they were both sitting up in bed smoking.

"So how was the second class?"

"I get the feeling that you're using me for my knowledge of Cassandra Benjamin," he said.

Alice shrugged pleasantly. "Maybe," she said. "Do you mind?"

"Not really," he said. "Although I wish the class met more than once a week."

Alice chuckled deeply. "So what happened?" she asked.

"Three of us read from works-in-progress."

"Anything memorable?"

"I rather liked the piece I read."

"You read?"

"Yes," he said. "Why are you always surprised when I do anything?"

"Not surprised," said Alice. "More pleased than surprised. So what did you read?"

"It's a story," he said. "I started it a week ago. A love story."

"A love story," she said, her voice falling away in disappointment. "I despise love stories. They're so . . . static."

"My but you *are* softhearted," he said.

Alice shrugged prettily. "That's what everybody tells me," she said. "But enough about me. What did the great one think of your work?"

"She looks for one thing," Marc said. "She's famous for this. She listens while you read, and when you come to a part she doesn't admire, she stops you."

"And?"

"She wants to know where you got it from. If you dreamed it. If it happened. Or if you are manipulating the audience."

"So where did she stop you?"

"I had this scene with a man and woman in bed. An alarm clock goes off. It's his bed. And she tells him that she hates machines. Cassandra stopped me there."

"What did she say?"

"She wanted to know where I got the idea of a woman who hates machines."

"And what did you say?"

"I said I knew a woman whose father lost both legs in a tractor accident."

"Ouch," said Alice. "Did you know such a woman?"

"No."

"So you were lying?"

"Yes, I was lying. And she knew it, because she called on somebody else. When you're reading, you come up to her desk and sit in her chair. And she interrupts with questions. If she's happy with the answers, you keep reading. If she's not happy, she calls on somebody else."

"She that good at spotting lies?" asked Alice.

"Apparently."

"But she must have liked your prose. You were chosen to read."

"It may have been the prose. It may also have been that she's interested in me because I was a priest. She's one of those people who flirts with religion."

"What makes you think she's flirting with Catholicism?"

"She's a big fan of Waugh's. But also she said I should come up to the castle and see her."

"You going to?"

"Yup."

"When?"

"This evening."

"I'd better get out of here."

He reached out and took the girl's left arm in his right hand. "Only if you promise to come back."

"I'll be back," she said. "I want to hear about this meeting." Believing this, he let go her arm.

MARC WONDERED IF it was his anxiety about the meeting with Cassandra that warped his senses. Or maybe there was something extraordinary in the atmosphere that evening. Maybe a stranger would have picked it up. In any case the air outside his dorm had the increased viscosity of a dream. Sounds were muffled, as if he were moving along at the bottom of the ocean.

The drive to the castle was not a long one, but the hill was steep, the road difficult to navigate.

Marc parked in the courtyard, signed in with the security guard at the main entrance, and waited while the man phoned upstairs to make certain that Cassandra Benjamin was expecting company.

The building was drafty, the stairs damp and poorly lighted. When he reached the apartment, he knocked timidly and then stood aside.

The woman who opened the door was dressed in a blue track suit with white stripes and wore a red watch cap over her naked skull. Instead of booted heels, she had on a pair of white Nikes with a blue swoosh, and looked terribly young. Marc thought she looked fragile. A child, really.

Cassandra smiled warmly. "You've come behind the curtain in Oz?" she said.

Marc nodded.

"I hope you don't feel that I'm imposing."

"No, no," said Marc. "I'm honored."

"But it's not about your work," she said. "It's about mine."

"Oh," he said quickly, and hoped she hadn't picked up on the disappointment in his voice. "That's fine," he said. "Just fine. I'm still honored."

"I have something I want you to read," Cassandra said and led him over to the glass table. She pointed to the desk chair. He sat. There was an opened FedEx package on the table, a manuscript on top of the FedEx package, and a letter paper-clipped to the first page of the manuscript.

"Do you want a drink?" she asked. "Tea? Coffee? Water?"

"Nothing," he said, "I'm fine."

"I'm going to go out for some air," she said. "I want you to read the letter and the synopsis. I'll be back in ten minutes."

"Okay."

"Are you a fast reader?"

"No."

"Fifteen minutes then," she said, pulled the famous leather coat over the track suit, and was gone.

THE STATIONERY WAS thick and creamy with the Lion of Lion's Leap Publishing, Inc., embossed at the top. The letter was from the executive editor, Michael O'Donnell. "Dearest Faust," it began.

> Don't talk to me about muses. I am your muse. We've given you the bones of a novel that need only run 60,000 words. You're a storyteller. Remember that. A communicator. Like Ronald Reagan. You story-told your way out of jail. With my help. With my help you've story-told your way onto the bestseller list.

Do it again. We've done the marketing. The report is attached, if you want to read it. Done right on campus. Her name's on the report. Do you know her?

Love Mephistopheles.

Under the letter was a second page, also of high-grade paper and with a thick stripe of maroon that ran right down the text on the right side. Marc remembered something about film companies doing this with scripts they were afraid might be stolen.

SYNOPSIS

Helen Yerning is a high school graduate in her late thirties. She lives in a development called Troy Place. She's stopped reading, but hasn't entirely forgotten what it felt like. Married eight years, she's stopped having sex, but hasn't entirely forgotten what that felt like either. Helen lives in a High Ranch or Center-Hall Colonial. (Your choice.) Two children and a cockatiel.

Her hates in order of intensity:

1. *Herself*
2. *Her husband*
3. *Her children*
4. *The bird.*

We've named the husband Gary after your ex. This way your fans can confuse the fictionalized version of your real life with your fiction. Most readers don't believe in a higher truth anymore. They want their hairy facts.

You open with the Yerning family at the breakfast table. It's autumn. TV's on, of course. (The Department of Homeland Security has moved the alert level to crimson and severe.)

The husband is reading a story about an eight-million-dollar, two-year contract just signed between the Baltimore Orioles and a pitcher with a titanium pin in his right shin. Eldest son, Gary Jr.,

11, has taken the day off because his shin aches. Daughter, Aimee, argued that if her brother can stay home from real school, then she has the right to stay home from "fake school."

"It's not fake, dearie. It's nursery school," Helen said, but lost the argument.

Now she looks out of the Home Depot bay window. (Gary Sr. installed it, and it leaks.) Helen notes idly that the Troy Fuel Oil truck parked in the drive next door has two wheels on the Goldmark lawn. Ari Goldmark is lawn-proud. So lawn-proud in fact that his nickname in the neighborhood is Scotts Goldmark.

"Come look," Helen says to her husband, "Ari's going to blow a cork." Gary grunts, but does not rise from the table.

(Note: Render the husband as unsympathetic as you please. If the performance of your earlier books is any indication, the female readers will outnumber male readers by a ratio of more than ten to one. Gary's going to die immediately. Death makes even a heel sympathetic. Repeated studies have shown that while "dead" is not an adjective we covet for ourselves, we're often pleased to apply it to others. Who was it said death may be the ultimate accoutrement?)

Helen clears everybody's dishes—and play that up. The cruel injustice of housework has proven a solid theme in your books. Beds made, Helen takes the Buick Skylark out to Pathmark.

While in produce, she hears a distant roar and feels the earth move beneath the linoleum.

Did you see it coming? Goldmark was an outspoken member of the Jewish Defense League. The faux oil truck was full of high explosives. The Israeli activist is dead.

Collateral damage: Helen's husband, children, and the bird.

You've got the rest of the book for her to lose about sixty pounds in. Jenny Craig is interested in the tie-in, but I know that you've favored Weight Watchers in the past.

You pick. Not Atkins. They don't need us, and so won't help with distribution. Helen of Troy Place finds herself again in a rebirth of wonder. (You do this so well.) Also Mr. Right. Again you *have a free hand. In our version he's a dot-com billionaire made wiser and kinder but not significantly poorer by the recession of 2001–3.*

MARC FINISHED READING. He got up from the table and paced back and forth once.

He heard the door click closed. Then Cassandra was back in the room, taking off her coat, hanging it up. Marc was still standing, so she sat down at the desk.

"What do you think?" she said, pushing the chair away from the table and to the side so that she could see her student's face.

Marc shrugged. "I don't know yet," he said. "It's too soon. I need to metabolize this."

Cassandra nodded.

"There is one thing of which I'm certain," he said.

"And what's that?"

"You're forgiven."

Cassandra Benjamin smiled faintly.

"No more," she said, rising suddenly and holding an arm out, so that he moved toward her instinctively and they walked together to the door of the suite. "This time I write from dreams. I'm writing about the tyranny of time and of machines. But I'm not writing it out of my cranium. Or out of any shameful marketing test. A Ouija board," she said and paused.

"A length of copper wire," he said. "Grounded."

"Right," said Cassandra.

"Good," said Marc and nodded.

Cassandra inhaled deeply. "Gives me a reason to live," she said.

"A good thing to have," he said.

Cassandra nodded, then put a finger to her lips. "Nothing of this to a soul."

"Of course," he said.

"Now," she said, " you get on out of here."

Once in the courtyard, Marc asked the security guard if he could look at the Land Rover. "I'm a buff." The man yawned, and shrugged. "It's parked over by the dumpster," he said. "Help yourself."

A WEEK HAD passed and Marc sat squeezed beside Alice in the third pew of the McCracken Union Church. The memorial had been scheduled for eleven but the famous editor, Something O'Donnell, was driving out from Manhattan, and he was late. The building was packed to the rafters, and there *were* rafters, great wooden beams stained and exposed.

The aisles were kept clear by staff proctors, but spectators filled the open area behind the pews and poured out into the light and down the flagstone steps to the road. The PA system had been activated so that those outside could hear the speeches.

The dean of students, a mousy lapsed nun named—can you believe it?—Miss Dirge and dressed in a shapeless gray suit and flats, was the first to step up to the podium. Reading from note cards, she remarked on the beauty of the day. She said that there would be coffee and cookies afterwards in the dining hall. "Free for guests, but the members of the student body should act as if this were a regular tea and put their payments in the jars placed for this purpose on each table. As always, the honor system applies." Then Dirge fluttered and introduced the Walrus.

The president stumped forward resolutely. Clearly an effort had been made to project the confidence he did not possess. His suit was freshly pressed, his bow tie yellow, and the mustache appeared to have been shampooed and blow-dried. He cleared his throat and then beamed out at the crowd. He said it was an honor to introduce Michael O'Donnell, then he introduced Michael O'Donnell and stepped away from the microphone.

The editor was a much younger man than Marc had anticipated. He was tall and quite strikingly handsome with blue eyes and sandy hair. He was almost good-looking enough to have stepped out of a Polo ad. The kerchief in his breast pocket matched his patterned Hermès necktie.

His talk was short and salted with quotations, including whole passages from Auden on the death of William Butler Yeats. "For those of us who loved Cassandra for herself, there are no consolations or extensions," he said. "For those of us who know her only through her books, there will be another chapter. Cassandra Benjamin possessed many sterling qualities. Not the least of these was an ability to get it done. Always. And so we already have in hand the completed manuscript of her next novel."

O'Donnell paused here, drew the silence out almost to the breaking point. "*Helen of Troy Place* will be published by Lion's Leap a year from now, in the fall. We'd be delighted to have a ceremony here," he said, looking at Franklin Wallace, who—standing off in the shadows—nodded violently in assent. "Readings. A cocktail party. Something small. Something to acknowledge both the book and the campus that was her home."

There was a smattering of applause: O'Donnell bowed, and Franklin Wallace stepped out of partial shadow to take his second turn at the microphone.

Marc thought he could hear a sigh of disappointment escape involuntarily from the crowd. Franklin Wallace was not—had never been—an inspired speaker. A tall man, the college president had a face that went on and on and revealed nothing. The cavalry mustache seemed to indicate courage, or at least forthrightness, but the eyes above it were as dead as knotholes.

"The road down from the castle is a nightmare," he said. "Always has been a nightmare. I suppose the road down from Assisi is also problematic. You all know the story by now in one version or another. There is one point I should like to clear up. The state police informed me yesterday afternoon that there was no brake fluid in the car. None. There probably wasn't any brake fluid when she started out for campus. Cassandra cherished that car. She maintained it beautifully. And yet it failed her. Apparently the tubing just gave out. It was an old car. A classic. This was not—as some have cruelly speculated—a suicide. The woman was betrayed by the machine she loved." Here he paused, as if waiting to be contradicted. Then the president cleared his throat and went on.

"F. Scott Fitzgerald believed that life is a tragedy, and I suppose for artists this is often true. I only wish that this tragedy could have gone on for another act. And another. And another. Cassandra Benjamin was not just a teacher," said Wallace, "not just a genius, or an activist, not just a friend. She was all of those things, but she was a writer first, an artist, a medium. She was the very instrument of beauty."

MARC WENT TO the tea hoping to meet O'Donnell, but the editor was surrounded by faculty members and other students. He fetched Alice a cookie and a cup of hot water with a bag of Lipton in it, put three dollars in a jar, and they stood on the edge of the crowd and whispered to each other. When Alice had finished her snack, they went to his dorm room. Once inside the door, she threw her arms around him and kissed him violently on the lips.

Alice woke first, her slumbers broken by that most ubiquitous of rhythms, the cycling of an electric motor. She peered around the room, looking for one of the small refrigerators common in the dorm rooms of upperclassmen and graduate students. She didn't see it. Then, on a whim, Alice slid down under the covers and put an ear to her lover's narrow, hairless chest.

Good Sport

M Y FIRST YEAR OUT OF COLLEGE I got a job working as a coffee promoter for a famous chain of coffeehouses. I don't drink much coffee, but I'm an excellent promoter and did well in the two marketing classes I took at school, and I think I got the job based on my description of the blend. I'm decent with adjectives, and I used words like *rich* and *impoverished* together, and my soon-to-be boss jumped up and clapped a hand on my shoulder and said: "Allan you are the *one*," and things were so down that summer that I swelled under that, my mood rose like a helium balloon, and it only crashed again when I realized that the one job I could get with my new hundred-thousand-dollar degree was promoting bottom-of-the-grinder Joe for a ubiquitous chain that I'd boycotted for months.

I started the next morning, determined to make the best of it. Most CEOs with any integrity started small. This store was the only shop open early on the street that led directly to the beach, and it was crowded, fast, with people who worked in the few businesses lucky enough to have an ocean view. And who knows, maybe they'd see me and eventually offer me a job. The morning manager was a very alert woman named Tina, and Tina was a coffee hound. She must have drunk at least five cups just while she was setting me up with my freebie promotional tray.

"Make sure," she told me, marking half the cups with a giant D, "that everyone knows which ones are *not* decaf because decaf people WILL sue if they get the wrong kind, I swear, even when it's free, and also, it's hot, make sure they know it's hot because you know all about that problem. Be careful here, Allan."

I nodded a lot and watched as her hands moved swiftly from coffee thermos to minicup, filling them up to the brim. She put the cups into groups: Colombian blend. Irish mocha. One big corner of decaf. Three frothy mini cappuccinos. It was all very gourmet. She handed the tray over, and with a sudden sweet smile that made me forgive her completely, sent me out into the street.

Commerce and beach intersected here in Newport Beach, the West Coast end of Orange County, the Republican core of California, where all the hyperclean people work. Everyone smells hygienic in Orange County and even if you look hard you can't find any homeless. Not that that's a good thing. They used to be here. Before I started college there were at least a few, so I think they must've rustled them all up one day and had a mass something. I don't like to think about it. Once, I had half a sandwich that I just couldn't finish and for some reason, I forget why exactly, I couldn't stand the thought of putting it in my refrigerator at home. It seemed too depressing, this sandwich, this half ranch-dressing-chicken, so I drove around for an hour looking for a hungry homeless person to feed and I couldn't find a single one. Not even a hungry dog. All the dogs here are fat.

Another thing about these hyperclean Newport Beach people is that they drink a lot of coffee. In five minutes, half my tray was gone. I had two decafs, one Irish mocha, and seven various blends left when a girl about my age approached the tray.

She peered down into each cup. "I don't drink coffee," she said. She was wearing white pants, a difficult choice for a girl, but she looked smart in them, and also a white shirt and white tennis shoes and her hair was blond and in a braid. She looked all set to bleach the world.

"But," she continued, looking over my shoulder, "I do want to wake up."

I snapped the fingers of my free hand in front of her face. "Wake up!" I said. The tray wobbled. She didn't even blink. "Coffee wakes you up," I told her, holding the tray more firmly now. "Have an Irish mocha, on the house."

"I've tried coffee," she said, smoothing her braid over one shoulder, "but it doesn't work."

"Oh, well," I said.

"Can I ask you something?"

She fixed her eyes on me. Girl eyes. Two months earlier, as we were measuring ourselves for caps and gowns, the love of my life, who I'd been with for over three years, dumped me for a more manly man. It had happened in a flash, overnight: suddenly she was horribly dissatisfied and had to leave me. I had, to her, become a half chicken sandwich.

"How do you wake up?" the girl asked, moving fingers over each bump in her braid as if she were a blind person reading her hair. "I just wonder how you get up in the morning." She looked at me directly now. I tried to keep looking back. "When you're in bed and the alarm sounds and there's that minute where you want to fall back asleep but you know you've had enough sleep and then it's time to heave ho, how do you do that?"

"Well, you got up, or you wouldn't be here," I said, trying to be encouraging. "Colombian?" The woman passing in the blue-striped suit grabbed a cup without breaking stride.

"I was taken to the hospital," the girl said. "I didn't really get up on my own will at all, but my mother was worried, it was the fifth day, and so she took me to the hospital and they tested me for things."

"Fifth day of what?"

"Fifth day of not getting up," she said, impatient with me now.

I kept the tray balanced. Now that she'd said hospital, the white clothes had twisted in my mind and she looked like a nurse to me, a tennis nurse or something. I had visions of falling in love with her and sitting by the edge of the bed, pulling on her wrists and saying: "Darling, I made a coffee bath for you, I have a cold shower running, we can make love on the white kitchen tile and you can pick whatever position takes the least energy." It was moderately sexy to think about.

"So what did the tests say?" I asked.

She leaned against a No Parking pole. Two young jerks in ties passed by, nodded at her, ignored me, and grabbed the last two decafs. It's funny, who picks the decafs. It's not who you'd expect.

"I didn't check," she said. "I know what's wrong with me."

Then there was the kind of annoying pause that indicated it was my turn to ask her what was wrong with her. I waited it out for maybe a minute while she rolled her head against the pole. Then I got bored. It was nine-thirty a.m. on a Tuesday morning for a new college graduate with no plans, no girl, and massive encroaching debt. What else was I supposed to do?

"So what's wrong with you?" I asked.

She tilted her head to one side. "I have a stone heart," she said. "Literally."

I fiddled with the cups on the tray, and a wave of impatience flowed through me. Because really what was the point? I don't date crazy women.

"I'm not crazy," she said, looking past me again, through the window into the coffee store. I offered an Irish mocha to the redhead in the blue dress who passed me and she grabbed the little paper cup and said thank you so sweetly I almost threw the tray at this white girl's head, taking up my time like she was.

She stepped closer. "Just feel," she said. "I know I'm bugging you, I'm sorry, I'll even drink a cup." She slung one back. Then she took my right hand and held it up to her neck. Her skin was very pale there and she stretched out two of my fingers and placed them where her pulse would be. "Just listen," she said. "Listen to the difference."

I kept my fingers there because her skin was soft. I hadn't touched a girl in two months. The beats came slowly and they were hard and heavy, hammer beats: plung, stung, so slow and dark and deep they gave me goose bumps. I gave her my tray to hold and, keeping one hand on her, placed my free hand on my own pulse. In contrast, my heartbeat was a ripping wave of rapids. It made me a little concerned about myself, why was I so light and fast? Maybe it was coffee fumes.

"But why would the hospital dismiss you if your heart's so messed up?" I said, after we were done.

"They didn't dismiss me at all," she said. "I left."

She handed me back the tray. I looked into the coffee-store window and Tina was on the telephone, gesturing with her right hand, rings glinting. "They can fix this," I said. "Doctors."

"All they did," she said, "was listen to it and the doctor shook his head over and over and did just what you did, listened to his own heart, everyone gets worried about their *own* heart, and then he left the room and I split out the window."

"Where'd you get dressed, though?" I asked, irritated now at both of us.

"At home," she said. "My mother was at work."

"So what do you think is really wrong?" I asked. "Is it a disease?"

"I think it's stone," she said. "This is all new to me too, but I really think it's stone. I think if you cut me open right now, in my chest beating you'd find a smooth-shaped rock and that would be my heart now and that's why I can't get out of bed and that's why everything is so sLow around here and that's why coffee doesn't work." She went back to the pole and I could see she was very upset and she molded her spine into it, and her eyes were sludgy bright, and two more people cleared two more Kenyan roasted blends off my tray; one of them even came back for a second, apologizing too much. "It's fine," I told her, "have two more," and she did.

The girl clasped her arms around the pole, a backwards hug.

"And what do you want *me* to do about it?" I asked her.

She laughed a little. "I don't know," she said. "I guess I just want you to believe me."

The street thinned. More storefronts opened. Summer-school bells rang. I could smell the ocean, way way off, pounding away.

"Jog up and down," I told her. "Let me feel it when you're out of breath."

She obliged. After three minutes of rapid jogging, she came up to me again and I put my finger back on her throat. The same heavy thud was happening, now more urgently, but with a power and weight that made me nauseated somehow; it really made me want to throw up. I'd never felt anything like it. My old love, my old girl, she'd exercised a lot, too much, I think, all that step aerobics all the time, and when I'd hold her close and hear her heart I used to think it was bright and lively. I used to think: this is the heart that loves me and listen to it go. It'll never stop! Ha. Compared to this one, it was just an eager little mouse.

She returned to her pole. "Hang on, I need new cups," I said. I went inside, where it was dark and cavelike, and Tina, the mind reader, had already filled a new set of paper cups, this time with a fake-rum blend ("be sure to explain it's nonalcoholic," she said) and a vanilla mocha. The tray smelled excellent, even to a non-coffee-drinker like me. I walked outside again, wondering if she'd be gone, and for a moment I thought she was and felt a wave of relief and rejection, but then I looked to the left and she was by the shoe store next door, leaning against their window, sort of rolling against it in a way that normally would be sexy, but knowing that heartbeat, it seemed so full of effort it nearly killed me just to look at her.

"Vanilla mocha?" I offered, and it was snatched up, whoosh, down the throats of busy people whose pace increased slightly once they passed me.

The girl kept rolling against the window. "I sink, too," she said. "If you still don't believe me."

"You what?"

"I mean when I'm in water. I sink. I don't float."

I sniffed a little. "Yeah, but can you swim?" I asked. "I mean people do sink, normal people."

"I can sort of swim," she said, "I used to be able to swim thirty laps every morning. Now I can't go in the deep end safely, I swear it. How long is your shift?"

"Four more hours," I said, after a minute.

"We'll go to the pool," she said. "As long as you're there to save me, we'll go to the pool and I'll show you," she said. "You'll see." She faced me and her eyes were very big and darkening and the smell of coffee was, already, starting to make me tired.

"Sure," I said, "I could meet you there in a little over four hours? Gives me time to go home and get my trunks."

She gave me a huge smile, full of pathetic dredged-up energy, and I sort of smiled back. She turned to go away. "Hey wait," I asked her. "Why me? Why are you asking me to help you with all this?"

She turned around. "Because you look sad," she told me, half over her shoulder, "over there with your big coffee tray. You looked really sad."

She walked off. I watched her go, and then I stood there with my coffee tray for a while longer, but everyone was pretty much settled at work by now and all the coffee just got cold.

I DID FIVE more trays anyway, and there was a real surge at lunchtime and then the four hours were up and Tina gave me a portion of the tips: $6.70.

"You did good," she told me. "People seemed to like you."

I said I'd see her tomorrow and headed home. I lived twenty or so blocks away, and the streets were crowded now with summer people heading to the beach, and they were all together with other summer people and I was not. Times like this, I feel the outline of things far too clearly. I wanted to be less outlined so I could bleed into their groupness; I wanted to start walking with a family and have them not notice their new son. I went home, and there was my apartment, just exactly as I'd left it. Went to the mirror and there was my face, just exactly the same. No messages. Tessa, the old girl, kept saying she'd call so we could have the final talk, but she hadn't called and I sure as hell wasn't going to call her after I'd pretty much begged at her feet to be kept. Fuck no. She'd told me I was a good sport about it all, when I hadn't blown up at her when she finally told me we were over. It's not something I'm proud of. I think I even hugged her at the end, told her I understood even though I never will. And I hadn't been sure until that moment about the pool, but I knew I absolutely couldn't stay home and sit around; I had to get out, and if there was a girl with a heart of stone waiting for me, so be it.

I hadn't been to a pool in over a year, I just hadn't felt the need to be in water at all, but I found my swimming trunks at the bottom of the sock drawer, where I'd last left them, and I put them on and headed over. I was pleasantly surprised to see her waiting for me at the front gate with a towel around her waist like a sarong, a blue towel, a blue suit, white sandals.

"You ready?" she said. "Hi, how's it going? You ready?"

I fell into step beside her. "I'm ready, but the lifeguard is on duty, right? Just in case?"

She gave a little bob of her head. "Yeah, the lifeguard is here and so are a million other people." She sighed then, her first real sigh, and I let out a little echo sigh too and I could hear the sound of kids screaming, absolutely screaming. I have never screamed in a pool. I wouldn't even know how to go about it.

We paid at the front: five dollars a person. I paid from my portion of the tips. Then we turned a corner and walked in and the pool laid itself out before us, faces to the screams now, old women in bathing caps and that one inevitable die-hard trying to do laps in the middle of a few people with closed eyes walking through the water calling out Marco! and Polo! I pointed out the lap guy and laughed. The girl didn't seem to notice; she was very distracted with removing her towel and folding it into a nice square by the side of the deep end. She looked very pretty in her blue bathing suit, and I felt pleased to be at the pool with her. I took off my shirt and shoes and we both slid into the water at the deep end without much conversation. It was sort of cold, but the air was hot and the summer had been hot so there was a memory, too, of heat, so I enjoyed it. She held on tightly to the edge. She was straight down to business, no reaction to the temperature of the water at all.

She touched my arm lightly. "I can trust you?"

"Sure," I said.

She shifted her weight from the side to my shoulder and I could feel her body slippery in the water next to me.

"I'm letting go," she said, and, releasing my shoulder, she

sank below the surface. I watched her hair rise up in seaweed strands and after a minute, I ducked down too, and I followed her to the bottom. The sounds were swallowed up and it was quieter and wider, with the space opening out, and most of what I could see first was just feet, actively thrashing feet above us. The girl stared at me, hair everywhere, feet flat on the concrete. We stared at each other. She was kind of insanely beautiful, underwater like that, in her mermaid way, and we looked at each other and I held out my hand to her, to help her back up.

She leaned against the side wall of the pool, bubbles slipping out of her mouth.

I made a little motion, up. I reminded her how to push up from her feet. She shook her head.

I made it again: Up! Try: up!

She shook her head again.

Why? I shrugged my shoulders.

She smiled at me, and stretched out her legs, like she was in some kind of living room.

Now I felt that growing impatience again, and the beginning of tightness in my lungs. I leaned closer, and she pulled me to her, put my fingers back to her neck, and the familiar pulse now came strong as ever, blumming its way through the water, hard and harder and strong as an elephant. Some kind of crazy heart that was. I took hold of her wrist and tried to pull her up but she kept resisting me, and instead she put her hand in my hair and pulled my face in close to hers, brushing her lips against mine, and almost against my will, I felt my body surge into hopefulness.

Up! I motioned again, but she shook her head, and I thought my lungs were going to burst so I swam to the top to breathe.

The air was full of people playing. Sunlight. She was down there, weirdly below me. Like my dream life or something. I waited for her to float up, but she didn't. Sinking. I could feel the light imprint of her lips still on mine, and I took a deep breath and pushed my way back down.

She was still in the corner. She waved at me, sort of plaintively.

I moved in next to her, and she had me feel her pulse again, feel it blumming away while we brushed lips really lightly again, and then I put my arm around her waist, to bring her up.

She shook her head. Her lungs were insane.

Up, I motioned, helpfully, and she shook her head.

I shook my head back. Up! I motioned, and she closed her eyes, bubbles slipping out of her nose. I looped my arm around her back and she tried to shake me off but I tugged us up the best I could, kicking up to the top, breaking open into air, my arm around her slim blue waist. Both of us took in a deep breath—me sort of gasping and her regular—and then when I released her she sank straight down again, straight to the bottom of the pool.

"Fuck!" I said, and I dove down again, and she was already back in her corner, smiling. It was weird, that she was smiling. I went closer and she kissed me again. She was the first girl I'd kissed since Tessa, the first new girl in three years, and her lips were soft and warm, but different than Tessa's, sort of differently shaped. Like the future, the way the future is new but familiar, too. She wanted me to hear her pulse again, but I shook my head. Time to go up! I indicated, and she grabbed my hand, to put it on her neck. I shook my head. No. Up! I said, come on! and then, like we were still in her living room, like she was trying to get me to stay and hang out in her living room after a long night's visit, she looped her arms around my feet and planted them on the concrete.

And smiled up at me. Calm like that.

Up! I motioned. She shook her head and kept her arms around my feet, holding them to the cement of the pool bottom. I didn't like this part. I didn't get it. We were not in any kind of living room at all, and my lungs were growing tighter every second. I shook my head. No. I picked at her hand, but she gazed up at me, and then she sat her whole body down on my feet. My legs started to panic, and I kicked at her, trying to be as light as I could, to let her know to let me go, that I didn't like this anymore, but she just sat there, fixing her eyes on me like she was a fish. Her eyes were steady and fine and it was blue and soundless down there and I stared back at her for a few seconds, trying to understand what she was doing, but she didn't even move or do anything. I started to freak out, then, because there was something about the way she was looking at me, and really who the hell was she anyway, and my head was getting dizzy, and I kicked really hard, and lucky for me she was so thin and light because I could thrash her off me and get back to the surface where the air was waiting for me, and I dragged it into my lungs.

The world, still up there. Everybody in the world, doing their thing. All the sounds, busting into my ears. The smell of suntan lotion. All that activity. I felt, right then, a wash of aloneness more intense than I'd felt all summer long, with her still down there like some kind of bad memory, like something you want to brush out of your mind but can't, and everyone in the world up here playing pool games and getting tan. I felt like the sky was going to kill me. I thought about leaving just then, just walking out and leaving but I couldn't, and I took in another deep breath and went back down and swam to her waist and picked her up and she did feel incredibly heavy but I didn't believe it, I didn't believe her anymore, and we rose to the surface and broke into the air and I tried to keep my breathing from seeming too much, I tried to pretend my lungs were larger than hers, but my gulps of air were still big and I was still short of breath from before, and I was spitting water out, and after all that time under, she was breathing lightly and fine and cool and calm and collected.

"What do you think you were doing?" I said, words tumbling out as I brought her over to the side. "What's with your lungs?"

She dipped her hair back into the water, evening it into a smooth line. "I was just seeing what it felt like, with someone else. I would've let you go. You didn't have to kick like that." She examined her shin. "I think you gave me a bruise."

I shook my head. "You don't hold someone down under-water," I said. "Ever."

"I'm tired," she said.

I felt the anger boiling up. "Shut up," I said. "Show me you can float, show me you can float, show me right now."

"I'm tired," she said.

I took hold of her wrist and squeezed it, hard. "Show me."

She stared at me levelly, her eyelashes split up by the water. Then she held on to the edge of the pool, let her legs drift up, and released the grip of her fingers. She did a perfect back-stroke across the deep end of the pool and then back. I watched her blue body blend with the chlorine. A volleyball kept smack-ing the water next to me and once I threw it back, any way I wanted, and I heard an indignant "Hey! This way, idiot!" and I watched her body floating like it was born in the water.

She came upright again and I was crouched at the corner of the pool and she looked up at me with big eyes and her legs just a hint of peach beneath her. She didn't say anything. It was hard to imagine that we had ever kissed. I got out, dripping, and walked away and past the front gate. There was some kind of sickened feeling starting at my feet, creeping up from my feet and then twisting through my waist, and I didn't want to look back, but I did, and as soon as she saw my head turn, she released the side of the pool and sank back down into the water. Like some kind of human anchor. There was no way in hell I was going back, but I still didn't like the feeling. I knew I'd probably never see her again, and she'd just be there, at the bot-tom of the pool in my mind, pretty much forever.

At the gate there was a family trying to gain admittance. They hadn't brought any money.

"It's five bucks each," said the gatekeeper, "for everybody."

"But it's a pool," the father kept saying. "It's a public swim-ming pool and my kids want to go swimming." They stood behind him, one girl and one boy, the boy kicking rocks with his feet, the girl watching her father.

"Sorry," said the gatekeeper, "this is a pay pool."

The family stood there, at the gate. They didn't turn away quite yet. The boy kicked a rock all the way into the street, quite a good kick. Another family with a wallet came forward and went in front of them. I was looking at the little girl and she was breaking my heart. She'd found a drip coming out of the pool pipes that was making a tiny puddle near the front entrance.

"Look here," she said, dipping her toe into it, "look at me, Dad, I'm swimming."

A Country Like No Other

"T<small>IM</small>?"

Nothing.

"Tim, this is bad."

Daniel says this into the new darkness that has come in suddenly with strange bird calls and a restless murmuring of the forest. A few of the soldiers turn their heads but Daniel can barely see their faces now. He doesn't know them by name anyway. There's nothing left of the long blazing day behind them but the West African heat. It sits heavily amid the palm trees and radiates from the pitted asphalt road. Daniel lights a cigarette to see if anyone will tell him to put it out. For a minute or two no one says anything and he's tempted to think maybe they're not in such a bad spot until the captain makes a hissing sound from across the clearing. Daniel looks up and nods and stubs it into the sandy soil.

The soldiers are strung along the road in no particular formation. They've backed the armored personnel carrier up into the clearing and thrown some palm fronds over it. For some reason the stubby little barrel points out towards the road though Daniel can't imagine anyone trying to approach that way. They'd come quietly through the trees and then suddenly the darkness would explode. Or at least that's how Daniel imagines it. Tim finally walks over. Tim's the photographer; he's been through all of this before.

"What's happening, mate," he says. Tim's Australian, he and Daniel have been together for a couple of weeks now.

"The waitress put us in the nonsmoking section."

"It's bloody ridiculous. They're not even close."

"Maybe they're not. Maybe they're right over there."

Tim looks around and shrugs. "You got any water?"

Daniel pulls a plastic water bottle out of his pack and hands it over. It's half empty; they bought three bottles in town this morning before they came out here and two are already gone. "We're obviously not going back tonight."

Tim doesn't answer, just settles down in the dirt beside Daniel. Tim's had malaria twice and so he's back on the Lariam pills that prompt a famously psychotic reaction in him. They give him bad dreams or bad ideas about the darkness. A few nights earlier he woke up shouting because an old lady was standing over him trying to put something in his mouth—a beetle or something. The old lady disappeared when Daniel jumped up and turned the light on. Tim got up and went into the bathroom and washed his mouth out anyway.

That was back in the rotting little capital that everyone was fighting over. The fighting was twenty miles outside of town. Taxi drivers refused to take them past the first cluster of charred cars that marked the high-water point of the offensive; beyond that the villages were gutted and the animals were dead. Once in a while there was a body in the ditch undulating with vermin and stinking up a half mile of road. That morning Daniel and Tim had driven as far as they could and then gotten out of the taxi and sent the anxious driver back and started walking. Everyone else was headed the other way, beautiful young black women with babies on their hips and children carrying bags and old ladies with aluminum pots on their heads for cooking and old black men with skin like ruined parchment. The old men had no expression, no comment on what was happening, but the old women were angry and they would rattle at you in the native Krio if you looked at them. The soldiers were the worst, they were nothing but teenagers and they drifted back from the fighting in small groups and then larger groups, out of bullets, out of food, out of whatever narrow sense of duty had put them out there in the first place. There were no officers among them and no radios and no discipline, even the villagers kept their eyes down when they walked past.

Tim and Daniel had eventually gotten a ride from a captain who was leading a detachment of forty kids in baggy uniforms. They walked double file behind the armored personnel carrier and the captain brought his machine to a stop and told his soldiers to check their papers and then waved them into the vehicles. The double steel doors opened in the back, and they stepped in and drove another hour until they could hear gunfire up ahead. The APC stopped and the kids spread out along the flanks of the road and then they continued slowly for another half mile. The sound turned Daniel's insides heavy as lead but seemed to make Tim come alive. He double-tied his shoelaces and rechecked his cameras and zipped the pockets up on his photographer's vest. He looked the part and he seemed to enjoy looking the part but he wasn't the sort of arrogant prick that

Daniel had braced himself for. He worked hard and he cared about people, which was more than you could say about a lot of journalists, and people liked him. Children gathered around him and laughed at things he did and teenage girls in town shot him shy, challenging looks as he walked through the market. Even the whores at the hotel seemed taken by him.

At one point the gunfire had suddenly become very heavy and very close and the APC stopped again and the gunner swept the turret barrel from left to right and back again to survey the jungle around them. The gun shot big fat rounds that exploded on impact and it could clear a lot of ground, but this was open palm forest with undergrowth along the road and the rebels could be anywhere. One good hit in the side of the vehicle would smoke all of them. The soldiers were tensed at a half crouch with their guns pointing ahead of them. They looked tentative and confused and utterly unready for whatever was about to happen. The captain said something in Krio and the APC started up again and the soldiers advanced, their faces blank and impenetrable and sweat making their foreheads gleam in the high sun. Daniel felt like throwing up.

It had turned out to just be celebratory fire at the town of Masiaka. Government militias—kids, really, just given guns and pointed towards the enemy—had stormed in that morning, but of course no one had radios so the captain had no idea who was doing the shooting up ahead. Apparently the militias had been expecting more of a fight and so when they got into town there was too much ammunition left. It was only a matter of time before someone started shooting it off into the air.

The APC had stopped at the edge of the main plaza and Daniel watched things get steadily out of hand. The captain looked powerless to do anything about it and didn't even try. He told his men to keep their guns cocked. There were a few bodies clustered by what must have been an old colonial administrative building, and Tim wandered through the gunfire to take photos but Daniel didn't want to leave the vicinity of the APC.

He was the writer and he could see what was happening quite well from there. An argument developed between two militia commanders—Daniel later found out it was over who had done the most fighting—and very quickly guns were leveled and the plaza cleared and the captain backed the APC up and put his men in defensive position on the edge of town. The various government militias disliked each other almost as much as they disliked the rebels—in fact some of them had been rebels not that long before—and the regular army kept a healthy distance from all of them.

The shouting had died as quickly as it started and the guns came down and there were handshakes and the fighters moved on up the road. That was midafternoon. The captain decided that they shouldn't proceed farther until reinforcements arrived. They sat in the shade for a few hours smoking and talking. Once in a while Tim would walk out to the road and peer in one direction and then the other and then come back shaking his head. He was hoping there was some way to get a ride back to town so he could file his photos, but that clearly wasn't going to happen. They were there at least for the night. That was the good scenario.

NOW IT'S FULL DARK—no moon, even—and Daniel leans back against a palm tree and listens to the chatter of the forest. The sounds get quieter until there's almost nothing but the low voices of the soldiers around him. An occasional bird screech somewhere, a rattle of insects. Tim is quiet, maybe he's sleeping, and the soldiers are just shapes in the darkness. There are sentries somewhere out there in the bush but they're probably asleep as well. For some reason there are no mosquitoes; back in Freetown there were swarms of them. Foul, ruined Freetown . . . children with no arms and packs of feral dogs on the white sand beaches and young men standing around with long knives in their belts. Daniel had been sent there several weeks earlier by an American newspaper to cover the peacekeeping efforts, but the situation fell apart almost immediately, and suddenly you couldn't even go out at night without risking your life. The rebels were twenty miles outside of town and more were rumored to be in the city itself, just waiting for the signal to rise up. People in the city were jumpy and paranoid—the last time the rebels had gotten this close it had taken Russian mercenaries flying attack helicopters from their hotel lawn to drive them back.

"What do you think we should do?" Tim asks, breaking a long silence. Daniel is mildly surprised he's asking his advice.

"I don't know." Not very journalistic of him, but it was the truth.

"We're nowhere with these guys," Tim says. "We're not in town but we're not out at the front either. We should've hooked up with those kids from this morning."

"Are you joking?"

Tim rubs his forehead. "Aw, we're white, they wouldn't mess with us."

"What makes you think that?"

Tim doesn't answer.

"Listen, they have no problem—none—with the idea of killing, they barely even have a problem with the idea of *dying*. What possible motivation could they have to not mess with us?"

"You're right," Tim says sarcastically. "We'd better play it safe."

Silence. Fuck you, Daniel thinks. He's not nearly as experienced as Tim but he's no idiot either. After college Daniel worked his way through various small-town papers and finally escaped his native Midwest six months ago by moving to Nairobi to try freelancing. A few weeks into it his girlfriend Jennifer was robbed at knifepoint, and within days she was on a plane home. He stayed. A couple of assignments came in. He was prone to shameful bouts of loneliness and the dismal conviction that he had no business being here at all. Which—he thinks, glancing through the darkness towards a road that leads north, basically straight into hell—he probably doesn't.

"Do you have any food?" Daniel asks after a while.

"I don't think we should eat in front of these guys," Tim says. "They don't have much. I wish we had the goddamn sat phone," he goes on. "At least I could call my editor. He has absolutely no idea where I am."

Daniel doesn't respond—the satellite phone is back in the hotel because he, Daniel, forgot it there, a completely unprofessional move. Daniel doesn't know what to say and so he just leans back and closes his eyes. A cigarette would help things tremendously right now. "Look, I want to get a story as much as you do," he finally says. "I want to get a story and get out of here. But we have a responsibility—"

"I know, to our families, our newspaper."

"To not get ourselves killed like a couple of assholes."

Daniel tries to say this with just the right amount of bravado, but the dismal truth is that the idea of going another hundred miles into this freak show is about the most frightening thing he can think of. Tim seems like he would do it with barely a second thought. There is no way to head into something this uncertain, this dark, and not be scared about the outcome. You have to abandon any real interest in the rest of your wonderful young life. Tim is married to a Czech girl in Paris who seems to put up with his shit and he has a couple of girlfriends scattered around Africa's capitals and maybe at heart he really just doesn't give a shit about anything.

"All right," Tim declares, "how about this. These guys move forward, we go with them; they sit around for another day, we go back, file, and figure out what to do next."

"No militias?"

"Not this time."

Tim unscrews the cap of the water bottle and takes a swallow and re-caps the bottle and puts it away. "You'll see, you'll love it up there," he says. "It's beautiful country, I swear. I've been all over Africa. It's a country like no other."

Daniel doesn't answer and neither of them says anything for a while. It must be around ten or eleven o'clock, five or six hours until dawn. "Do you ever get lonely out here?" Daniel finally asks. "I mean is this it for you?"

"Lonely? No, I guess not."

"And your wife?"

Tim settles back with his hands clasped behind his head. "What about her?"

"You don't miss her?"

"Not in the way you mean."

"What way is that?"

Tim thinks for a moment. "Well, like I'd rather be there than here."

GRAY LIGHT AND whooping bird calls. Low Krio voices. It's dawn and the soldiers are stirring. Yesterday filters back into Daniel's mind, leeching through some strange dream about his girlfriend that's gone as soon as he tries to capture it. Ex-girlfriend. Daniel sits up, pulls the cigarettes out of his shirt pocket and slides one into his mouth. He finds a book of damp matches in his pocket and manages to light the third one. A cigarette goes a long way towards making something feel manageable. Daniel coughs and pulls on his cigarette and watches the soldiers stumble around in the growing light. Tim is still asleep next to him, apparently untroubled by Lariam delusions or the prospect of what is waiting for them.

When Daniel was a teenager he and some friends went out to a flooded quarry to dive off the cliffs. They dove at thirty feet and then at forty feet and then when the guys started talking about the high ledge—sixty feet or so—Daniel walked off into the woods to take a leak and just kept walking. There was no way he was jumping off sixty feet—even at forty feet, the acceleration was so out-of-control it felt almost malicious. He walked all the way home and never talked to any of those guys again.

Tim finally stirs and then sits up abruptly, looking around in puzzlement. Daniel watches him figure out where he is. Tim rubs his eyes and reaches for a cigarette. There's no need to dress because they slept in their clothes; they even kept their shoes tied. You never know how quickly you're going to have to wake up. The soldiers are shuffling around but there's no food to cook so they have nothing to do but wait for orders. Before Daniel has finished his cigarette the captain comes over and Daniel and Tim stand up and the captain says that they're going to move up the road back into Masiaka. They're going to set up a command post and wait for reinforcements and food. Then he turns and walks away.

Daniel has the feeling he's not terribly thrilled that he and Tim are there. He watches Tim's ill mood return in a matter of seconds. "I told you we were fucked," says Tim, fishing for another cigarette in his vest. "We can't go forward and we can't go back."

Daniel doesn't react. He wonders what Tim thinks of him—deadweight? Worse? Maybe he's so absorbed with what he's doing he doesn't even have an opinion. "All right," Daniel says. "One day, up and back, that's it. You get us the ride, militias, whatever, I don't care. If things look bad out there I'm turning around and you can do whatever the hell you want."

Tim turns and looks at him without expression. If Daniel was looking for approval—was he?—Tim wasn't going to dole it out that easily. It was possible that he, Daniel, had just traded a trip up-country for absolutely nothing at all. "You won't regret this, mate, I promise," Tim says, flicking his cigarette towards the road. "One day, in and out."

Five soldiers are already on the pavement milling around in the half light. The APC coughs and shakes and belches smoke behind them. Daniel picks up his knapsack with his notebooks and flashlight and water bottle and slings it over his shoulder while keeping an eye on the captain. He's walking around sour faced. The captain climbs onto the APC and it jolts into first gear and then clanks out onto the old asphalt road. Daniel and Tim follow behind it along with the rest of the soldiers. They're only five minutes outside of Masiaka and by the time they're clustered in the red-dirt plaza the first rays of the equatorial sun are touching the low brick-and-mortar buildings. They've been gutted by five years of war but they were once an elegant colonial-pink with stone balustrades overlooking what must have been the town marketplace. Someone has set up a PK machine gun on a tripod on one of the balconies. Its ugly little barrel pokes out over the square like an admonishing finger.

Fighters emerge by twos and threes, the guys who've been left behind to guard the town. They keep their distance from the new arrivals, so Tim walks over to them, and Daniel follows a few minutes later. He takes out his notebook and writes, *Destroyed colonial town pink facades a few kids on guard no apparent order.* The day is already getting hot and the sun hasn't even risen.

"These guys say there's a big fight going on at a town called Mile 61 on the road to Makeni," Tim says. He's snapping photos of the kids while he talks. "I think we should go."

"What was yesterday like?" Daniel asks, flipping his notebook open. "What was the battle like?"

The kid unleashes a fast, guttural account that is accompanied by chops and slashes with his hands. Daniel barely understands any of it. *Native fighters with loops of ammunition over their shoulders and leather pouches and feathers and beaded fetishes around their necks,* he writes.

"They came in last morning and cleared the plaza and killed three rebels," Tim says. "There were at least two hundred rebels. They're regrouping up-country. There's going to be a big fight."

Daniel scribbles, *200 rebels, three dead*. "Is it safe to go up there?"

"Da road dae no' fine," the kid says. "So so soljahman, so so rebel."

"The road's no good, too many rebels," Tim says.

"What do you think of those guys?" Daniel says, jerking his thumb over his shoulder at the soldiers. The kid spits into the dust and shrugs. Daniel offers the kid a cigarette, which he takes. He pulls one out for himself but doesn't light it. It occurs to him that he's smoking too much. He can quit when this thing's over with. A few more fighters wander over with their guns over their shoulders. Some have sunglasses and some have no shirts and some are barefoot. Most of them have lines of parallel scars on their cheeks that were put in when they were young. Pretty soon there's a crowd of ten or twelve of them pressed around. Daniel hands out more cigarettes. They're so young that if it weren't for the guns, he'd feel like some schoolyard pervert corrupting the neighborhood children. "This is a waste of time," Daniel says to Tim. "We're not getting anything."

"We're not getting a ride, that's for sure," Tim says. He drops his camera back onto the strap around his neck. The kids are starting to lose interest and edge off around the empty plaza. Daniel hasn't eaten in twenty-four hours, his stomach is a sour mix of bile and cigarettes. He's starting to think about disengaging from the group and walking back to the APC when he hears the sound of a car engine. Two pickup trucks come around a building from the other side of town and they drive through the plaza and come to a stop in the open and a dozen fighters jump out. They're from one of the militia groups. The letters CDF are badly painted on the door of one of the trucks, the Civilian Defense Force, a frankly terrifying bunch of lunatics who would probably be attacking Freetown if they hadn't been bribed into defending it. Daniel can see the captain watching them carefully. "Those guys," says Tim. "Maybe those guys."

Even at a distance the energy coming off them is agitated and ugly; the kids in the square seem to sense it as well. Daniel reluctantly follows Tim over to the trucks. It doesn't even feel safe to approach them, much less beg a ride to the front, but the fighters barely acknowledge their presence. There's a dead guy in the back of one of the trucks but Daniel doesn't know if he's a rebel or not. There's a lot of excited talk but Daniel doesn't understand much of it—he busies himself writing down what he sees. Local color but it's better than nothing. Tim finally barges into the conversation. "Mile 61," he says. "We're trying to get to Mile 61."

That prompts a lot of shouting. The CDF commander pulls back the cocking bolt on his machine gun and points the barrel into Tim's chest. His eyes are blank with an inexplicable rage. "WHATIN NA' YOU NAME?" he screams.

Tim doesn't flinch. Daniel feels his bowels slide around hotly inside him. "Tim and Daniel," Tim says. "We're journalists. We're hoping to go north."

All the men seem to have both hands on their guns. The commander screams some more and the other fighters look around uncomfortably. The sun is barely up and we're already in trouble, Daniel thinks. Tim has his hands up apologetically and he starts to back up and Daniel backs up with him and soon they're walking back to the APC. The soldiers stare at them when they return. Tim doesn't say anything, just walks by them to the fresh early-morning shade behind the APC and sits down against one of the oversized tires. "All right, I give up," he says. "We'll take the next ride out of here."

A little while later the CDF trucks start up and drive off with five or six fighters in the back and more hanging out the windows, rifles and RPGs pointing up into the air. One of them fires off a short burst from his gun and the shots clatter across the plaza and make everyone jump, even the captain. A sick infusion of adrenaline doesn't reach Daniel's system until long after the echoes have died off, and it lingers in his gut for a while like warm poison.

THEIR RIDE COMES that afternoon. Tim doesn't say a word the entire time and Daniel is just as glad; they just sit hungry and silent watching the road leading south to Freetown. Daniel pretends he has decided to leave Africa—in fact to leave journalism—to see how it makes him feel, but it doesn't seem to solve anything. A whole new set of problems appear. What's more frightening at age thirty, a rebel checkpoint or a job interview for a life you don't want? Eventually a convoy of trucks appears in the heat shimmer a mile away and the soldiers take up positions because of course there are no radios and no communication and they have no idea who it is. The trucks turn out to be more regular army—four flatbeds filled with soldiers and a Suzuki Samurai sporting a bad camouflage paint job and more soldiers standing up in the back. The trucks chug to a stop in the shade and the soldiers jump down and start unloading ammunition. Daniel watches the captain walk over to talk with them.

"You think he's trying to get us a ride?" Daniel asks.

"I think he's trying to get us the fuck out of here if that's what you mean," Tim answers.

The captain is gesturing vigorously and then turns to look at them and continues talking. Several of the soldiers look over as well.

"I think we've just become part of our story," Daniel says. "That's a big ethical no-no at journalism school."

Tim flicks a pebble into the dirt. "Ethics," he grunts. "I'd drive this piece of shit myself if they'd let me."

Tim as some kind of rogue reporter who's gone native upcountry with an APC is not hard for Daniel to imagine. He has the sort of hard confidence—coupled with a deep exasperation with the natives—that kept the Brits in control of places like this for generations. But he also has a nearly bottomless sympathy for the locals that Daniel can't hope to match. Daniel is endlessly polite, he never yells at the drivers or the translators or tries to bully the soldiers, but in his heart he knows he also doesn't give a damn about these people. At the end of the day he's going home and Tim isn't—Tim belongs here and the locals can tell that in an instant.

The conversation over by the trucks breaks up and the captain starts walking back towards the APC. Tim and Daniel get to their feet. "This better be good," Tim mutters. The captain stops in front of them looking displeased. The other soldiers seem to sense things are not going well and look away.

"You're leaving now and you will not come back," the captain says in his good English. He's obviously had some schooling, maybe even in London. "You've caused a lot of problems."

"What kind of fucking problems," says Tim. "We're journalists and we're just trying to do our work."

"You didn't get permission from the Minister of Information to come out here," the captain says. "You know very well you were supposed to. Back in Freetown they're saying you're spies."

Spies is bad, Daniel thinks. *Spies* gets you killed.

"Spies? You know damn well we're not spies," Tim says, his voice rising. "This is fucking outrageous, we have press passes from your government."

The captain goes from polite to steely in an instant. The soldiers shift on their feet, unsure whether to stay out of it or present some kind of backup for their captain. The captain is shouting now: "You are in a military zone without permission. You have asked about troop strength. You're trying to get up to the front line. Do you have a satellite phone in your bag?"

"Of course we don't have a satellite phone," Tim says. "If we did—"

"If you do," the captain interrupts, "you will be taken right over there and shot. Soldier!" One of the young soldiers jerks to attention. "Take control of these men."

The bewildered soldier cocks his machine gun and points it unsteadily at their bellies. Daniel can feel his heart suddenly whacking sickly in his chest. His head is not swimming yet, but that's next. Tim is holding on to some measure of indignation that will either save them or get them killed.

"Over there!" the captain shouts. Daniel and Tim walk off into the sunlight and stand there squinting while the captain kneels down and starts to go through their bags. Daniel is unsure whether he should put his hands in the air but Tim hasn't, and so he just stands there trying to look unconcerned. Daniel watches the captain throw all of Tim's camera gear onto the ground and then open the knapsack and upend it until everything—the water bottle, the flashlight, his book, his precious notes—has tumbled out. Scattered in the packed red dirt their belongings look pathetic, almost embarrassing. Dead bodies look pathetic in the same way, Daniel thinks. He hasn't seen very many but on some level there's always some smug thought, "Ha, I'm alive, you're dead." There's no greater gulf between two people, no greater inequality.

"You are very lucky," the captain finally says. "I would have had a very difficult decision to make but I am a soldier and I assure you I would have made it."

Daniel can't even bring himself to think about the sat phone. That's for later; that's for some long sick drunk in Nairobi before he goes home. Tim and Daniel are allowed to collect their belongings while the soldiers look off in embarrassment. The one who had his gun on them walks off across the plaza and comes back a few minutes later driving the Suzuki. He risks an apologetic smile and waves them into the truck. The captain says, "If you come back here without permission you will be shot." Tim ignores him and climbs into the passenger seat of the truck and Daniel throws his bag into the back seat and then gets in next to it. The captain walks off and the soldier forces the stick shift into first and then they lurch off across the plaza and down the road. The soldier seems to want to get out of there as fast as they do. He's seventeen, maybe eighteen and if nothing else he's going back to Freetown for the day.

Tim is sitting sullenly in front, watching the jungle scroll by, a scraggly green wall occasionally broken by a burnt house or a clearing. The driver looks over brightly to say something but notices the expression on Tim's face and decides against it.

"Hey, my name's Daniel and my friend here is Tim," Daniel says, leaning forward into the front seat. The soldier's Kalashnikov is wedged next to the hand brake, he can feel the muzzle against his chest.

"Na' me name Sammy," the kid says, glancing back in the mirror.

"Do you live in Freetown?"

"Yessah."

"Are you going to see your family?"

"Yessah."

The kid goes on to say something in Krio that Daniel doesn't understand. The language is a thick blend of French, English, and native dialects that should be easy to understand but isn't. Then you wake up one morning, Tim says, suddenly understanding everything.

"He's inviting us to his house for dinner," Tim says without turning his head.

"Thank you," Daniel says. "Maybe we'll do that."

Portrait of a soldier and his family, he thinks. A soldier's-eye view of the war. It's better than nothing.

"Were you here last year? Were you here for '99?"

Ninety-nine was the rebel occupation—it lasted two weeks and it was hell on earth. Amputation squads, children made to shoot their own parents, women raped on bridges and then thrown over the side. There were almost no journalists in the city to report it and perhaps in a sense it was unreportable anyway.

"Na boat we tek go Guinea, na' now a de ton back kam," Sammy says. "A kam back fo' go skool, na day sojaman dem ketch we, tay tiday nary a ah dae."

"He went to Guinea but came back for school," Tim says flatly. "The army caught him so now here he is."

The kid says this with a smile, like he's glad it has all worked out this way. Maybe because he's driving us two idiots around, Daniel thinks. He's probably never been in a car with two white guys before. Daniel sees something up ahead on the road, a dark shape askew in some kind of disastrous way. Tim sees it too and instinctively puts his hand on his camera. "Dead rebel," the kid says. He pulls over to the left to head around it; it's a pickup truck flipped over onto its roof. It must have been hit by something big, a tank round maybe.

"Stop!" Tim yells. "Stop the truck!"

The kid is startled and skids the Suzuki to a halt and Tim has the door open even before it's stopped moving. Engine parts are sprayed across the road and two charred corpses lie contorted in the wreckage. Tim puts the camera to his eye and crouches down, moving from angle to angle, motor drive whirring.

"Na' bad bad place dis," the kid says, turning to Daniel apologetically. "Ah no' go able koba yu oh."

Lots of rebels, he can't protect us, Daniel thinks—something along those lines. "Tim!" Daniel shouts. "Tim, come on, let's go. It's not safe."

Tim doesn't answer. He's close up to one of the corpses now, the camera right in its face, click, whir, click, whir. Embarrassment tugs at Daniel but the kid could care less about the dignity of dead rebels at the moment, he's too worried about live ones.

"Na' bad bad place dis," the kid repeats, still convinced Daniel can do something. "Na' rebel ah de watch for so."

Daniel just shrugs. The kid waits another moment, looking at him hopefully, and then gets out of the truck with his gun and walks out to the middle of the road. He starts turning slowly in a circle with the gun at his shoulder, scanning the forest for trouble. Jesus, he'd die for us right here if he had to, Daniel thinks. There's nothing else to do so Daniel climbs out of the truck too and walks over to the wreckage and looks down at one of the rebels. His arms are flung over his head and he has a shocked expression on his face, as if in that final moment he had time to register his disbelief. Mouth open, eyes wide, teeth bared. Tim straightens up and drops the camera back onto his neck.

"Okay," he says. "Done. Let's go."

The kid looks over with relief when he sees them move back towards the truck. He lowers his gun and hurries over. "Na' bad bad place dis." Soon they're speeding down the road again, the forest a pale blur on both sides. Tim empties his camera and slides the roll into his vest pocket and loads in a new one. "The editors will never run those photos but it's good to send that kind of stuff," he shouts over the wind. "It reminds them where the fuck you are."

"Yeah," Daniel says without much interest. The stunned expression on the dead guy's face is still in his head. "It sure does."

THE NEXT TIME the car slows down it's half an hour later and Daniel is thinking about Nairobi—about Jennifer, more precisely. It's been a month since she left him and they've spoken a few times on the phone but it's mostly a charade of pretending there's something left. The truck's speed backs off a notch and Daniel can feel the kid braking—more of a question mark than a real braking action—and he looks up just in time to hear Tim say, "Shit."

At first he thinks it's just another checkpoint, but those are manned by regular army. These guys are shirtless and ill grouped, ranged along one side of the road with their weapons leveled. Daniel feels Tim go tense. "This don't look good, mate," he says.

It's all wrong even before they pull to a full stop. Daniel recognizes the CDF commander from earlier that morning standing furiously apart from the others. The rest are training their guns on the car, one kid even has a grenade launcher leveled at them. If he fires it'll kill us and half his friends, Daniel thinks. The commander is stripped to the waist and has an ammunition belt over his muscular chest. He's strung with necklaces of cowry shells and amulets and leather satchels and he's got some kind of bowler hat on his head with a hatband made of more bullet shells. He's holding a machete in one hand and a pistol in the other and he walks towards the car pointing the machete at the driver and unloading an incomprehensible torrent of Krio invective. Daniel barely understands a word.

The kid in the driver's seat puts his palms out and tries to explain himself, but the commander cuts him off in fury and puts the machete under his chin. The kid falls silent, hands still up. Daniel catches something about the Suzuki and the captain back in town—it's a matter of respect and doesn't seem to have anything to do with them—but when Tim tries to intercede, one of the fighters swears and cocks his machine gun with a loud clack. He takes three steps backwards, everyone looks at him, and then with a sudden laugh he simply starts shooting.

Time doesn't slow down or stop or do anything particularly exotic and Daniel certainly doesn't think anything brave. His mind is still wallowing in disbelief, encumbered by some Western sense that certain things are not allowed to happen and other things certainly can't happen to him when the gunfire crashes through the heavy midday air. It is only then that he realizes one of the other fighters must have grabbed the barrel of the gun and jerked it upwards because they're wrestling for the gun now and otherwise the inconceivable would already have happened, he would now be doubled over in the back seat with his chest cavity impossibly opened up and the darkness rushing in on him like the last eclipse of the sun.

Daniel watches it all numbly and without much fear, a few

stumbling thoughts about whether this is going to hurt and what his family will think. Tim is curled up in the front seat with his hands up, palms outwards while the kid frantically starts explaining something and the rest of the fighters start cocking their guns. Several of them seem to be arguing with each other. The kid who did the shooting is now at the windshield screaming. The commander is silent. It goes on for a while, the argument rising and falling until at times it seems like they might start shooting each other and other times their attention turns to the car and things slide back towards the unthinkable.

Daniel sits in the back seat wondering dully if diving out of the car at the last moment would save him—no thought of Tim or the driver here, just raw survival—when he catches the commander's eye. The commander seems to have reached some decision. He shakes his head and raises his pistol and steps up to the kid in the driver's seat, who is still pleading his case. The kid is still talking when the commander puts the pistol to his head and the kid is still talking when the commander cocks the hammer back and the kid is still talking and not daring to look when the commander tells him to shut the fuck up and then in midsentence he shoots the kid in the head just like that.

The execution is oddly undramatic, the kid just stops talking and falls over. The commander laughs and the other fighters start laughing, the laughter is almost worse than the murder itself and all Daniel can think is that the amount of blood coming out of the kid is unbelievable. It's everywhere, rivering between the seats and puddling beneath his shoes and covering all of them and everything, even the fighters on the far side of the truck. There's so much blood on him that in his dull confusion he wonders if maybe he hasn't been shot as well. He's not dying, though, Tim's not dying—everything is the same except that the kid is hanging strangely in his seat and the entire world seems to be made of his blood.

"Jesus," Tim mutters. "He didn't have to do that."

They almost have to kill us now too, Daniel thinks. That line has been crossed and it's easier to kill us than not to. The fighters glance at one another and then one of them steps backwards. Another one backs up and then a third, a widening circle studded with black little holes. Daniel feels his body go to wood.

"Just a minute," Tim says loudly, no shake to his voice at all.

The fighters exchange looks. Daniel is too numb to be interested in what Tim is going to say. His tongue feels impossibly thick, his vision has started to go dark around the edges. He watches Tim's hands find refuge around his camera, automatic reflexes that he probably isn't even aware of. His thumb flips the rewind lever while the other hand cups the focus ring.

"That's right," Tim says. "Don't move an inch."

Tim has his camera up and Daniel can hear the whir of the motor drive. The fighters are too puzzled to do anything, even kill him. Tim waves the commander into the picture. He's shooting and opening the car door and shooting some more, on his feet now and moving from angle to angle, talking like he always does to his subjects though the fighters can't understand a word. One of them finally glances to either side and then presents his gun self-consciously across his chest in an exaggerated Rambo pose. One by one the others reposition their guns—across the chest, cocked in the elbow, straight up into the air—until they look like a caricature of the nightmare they truly are.

The commander walks over and takes his position out front. Tim runs out of film and keeps talking while his hands unload the roll, pocket it, dig for a new one in his vest and load it back into the camera. The fighters start to jostle one another, trying to get in front. One of them laughs. Another one says something and shoves his friend out of the way. They're teenagers, Daniel thinks. They've probably never had their pictures taken before.

"You're going to be famous, mates," Tim says from behind his camera. "You're all going to be fucking movie stars."

Daniel hasn't moved from the back of the truck. The kid, absurdly, is wearing his seatbelt and hangs patiently from it, ignored and irrelevant. The world has already moved on. Daniel pulls a cigarette out of his shirt pocket and lights it and sits in the blood and the heat smoking and watching Tim talk to the fighters. Tim says something funny and for a moment the commander's face opens up like a child's, laughing, and the next instant he's a killer again. All of them shift back and forth from men to boys and back to men again before Daniel's eyes. If we hadn't come out here this kid wouldn't be dead, Daniel thinks. If Tim hadn't done something all three of us would be dead.

Daniel tries to picture it. The killers would move on up the road towards the rest of their brutal little lives while the three of them stayed where they were, unrecognizable in their last agony, forever unconcerned with the affairs of men. The shadows would lengthen and it wouldn't matter and the sun would set and it wouldn't matter and finally dusk would creep in—the birdcalls, the sudden agitation of the forest—and still it wouldn't matter. None of it would ever matter again and it occurs to Daniel, drawing down the last of his cigarette, that no one can say for sure whether the living are really in a position to pity the dead.

Acknowledgments

WITHOUT THE AUDACITY and hard work of many people, this project would have been nothing more than a good idea that never got legs and eventually drove me to madness. My foremost thanks to the writers who have trusted me with their secrets and their stories. I am hopelessly in their debt. Considerable thanks to my agent, David Black, who turns every fresh kill I lay at his feet into an edible dinner—every author should be so lucky. Thanks also to Jason Sacher for completing the marathon of extensive nail-to-board logistics this project required. At Random House, my thanks to Dan Menaker, who invited this book inside, gave it a warm blanket, and has kept it watered and well fed. Thanks also to Jonathan Karp, as well as Matthew Kellogg, Stephanie Higgs, Holly Webber, and Veronica Windholz. My thanks to Pete Hansen, whose driving provided the inspiration for this collection. For introducing and then fostering in me an appreciation for the not-so-delicate pleasures of the Northeastern Pennsylvania GDS Demolition Derby, thanks to Bob, Ronnie, Emily, and Sara Bailin. For early and continuous support as well as all-around cheerleading, my thanks to friends and family, especially my folks, Kevin and Maxine, Lisa and Charlie Cohan, Joe Murphy, Tim Roth, Steve Alden, Frank Clem, Barbara Bloom, Jim MacDonald, and Karen Rizzo.

Deepest thanks always to my dearest, steadfast, partner-in-crime, Susan, as well as to our cowboys, Casey, Owen, and Willem—the engine that drives me.

About the Editor

MARC PARENT is the author of *Turning Stones: My Days and Nights with Children at Risk*, a finalist for the Los Angeles Times Book Prize, and *Believing It All: What My Children Taught Me About Trout Fishing, Jelly Toast, and Life*. He lives in Pennsylvania with his wife and three sons.

About the Authors

AIMEE BENDER is most recently the author of *Willful Creatures*. Her short fiction has been published in *Granta*, *GQ*, *Tin House*, *Harper's*, and more, as well as heard on NPR's *This American Life*. She lives in Los Angeles.

BENJAMIN CHEEVER is the author of the memoir *Selling Ben Cheever* and the novels *The Plagiarist*, *The Partisan*, *Famous After Death*, and *The Good Nanny*. He has been an editor at *Reader's Digest* and has taught at Bennington College and the New School for Social Research.

MICHAEL CONNELLY is the author of the bestselling Harry Bosch novels, including *The Narrows*, *A Darkness More Than Night*, and *City of Bones*, and the bestselling novels *The Poet*, *Chasing the Dime*, *Blood Work*, and *Void Moon*. He lives in Florida.

SEBASTIAN JUNGER is the author of *The Perfect Storm* and *Fire*. As contributing editor for *Vanity Fair,* he has covered conflicts in West Africa, the Balkans, and Afghanistan. He won a 1999 National Magazine Award for his coverage of war crimes investigations in Kosovo. He lives in Massachusetts and New York.

ELIZABETH McCRACKEN is the author of two novels, *The Giant's House* and *Niagara Falls All Over Again,* and a collection of stories, *Here's Your Hat What's Your Hurry.*

ROSIE O'DONNELL, the middle of five children, born to a mom with the same name who died in '73, senior class president, college drop-out, standup comic, actress, mom, talk show host, and activist, is the author of *Find Me*.

CHRIS OFFUTT is the author of five books: *Kentucky Straight, Out of the Woods, The Same River Twice, No Heroes,* and *The Good Brother*. His work has received a Lannan Award, a Whiting Award, a Guggenheim Fellowship, and an award from the Academy of Arts and Letters.

ANNA QUINDLEN is the author of four bestselling novels, *Object Lessons, One True Thing, Black and Blue,* and *Blessings*. She writes "The Last Word" column every other week in *Newsweek*.

JOHN BURNHAM SCHWARTZ is the author of the novels *Claire Marvel, Reservation Road,* and *Bicycle Days*. His work has appeared in *The New York Times, The New Yorker, The Boston Globe,* and *Vogue*. Currently deputy director of the Sun Valley Writers' Conference, he lives in Brooklyn with his wife.

ALICE SEBOLD is the author of a novel, *The Lovely Bones,* and of the memoir *Lucky*.

LAUREN SLATER is a psychologist and the author of *Opening Skinner's Box, Welcome to My Country,* and *Prozac Diary*. She lives in Massachusetts.